Where Death and Danger Go

V. M. Knox

9

For Tom, Eloise, Ben and Charlotte

Also by V. M. Knox

In Spite of All Terror
If Necessary Alone

"Honours should go where death and danger go."

Winston S. Churchill
Speech to the House of Commons
24th July 1916

Great Britain 1941

1

Oxfordshire, England, Sunday 25th May 1941

Clement pushed back his jacket sleeve and stared at the reddish-purple scar. While the injury had healed, the memories were still raw. He'd survived. That was all he needed to remember. He lifted his head and gazed at the clear evening sky, breathing in the heady scents of the season. The panacea of spring in Oxfordshire was beginning to take effect on his subconscious and with the warmer days had come calmer dreams.

The telephone ringing interrupted his thoughts, the persistent noise bringing him back from the past. Hurrying, he ran into the house and along the front hall then lifted the telephone receiver.

'Would I be speaking to Reverend Clement Wisdom?' a male voice asked.

'Speaking,' Clement said. He felt a wave of relief. It wasn't the call he was expecting. 'How can I help you?'

'Clement, this is Superintendent Arthur Morris, previously Chief Inspector of Lewes Police. I am sorry to disturb, but I think I may need your help.'

Clement's mind went back to other times and Fearnley Maughton, his former home in East Sussex. Even though almost a year had passed since he'd last seen Morris, Clement found himself smiling. 'You knew where to find me then, Arthur?'

'One of the benefits of being a policeman, Clement.'

'Congratulations on your promotion. Are you in need of a clergyman?'

'Not exactly.' Morris paused. 'I was wondering if you are still acquainted with certain persons in Whitehall?'

Clement's smile faded.

'I'll take your silence as a yes,' Morris said. 'Could we meet? Preferably somewhere outside Oxford?'

'When did you have in mind?'

'Would tomorrow suit?'

Clement thought for a moment. 'Ah, yes. I can do that.'

'Do you know the public house called *The Trout* at Godstow?'

'I do.'

'Shall we say midday?'

'Tomorrow then, Arthur.'

Clement replaced the telephone receiver. He had, of course, expected a call but the caller was a surprise.

Standing in his front hall, he visualised Arthur Morris, the relaxed, authoritative manner and quiet demeanour. Clement remembered the last time he'd seen Morris and for a moment he was back on the pebbled beach in the dark, only the English Channel between them and the enemy. Clement swallowed, his mind on the past. It had been the waiting he'd found most difficult then; not knowing whether either of them would still be alive when morning came. That mission had been successful but the victory had been soured by the revelation of the unexpected traitor. It had been the last, painful piece of the puzzle Arthur Morris had helped him to unravel. And now Morris was asking for help again. Clement felt a frown crease his brow. He wondered what could be troubling the Superintendent enough to make contact and yet despite the bitter memories, Clement liked Morris and looked forward to seeing the man again. They were about the same age and shared a similar past: both had had fathers who'd been vicars, both were now widowers and neither had had family.

Clement sauntered into his kitchen and stared through the window at the vibrantly coloured crocuses flowering beneath the trees. He shivered, the action involuntary. Despite the tragic experiences with Morris and his picturesque garden, it was the more recent memory of his mission to far northern Scotland that could, in an instant, turn his blood to ice.

He lifted his gaze and stared into the sky. The setting sun was highlighting the treetops. The translucent light of evening was descending. He continued to stare but he no longer saw its loveliness. A month in the relative safety of Oxford had made him almost forget that he was still an officer in His Majesty's Special Duties Branch of the Secret Intelligence Service.

Blinking, he turned away from the window, his mind on Morris's initial question about certain persons in Whitehall. He knew to whom Morris was referring: John Winthorpe, fellow cleric of the Anglican Church and currently, Captain of Naval Intelligence with the SIS. Clement thought on his former colleague from theological college; a man who, Clement believed, had found his true vocation in the labyrinthine corridors of Whitehall. Intelligent, charming, with all the right connections; John Winthorpe always turned heads.

Clement hadn't heard from his old friend in about a month, since Johnny had arranged his current living arrangements and employment; inhabiting a small house in St Bernard's Road, Oxford, and engaged as Assistant Archivist at St Edward's School not a stone's throw away. It was the most boring position imaginable but it had two main benefits: flexible hours and no questions asked. Clement's hand reached for the kettle and, filling it, he set it on the stove and lit the gas.

Placing the teapot on a tray, he took his meagre supper into the front room and turned on the radio. Richard Dimbleby's voice was telling the nation of the latest devastating bombing raids and their terrifying consequences but this night Morris was never far from Clement's thoughts. He wondered what had prompted the call. 'Don't get ahead of yourself,' he muttered.

An hour later, he switched off the wireless, the daily news giving little hope of a quick resolution to Nazi aggression. He returned the tray to the kitchen and tidied up. Standing at the kitchen window, his gaze settled again on the trees in his garden. He heaved a long sigh; such a tranquil scene. It was an illusion. The atrocities of war both in Britain and elsewhere were many and varied and the secret, shadowy world he inhabited was never far away. He felt its icy finger tapping his shoulder. Drawing the blackout curtains, he went upstairs.

Clement stood in the doorway to his bedroom and looked at the suitcase on top of the wardrobe. He'd almost forgotten it was there in the month that he'd been in Oxford. He pulled it down, retrieved the key from the lowboy and sprang the lock.

Inside were two items neatly wrapped in an oily, linen cloth: his Fairbairn-Sykes commando knife sitting in its scabbard, and his pistol. Lifting the dagger, he withdrew the double-edged blade from its sheath. It fitted snugly into his palm; the feel of it unsettlingly familiar. Images, dark and bitterly cold, flowed from his memory. Taking a long breath, he pushed the knife back into its sheath and placed it on the bed. His gaze shifted to the Welrod pistol and several magazines of ammunition wrapped neatly alongside it. 'You're getting ahead of yourself again, Clement Wisdom,' he whispered. He put both weapons back in the suitcase but he felt the tightening in his chest that always heralded a mission. Relocking it, he lifted it back onto the wardrobe.

Clement woke to the persistent chorus of the blackbirds. He'd slept fitfully; dreams of Caithness resurfacing, triggered, he felt sure, by seeing the weapons of his wartime trade. He blinked several times, then rubbed his hands over the stubble of his day-old beard. Sitting up, he yawned, the suitcase in his peripheral vision. He glanced at the clock on his bedside table. Six o'clock. Early. Too early. But too late for further sleep. He reached for his dressing gown, his feet searching for his slippers beside the bed. As was his habit, he made his bed then went downstairs and opened his front door.

Bending, he reached for the morning newspaper on the step then tucked it under his arm and went to the kitchen. Tossing the newspaper onto the table, he drew the blackout curtains and set the kettle on the stove. The open tabloid caught his attention. A large photograph of devastated and bombed-out buildings occupied the front page. Sitting, he began to read. Hundreds had been killed and scores made homeless. How much longer could Britain hold out? It was an unanswerable question. Yet it was the one on everyone's lips. The intensity and relentlessness of it all coupled with never-ending uncertainty had made 1941 a dangerous and unpredictable year. And it wasn't over yet. The constant threat of death, of ceaseless bombing, of invasion and ruthless Nazi rule was undermining the nation's spirit and would,

Clement knew, inevitably erode resolve. The kettle whistled. He stood to make the tea then cut a slice from the last of his small loaf of bread and sat at the table with the newspaper.

As troubling as the photographs were, he knew his war was elsewhere. He'd made his decision long ago and it had cost him everything he held dear. There was no turning back. Folding the paper, he stood then poured some hot water into a bowl and carried it upstairs. Setting it on the washstand, he adjusted the mirror and reached for his razor.

The soap felt warm against his skin as he lathered the stubble. What had happened to make Arthur Morris call him? Clement chastised himself. One telephone call did not make for an undercover mission. He drew the razor down his cheek and along his jaw then wiped the blade on the towel. Perhaps it would come to nothing. He finished shaving, telling himself that he was worrying needlessly, then patted his face dry. His hand reached for the small mirror intending to replace it in the drawer but he caught his reflection. He stared deeply into his eyes. While his current occupation secretly terrified him, he knew he could do it. And, if he was completely honest with himself, widowhood had made it easier. Downstairs, he heard the key turn in the front door.

Fixing his clerical collar around his neck, he walked onto the landing. 'Is that you, Mrs Warrender?'

'Reverend Wisdom?' the housekeeper called back.

'I'll be down in a minute.'

'Not going to school today? Are you poorly?'

'Not at all; but thank you for your concern. I have an appointment out of town.'

'Should I telephone Mr Bainbridge for you and let him know you won't be in?'

'That won't be necessary, thank you. I'll call in to school and see him myself.'

'As you wish. Can I make you something to eat?'

'That's kind but I've already had breakfast.'

'I'll get on then. Will you be wanting me to leave you some supper?'

'Thank you. That would be helpful.'

'Very good.'

Clement heard the door to the kitchen close. Walter Bainbridge, the Senior Archivist at St Edward's School had recommended the housekeeper and Clement was grateful for her daily assistance but she was inclined to talk, and chat was something he avoided.

At ten to nine, he said goodbye to the kindly and somewhat stout Mrs Warrender and closed his front door. Walking to the corner of his street, he crossed the road and strode towards St Edward's School only a few minutes' walk away. Boys of all ages ran before him along the footpath. 'Don't run!' he shouted then smiled. Boys! Eager for life and adventure. He watched them run ahead. What future awaited them? The Nazis' attempted invasion the previous year had not succeeded but Clement wasn't so naive as to think they wouldn't try again.

Entering the main door of the school, he walked along the crowded, jostling corridor filled with raucous boys, the pungent smell of sweat-encrusted socks hanging in the air. The bell was ringing. Corridors emptied. He made his way to the stairs to his subterranean office, his footsteps suddenly audible in the now empty hallways. Surrounding him on every wall were the photographs of past students, their ageless faces staring out. Some were the stern-faced images of teams; cricket and rugby, of boys with rigid arms and tucked-in thumbs. Others were of boys on bicycles and teams of cross-country runners; photos taken before the war when boys of every nation attended the school on exchange programmes. That had all been discontinued with the coming of war and the German students in particular, hastily returned home.

Descending the stairs, he opened the door to a small basement office he shared with Walter Bainbridge. Bainbridge wasn't there yet. Clement switched on his desk lamp and started on the mountain of files awaiting his attention. He worked on the former headmaster's speeches for well over an hour before closing the file. Despite the quantity of files on Walter's desk, he still had not arrived and now Clement couldn't wait any longer. He checked his watch then wrote a quick note saying that he may not be in for a few days. Leaving it propped against the ink well on Walter's desk, Clement turned out the light and closed the door.

The bus stop on the Woodstock Road was only a

hundred yards from the school gate. Clement quickened his pace, the eleven o'clock bus due at any moment. At the bus shelter, an elderly man wearing a frayed tweed coat sat waiting. 'Morning,' Clement said. The man smiled in response but didn't speak. A minute later the bus drew up.

Standing back while the older man boarded, Clement heard him purchase a ticket for Enstone, some miles distance to the north-west. Paying his fare, the man then took a seat behind the driver.

'Where to, sir?' the bus driver asked Clement.

'Wolvercote,' Clement replied, searching for some coins. Paying the fare and pocketing the ticket, he walked to the rear from where he could watch his fellow passengers. Other than the man who boarded with him, there were six women with full shopping baskets, two small children, and ten airmen who chatted excitedly amongst themselves. As they left the outskirts of Oxford, an older couple joined the bus, the pair sitting towards the front. The woman didn't carry a shopping basket and they were well-dressed, so Clement decided they were keeping an appointment or visiting someone out of town.

Clement alighted in the village of Wolvercote about a mile from Godstow for his scheduled meeting with Morris at *The Trout*. As he did so, laughter floated towards him. Several children were playing a game of hide and seek on the nearby green. He paused, watching them. Never having had children of his own, he knew little about them but their laughter made him smile. The scene was so ordinary and care-free, so oblivious to the catastrophic events going on not too far away.

'May they never know the trauma of their city cousins,' he muttered, remembering the pictures in the morning paper. Ahead of him, the airmen gathered on the footpath, several lighting cigarettes. Clement guessed they were making for *The Trout* also. He hung back, their chatter and occasional laughter along with the aroma of tobacco wafting towards him.

He checked his watch. He was in good time and he would enjoy the walk after a morning in the stuffy basement office. Thirty-five minutes later *The Trout* came into view, a low, curved stone wall separating the road from the inn. Clement took the steps beside an adjacent bridge that led to the inn's front door. Opening it, he stepped inside. Through the windows he could see several groups of people sitting on the terrace by the river. No one was sitting indoors. He ordered two small ales from the barman then made his way outside.

The number of people there surprised him. The warm, late spring weather was encouraging people to sit in the sunshine. The scene was a welcome respite, a refuge of sorts from the daily unpredictability of war. Clement scanned the assembled gathering, searching for Arthur Morris but the phlegmatic, grey-haired man was not yet there. Clement made his way to a table by a low wall overlooking the fast-flowing river. Around him groups of friends chatted and laughed. About twenty feet away, a couple sat together, their hands touching, their eyes engaged solely on each other.

The airmen had taken a table by the river, glasses of beer already in their hands and behind them, three men sat huddled in conversation. Clement's gaze settled on the trio. One of the three appeared to be of advanced years. The other two men were young but he knew the type. Their clothes were a uniform of sorts; the tweed jackets and worn clothes of academia. Clement returned his gaze to the roaring torrent beside him as it tumbled past.

At exactly noon, the small door from the inn opened and the man he recognised approached him.

Clement stood. 'How are you, Arthur?'

'Good to see you, Clement. Thank you for the ale,' Morris said pointing at the glass.

'How can I help you?'

Morris took the seat opposite Clement. 'Do you have any commitments for the next few days?'

Clement visualised the files on his desk. 'Nothing urgent.'

Morris leaned forward, his voice low, his brown eyes flicking around the other patrons. 'I'll come straight to the point. About two months ago, just before Easter, in fact, the body of a man was found buried in a copse of trees in a field near the village of Ramsey, some thirty or so miles north of Cambridge. The pathologist confirms that the body had been in the ground about two months. Thanks to the severity of last winter and the boggy soil where he was found, the corpse is quite well preserved.

The deceased was a physically fit man in his mid-forties. His remains offered no identification and no one has come forward to claim him nor has anyone reported him missing. Whilst that's not a completely unusual occurrence in the cities these days, it is unusual in remote farming communities. Especially so in view of this particular man.'

Clement frowned. He wasn't sure why Morris was telling him about what he considered to be a police matter. He waited. With Morris, Clement recalled from working with him previously, there would be a good reason.

Morris went on. 'From the deceased's roughened hands, we believe he may have been a labourer or manual worker of some kind.'

'Who discovered the body?'

'The farmer's dog, actually. There'd been a lot of rain and some scavenging animal had been digging there. Charles Ward, the farmer on whose property the deceased was found, doesn't recognise him.' Morris took a long sip of his drink before continuing. 'And, something really unusual; there wasn't a single possession on him. Nothing in his pockets or coat. Nothing personal of any kind.'

'Do you suspect theft?'

'Not really. Thieves don't usually kill then bury their victims.'

Clement frowned. 'How did this man die?'

'He was shot through the heart at point-blank range,

facing his attacker.'

Clement felt his eyebrows rise. 'And no other injuries of any kind?'

'None. With the exception of a patch of scarred tissue under his upper right arm, there are no identifying marks of any kind. It remains an unsolved case.'

Clement stared at the gurgling waters. 'Sounds as though he knew his killer.' He frowned. 'Not even defensive wounds?'

'Nothing at all. No blood, flesh or anything else under the fingernails and no bruising or other injuries anywhere else on the body. Nothing, in fact, to suggest even the slightest resistance.'

'Totally unexpected. It sounds like an assassination, Arthur. You say you believe him to have been a labourer of some kind?'

Morris nodded then sat back in the chair and reached for his glass. 'You would expect there to be something under the nails. Even if there was no evidence of an attack, there should have been evidence of his trade.'

'Forgive me for saying, Arthur, but I'm not sure any of this is a security matter.'

Morris leaned forward and continued in a low voice. 'Quite right and on the surface it doesn't appear to be. However, something else happened at about the same time and in approximately the same location and what I don't know yet, Clement, is whether this death and the other incident are connected.' Morris took another sip of ale. 'You will recall a well-publicised incident that happened in late January near the village of Ramsey in Cambridgeshire.' Morris placed his glass back on the table, the brown eyes flashing once more around the assembled gathering on the terrace. 'Do you remember a German spy was captured in a field in Cambridgeshire in late January? It was in the papers. His name was Josef Jakobs.'

Clement frowned. 'I do remember. You think there is a connection between the deceased and this spy Jakobs?'

'I wouldn't have until two days ago. You may recall Jakobs dropped by parachute during the night of the thirty-first of January and landed in a field not a hundred yards from where our murdered man was found.'

Clement frowned. 'What happened two days ago?'

'Another gun was found in the same field not far from where Jakobs landed. It was only discovered because Mr Chisholm, the farmer on whose property Jakobs was found, is ploughing at present and the metal blades of his plough unearthed the weapon.'

'Do you know what it is?'

Morris nodded. 'A Luger. And it has been fired once.'

Clement frowned. 'Remind me about Jakobs?'

'He broke his ankle on landing and after surviving a long, cold night in the field, with morning's light, fired three shots into the air to attract the attention of some nearby farmworkers. At the time, one of the farmhands notified the local Home Guard who then contacted Ramsey Police. Both the police and the Home Guard attended the scene. Jakobs was then taken by horse-drawn cart to Ramsey Police Station. There was little doubt he was a spy; he had with him maps of Warboys and Upwood aerodromes, flashing lights, code books, a large amount of cash and a piece of really damning evidence, a radio transmitter - along with the Mauser pistol he'd used to attract the attention of the farmworkers. That was when they called me. But there are a few things about all this that don't quite add up. Ramsey Police interviewed David Chisholm at length who said that he'd heard four shots. Jakobs's Mauser pistol was found to have been discharged only three times. Chisholm was told he was mistaken and nothing more was said.'

'Did you call Special Branch about the Luger?'

'Yes. The day it was found. I spoke to a young man who told me to submit a report. Put it this way, Clement, I wasn't confident anything would happen any time soon. Perhaps they think it unimportant. Perhaps they think the Luger belonged to Jakobs and as he is already in custody, it doesn't warrant their immediate attention. But I'm not so sure. There are just too many things about this case that bother me.'

'You're quite certain the gun couldn't have belonged to Jakobs and that he threw it into the field?'

'I think it unlikely. Remember Jakobs had a broken ankle and the Luger was approximately thirty yards from where Chisholm says Jakobs landed. Of course, Chisholm could be mistaken, it was five months ago, but regardless, I don't think it plausible that Jakobs would

16

have both a Mauser and a Luger. And why would he keep the Mauser with him then crawl thirty yards with a broken ankle to dispose of the other and crawl back? Moreover, Clement, if Jakobs was the murderer, how did he manage it with a broken ankle? How did he bury a body single-handedly?'

'How far is it from where Chisholm says he found the Luger to where the body was found?'

'The deceased was found in a shallow grave in a copse on the other side of the field and on a neighbouring property. A distance of approximately seventy yards from where the Luger was found and around a hundred yards from where Jakobs landed. We also have the bullet. It was lodged in a tree trunk in the copse. The pathologist has confirmed it was fired from the Luger.'

'Is it possible though that whoever fired the weapon then threw it into the field, knowing Jakobs was there? What did Jakobs say after his capture? Was he aware of anyone else there?'

'I have a copy of the police and Home Guard reports in my office in Cambridge taken from Jakobs at the time. You're welcome to read them. There was little doubt he was a spy, based on what he had on him. A comprehensive list was made. Also, while he wasn't in uniform, he was wearing a flying suit and under this he had a suit with shirt and tie. As I recall the local lads said he was quite well-dressed. No identifying labels, of course. But as far as I am aware, no one has asked Jakobs about the possibility of there being another person there. While Jakobs's arrival in England is well documented, it's the unidentified murdered man who's of concern to me.'

Clement frowned, his mind processing the information. 'So, just to have it clear in my mind, Arthur, you think the deceased was shot and buried in the copse and the pistol used to kill him was thrown into the field where Jakobs landed. And that all this took place on the same night.'

Morris nodded but remained silent.

'Do you suspect Chisholm to be involved in any way?'

'No. He was at home with his wife. Besides, if Chisholm had seen the deceased, he would have thought him another spy and, I feel certain, confessed to killing him. Ramsey Police ruled him out as a suspect and I agree with them. Unless farmers have kept a souvenir pistol from the last war, they don't usually use them. Rifles are more their thing. And remember, the shot was fired at point-blank range. That requires a very cool personality.'

'The bullet that killed the deceased is definitely nine millimetre?'

Morris nodded. 'Yes, we have it and it has been confirmed that it was fired from the Luger.'

'I'm sorry to be asking so many questions, Arthur. I'm sure you have done a thorough investigation.'

'If I had, Clement, we'd know who this man was. I am by no means offended. Please feel free to ask as many questions as you like. It can only help.'

'Thank you. Is the neighbouring farmer a suspect?'

'No. Again according to Ramsey Police, on the night in question, that is January thirty-first, Mr Charles Ward was in Ramsey buying seed and stayed overnight. His alibi has been verified by the publican in Ramsey.'

'It would be good to speak with Jakobs. Do you know where he is now?'

'The last I heard he went to Canon Row Police Station in London. It may be faster, Clement, for you to find out his current location. Or if, in fact, he is still alive.'

'I'll try. It begins to look as though someone else other than Jakobs landed in that field in Ramsey, doesn't it?'

'That was the conclusion I came to.'

A burst of laughter from the airmen interrupted Clement's thoughts. He glanced at the group then looked back at Morris. As much as it began to sound like a security matter, Clement didn't wish to involve the Service if there was a simpler explanation. 'Is it possible that the deceased was a local who witnessed something. You know, wrong place, wrong time?'

Morris tilted his head, the eyebrow rising. It was his sceptical gesture that Clement remembered from when they'd worked together before. 'That would seem plausible but as no one hereabouts knows him, it doesn't seem likely.'

Clement frowned. 'The Luger suggests a second German spy but did he jump with Jakobs or after? Or indeed from a different aeroplane?'

'I did check with Home Security. I am informed that while there were seventeen air raids listed in the Eastern Sector for the thirty-first of January, there were, officially, no night raids recorded. It has to have been a single aeroplane.' Morris took another sip from his drink then, setting it on the table, leaned forward. 'Which means, Clement, if there was only one aeroplane, then two people jumped from it. If this second man and Jakobs are connected, and I think there's a very strong possibility that they are, then the identity of the buried corpse could be of national importance.'

Clement gazed at the river. 'Was a second parachute found?'

'Only Jakobs's chute has been recovered.'

Clement gazed at the tumbling waters cascading over the weir. 'Is it possible a local found the chute and has used the fabric?'

'I did think of that too, Clement. We have checked the marriage registers and none of the brides in the immediate area in the last six months have worn white silk.'

'Who else knows about this?'

'David Chisholm, he's the farmer in whose field Jakobs landed, the local police and local Home Guard know about Jakobs. But only Chisholm, Ward and my lads know about the unidentified corpse and the Luger. The farmers have been told to keep it to themselves for now.'

'What would you like me to do, Arthur?' Clement said, thinking it unlikely that a small rural community could keep that secret for more than a few days.

Morris leaned forward. 'If this deceased man is a German, the security forces should know about it. They may already. Or it may be a complete surprise. Either way, I feel they should be informed and soon. It shouldn't wait for Special Branch to decide if a Luger found in a sodden field in Cambridgeshire is important enough for them to investigate.'

'I think you're right, Arthur. I'll telephone my people and let you know. Are you stationed in Oxford?'

'No. Cambridge. But I'll stay in Oxford until I hear from you. You can reach me on this number.' Morris scribbled the Oxford telephone number on his card and handed it to Clement. Standing, Morris drained his glass. 'Thank you, Clement. Good to see you again.'

Clement took the bus back to Oxford. He wondered if he should return to St Edward's but it was already mid-afternoon and his mind wasn't on the former headmaster's speeches. Checking he had his ration card, he headed into town to buy some groceries before getting a bus home.

The clock on the kitchen dresser chimed four as he entered the house in St Bernard's Road. Carrying his groceries into the kitchen, he saw a note on the kitchen table beside his supper. Reaching for it, he tore it open. Mrs Warrender had left early, it said, to visit her ailing mother. Clement wasn't displeased. He wanted to think about what Morris had told him without any distracting chitchat. He put away his weekly rations then strolled outside to sit in his garden. Somewhere a bird was chirping. It was so peaceful. He sat in his chair in the garden and closed his eyes, the lazy aromas of spring filling his senses. He focused his thoughts on the unknown body found in Cambridgeshire and explored the possibilities.

If the deceased had also been a German spy and had jumped immediately after Jakobs, who had shot him? It seemed unlikely that Jakobs was the killer for all the reasons Morris had put forward. Nor a wandering local. Clement opened his eyes and stared at the oak tree at the bottom of his garden, the missing parachute on his mind. What would the man have done with it? There were as yet too many unanswerable questions. He decided to call Johnny Winthorpe in the morning.

The light was failing. Above him a bird sat in the branches of the oak tree. A few seconds later, it flew to another branch. He watched it flit around, jumping from branch to branch before flying away. His eye searched for the bird in the evening light, a squint forming into a deep frown. The bird had gone. He stared into the empty sky, his mind lingering again on a second man parachuting into England. Surely a second spy would have had spying paraphernalia with him, similar to Jakobs? Morris had said the man had no possessions at all. Did that mean he hadn't parachuted into England?

2

Oxford, Wednesday 28th May 1941

The bus door opened.

'Where to, Reverend?' the driver called to him.

'Woodstock, please,' Clement said. He took his ticket and walked towards the rear of the bus, glancing at his fellow passengers before taking his seat. On his right were four women and two men. Six other men sat on the left and there were five young children of varying ages. He didn't recognise any of the faces.

The bus door closed. Clement idly watched the passing suburban streets from the bus window as they left Oxford heading west. It perplexed him that while total carnage was taking place in the big cities, little appeared to have changed in Oxford. He didn't know why the Luftwaffe had spared the old town. Perhaps they had an historical conscience after all. He smiled. He doubted it. Whatever the reason, and he was sure there would be one, he didn't know it. His gaze returned to his fellow passengers as he recalled the previous day's telephone conversation which had resulted in the unexpected journey.

Captain Winthorpe hadn't been in his office in Whitehall and Clement had spoken instead to Johnny's efficient secretary, Nora Ballantyne. When he'd asked about any SIS activity in Cambridgeshire on the night of January thirty-first, she'd chastised him for talking about such matters on the telephone. While he'd always thought her manner to be brusque, yesterday she'd been almost dismissive. He felt a frown crease his forehead. He decided it was the war. With Johnny absent, Clement felt certain Miss Ballantyne would be busier than usual and what she'd instructed him to do seemed almost incongruous. He was to go to Woodstock and report his concerns to a Corporal Hughes. Clement shook his head. Surely he could have spoken to someone in authority over a secure telephone line. He stared at the passing countryside, his lips pursing. It was evident to him that Miss Ballantyne thought his suspicions about enemy spies trivial at best and deserving of nothing more than a parochial response.

He actually prayed she was right but his inner voice and the previous sleepless night was telling him otherwise. He'd thought of little else since his meeting with Morris. If Jakobs hadn't killed the man found in the copse, then a third person existed. Whoever this person was, their continued, undiscovered identity and whereabouts could have major ramifications for the nation as well as for himself. His gaze fell on a large field of some unknown crop growing on both sides of the road.

Above the sound of the bus's engine, Clement heard the familiar burring hum of fighters; low at first, then with each passing second growing louder until the noise suspended all thought. The increasing roar overhead was having a palpable effect on the passengers. The bus slowed then stopped, the driver pushing his head through the adjacent window. 'No need to worry, everyone. Little friends!'

An audible sigh spread through the bus as the driver restarted the engine. 'What brave boys!' a woman two rows in front said aloud. She recommenced her knitting as the thundering, burring sound of piston engines intensified above until the shadow of the returning squadron passed over them.

Kidlington airfield was off to his right. Clement silently thanked God for their safe return but his gaze was on the woman's knitting and the quick, rhythmic movement of the needles. The ordinary and the extraordinary; the repetitive click-clack of knitting needles and fighter aircraft of thunderous power that criss-crossed the skies multiple times every day were like something for a futuristic novel; almost unfathomable to comprehend. Everyone admired the pilots' bravery. Not so for Johnny Winthorpe and the thousands of others who did heroic deeds in secret. Theirs was a hidden world forever shrouded and unknown. Clement returned his gaze to the flat country and its unknown crop and what he considered to be the futility of this day.

He stepped from the bus and walked past the old stone cottages and shops that hugged the village roads and headed towards the large ironwork gate at the end of the thoroughfare. Beside the gate was a small, black wooden hut. A young man wearing a corporal's uniform stood on Clement's approach.

'Morning, sir,' the guard said. 'Your name?'

'Major Clement Wisdom. Are you Corporal Hughes?'

'Not me, sir. You are expected. Just follow the path ahead then when you get there, take the small door on the left to the basements. Can't miss it.'

'Corporal Hughes is in service here?'

The guard smiled. 'In a manner of speaking. Just follow the path and knock at the door, sir. You'll be looked after there.'

'Ah,' Clement said, now realising that Corporal Hughes wasn't so much in service as in *the* Service.

Following the gate corporal's directions, Clement walked along the gravel path, a light breeze carrying the fragrance of freshly cut grass. The driveway was long and the grand palace still far ahead. Off to his right was a vast lake and before him a stone bridge led on to the mansion beyond. Despite the picturesque scene that greeted him on the mild spring day, he wasn't there to see Blenheim's evident marvels. But he found himself smiling at the thought of the Secret Intelligence Services inhabiting the basements of the Prime Minister's birthplace.

The gigantic mellow stone building almost shone in the afternoon sunlight as Clement approached it. Fifteen minutes later Clement knocked at an insignificant door to the left of the grand entrance and within seconds a sergeant opened the door.

'Major Wisdom for Corporal Hughes, Sergeant,' Clement said.

'This way, sir.'

Clement followed the burly sergeant down a flight of stairs into a wide underground corridor. To the left and right were rooms with closed doors. At one time, the subterranean space would have been the domain of butlers and under-butlers, but now the whole place seethed with the palpable efficiency of military and security personnel.

Having served in both world wars of a troubled century, Clement had become accustomed to the ways of the military but even though he was now in the more unorthodox branches of the armed services, he had never seen a sergeant escort a major to a corporal. The sergeant preceded Clement up a flight of thickly carpeted stairs to a room on the next floor. There Clement was shown into an elegant drawing room, the sergeant leaving him in the quiet opulence.

Within minutes a shiny, wooden-panelled door opened and the man Clement recognised as *C* entered the room. 'We have never formally been introduced, I think, Vicar. I am Sir Stewart Menzies. Mostly known as *C*. Sometimes as Corporal Hughes. I understand you think we may have a German spy on the loose.'

Clement stood and shook hands with the man for whom he ultimately worked. *C* listened without interruption as Clement told him about his conversation with Morris and his own speculations.

When Clement finished, Menzies sat back in the gilt armchair. 'I think you're correct to be suspicious. There are, Major, aside from a good many airfields hereabouts, certain sensitive installations in this part of the country. Even where we are currently sitting is coveted by our enemy. We understand that Herr Hitler is intending to make Blenheim the Nazi Occupation Headquarters once Germany rules Britannia.'

'Audacious,' Clement said, no longer wondering why the sumptuous palace and surrounding villages and towns remained unscathed from Nazi bombers.

Menzies went on. 'Blenheim aside, if the enemy were to become aware of any of our secret installations hereabouts, it would be a disaster. And nothing short of catastrophic if they were infiltrated. Who else knows about this?'

'Only Superintendent Morris and myself. The local police are treating it as an unsolved murder.'

'I seem to recall a policeman named Morris met with Captain Winthorpe last year?'

Clement nodded and waited. Menzies looked deep in thought.

C looked up. 'I think this should be investigated and I'll arrange for you to speak with Jakobs on Friday. For now, however, I'd sooner your suspicions about German spies remain between yourself and Superintendent Morris. Whilst we will run it as an SIS matter under your control, it would be preferable for any curious members of the general public and any lower-ranking police officers for it to be seen as a routine police investigation.' Menzies stood and opened a nearby door. 'Would you come in, please Miss Ballantyne?'

Clement heard the brisk clip-clop of high heels on the polished floors.

Nora Ballantyne flashed a smile as she entered the room.

Clement nodded in response. He could see she was enjoying his surprised reaction. He had thought he had telephoned Whitehall when he'd spoken with her the previous day, but while the woman was the epitome of secrecy, he believed she was sharing a joke with him. Something, he felt sure, she didn't often do.

'I think you know Miss Ballantyne, Major.'

Clement nodded.

'Anything Major Wisdom wants, Miss Ballantyne. Anything at all.'

Nora Ballantyne beamed then turned on her heel and left the room, closing the door behind her.

'Stay in regular contact with Miss Ballantyne,' Menzies said. 'She will keep me up-to-date with your findings. I'd be interested to hear what, if anything, you learn from Jakobs. I want a thorough investigation, Major. We need to know the identity of the deceased and, more importantly, who killed him.'

Clement nodded to the guard on duty as he left. Walking along the street he headed for the bus stop hoping he hadn't missed the last bus back to Oxford for the day. Twenty minutes later one pulled up and Clement climbed aboard. He took his usual seat. He wanted to think. What he'd hoped for was a routine debrief to some obscure corporal. But with the personal involvement of the Head of the Secret Service and his own active participation, Clement knew this had the potential to take over his life for the foreseeable future. Leaning his head against the window, he thought about Mary. In his mind's eye he saw his deceased wife, her broad smile, her bright eyes and her slender ankles. While his grief would always be with him, time was beginning to blunt the edges of his anguish. It secretly worried and saddened him. He couldn't envisage a peacetime life without her. He rubbed his hand over his furrowed brow. Despite the endless speculation in some quarters of a negotiated peace deal with Hitler, he couldn't see an early end to the war. Moreover, if Hitler succeeded in invading Britain, Clement knew as an officer in His Majesty's Special Duties Section, he would not live long enough to worry about the future.

The squeal of brakes broke into his thoughts. Clement stepped from the bus at the intersection with St

Bernard's Road and walked towards his Victorian terraced house. Closing the front door, he hung up his coat and hat then went straight to his bedroom. Reaching for the suitcase, he placed it on the bed and sprung the locks then grasped the leather sheath of his Fairbairn-Sykes commando knife. Almost without thinking he strapped it to his inner left calf. The vicar in him winced at the thought. He couldn't philosophise anymore about his current occupation. Besides, self-doubt clouded judgement which inevitably led to procrastination. And that, so he had discovered first-hand, was as deadly as any dagger or pistol.

Standing on the bed, he wriggled his leg, his trouser falling over the concealed weapon. The feel of it against his skin was an instant reminder that the balmy days of Oxford for him were over. Not that he believed he would need the knife for a police investigation but he'd been wrong about such things before and he wasn't going to take any chances. His gaze settled on the other item in the suitcase. Unwrapping the oily cloth, he stared at the long, large-barrelled Welrod pistol and the magazine beside it. He lifted the holster from the suitcase. Tomorrow and every day thereafter, he would wear it.

Just after six o'clock, he telephoned the Oxford number Morris had given to him. 'Superintendent Morris, please. Reverend Wisdom speaking.'

Within seconds he heard Morris's voice. 'What news, Clement?'

'Where is our man currently?'

'Mortuary in Cambridge.'

'It would be helpful to see him.'

'I'll pick you up at six tomorrow morning. And Clement, delighted to have you with me.'

3

Cambridgeshire, Thursday 29th May 1941

Morris turned off St Andrew's Street and drove through the wide vehicular doors of Cambridge Police Station just on nine o'clock. He switched off the engine and together they entered the impressive stone building from the rear. Morris led Clement down some stairs to the basement where, at the end of a long corridor, there was an unmarked double door. They went inside. No one was there.

A strong smell of formaldehyde hung in the air. Clement wrinkled his nose, the smell an instant reminder of his time as chaplain at St Thomas' Hospital following the Great War. In the centre of the green and white tiled mortuary was a long metal table. Above it, a large domed light hung and against one wall there was a long metal shelf with two sinks where a swivel-head hose hovered above them like a predatory swan. Clement looked around; the business of death was perfunctorily detached and the silence, palpable.

The sound of a door opening made Clement turn. Two men pushed a trolley carrying the unmistakable shape of a corpse under a white shroud into the room and positioned it under one of the large overhead lights. The attendant then removed the sheet from the deceased and stood back.

'Thank you. I'll call you when we've finished,' Morris said.

The men left the room.

Clement stood next to the body. He had expected a more grotesque sight, then he remembered Morris's words about the corpse being well preserved by the boggy Cambridgeshire ground and a freezing winter. While Clement had seen death many times before, a corpse is always a confronting sight. Enemy or not, this naked man once held a soul that doubtless had hopes and dreams as well as a family somewhere. Clement said a silent prayer for the relatives of this man who would never see him again. 'How long did you say he's been dead?' Clement said, wondering why no one was missing this man.

'Pathologist says about four months. He was found on the eighth of April in a shallow and hastily dug grave just over two months after Jakobs was taken. Since then he has been in our mortuary. He would have been completely frozen but with the coming of spring, the body began to thaw. And, as you know, the farmer's dog found him.'

Clement's gaze returned to the corpse, his attention drawn to the neat hole in the man's chest.

Morris opened the file and handed it to Clement.

Clement read aloud. 'The deceased is male, aged in his mid-to-late forties, five feet seven inches in height with light-brown hair, fair complexion and was generally in good health. The musculature is well defined in the upper arms and legs, and is consistent with someone who was physically fit. However, the lower spine and the long bones of the arms and legs were beginning to show signs of epiphyseal wear that indicate a life of heavy manual work. His teeth are slightly worn but otherwise healthy. The stomach contents of fish and potato indicate that the man had eaten approximately ten to twelve hours prior to death.' Clement looked up at Morris whose only reaction was the characteristic raising of the eyebrows. Clement read on. 'There is a patch of keloid scarring three and a half inches in length and two inches wide under the upper right arm most likely caused by a contact burn occasioned sometime within the last twelve to eighteen months. There are no other physical abnormalities. There is significant compact stippling to the skin around the bullet's entry wound to the chest, with charring surrounding the hole, and a bright red hue to the wounded tissue formed from the expelled gases combining with the haemoglobin in the blood. It is estimated that the weapon was discharged within six inches of the victim. Death was instantaneous. The deceased has extensive lividity to the buttocks, shoulders, heels and calves, consistent with lying undisturbed in or on the ground immediately after death. There is indication of a past compound fracture of the right femur.'

Clement looked at Morris. 'Close range. Could even have been staring at his killer as he pulled the trigger.'

'So it would appear.'

Clement handed the file to Morris and reached for the deceased's right arm. Drawing it away from the torso, Clement stared at the patch of heavily scarred, roughened reddish flesh. 'A painful wound, deliberate or not.'

'You think it was deliberately done?'

'Could be. But if it were torture, why is it not more extensive?

'You think it was inflicted or even self-inflicted?'

Neither man spoke for some minutes.

'Do you have the bullet?' Clement asked.

'Yes and it's a match for the Luger.'

'What does the report say about the exit wound?'

Morris opened the file again. 'Not large but consistent with a soft bullet exit wound. So not subsonic.'

'Is there any possibility it was suicide?'

'While the shot was fired at close range, it was not directly on the skin as it most likely would be if it were suicide. Further, the bullet's path through the tissues would be angled, and X-ray has confirmed this is almost exactly straight. Difficult to do if holding the weapon oneself. And even more difficult to throw the weapon into the adjacent field after shooting oneself much less burying oneself.'

'Of course. Silly of me.'

Morris smiled.

'Anything unusual about the clothes?'

'These are interesting. Not only was the fabric hand-woven but the coat and trousers appear to have been handmade. And I don't mean by a tailor. His trousers even have turn-ups.'

'Made before the rationing of cloth. Don't suppose there are any labels in them?'

Morris shook his head.

Clement stared at the face of the dead man as he spoke. 'Is there any soil in the clothes?'

Morris walked to the door and called to the mortuary attendant. Five minutes later the man returned with a large bag and handed it to Morris who carefully placed the contents onto the nearby metal trolley.

'Quite a large amount of mud on the clothes, isn't there?' Clement said lifting the trouser leg and staring at the mud caked into the cloth. 'Is it a match for where he was found?'

'Yes. He was buried in fenland, Clement, so the amount of mud is not surprising,' Morris added.

Clement turned his attention to the boots. He lifted each in turn. 'Worn, old. But sturdy. Workman's boots.' Some dried dark brown mud still clung to the soles. 'Has this mud been analysed?'

'Same as the grave,' Morris added.

Clement ran his finger along the sole of the boot exposing the leather. A small clump of mud fell to the floor. Clement studied the footwear.

'See something?' Morris asked.

'A familiar staining.' Clement picked the encrusted mud off the boot exposing a long whitish line along the edge where the leather upper met the sole. 'I've seen this before on fishermen's shoes. It's from repeated exposure to salt water. I grew up on the Sussex coast, if you recall.' Clement lifted the corner of the coat. It was a heavy weave, and although not a tweed as such, it was thick, possibly homespun. Its only embellishment was a single blue thread that formed repeating stripes approximately six inches apart. Dried mud had mixed with blood and melting snow to form a muddy glue that impregnated the fabric most heavily over the shoulders and back where the corpse had lain in the ground.

Clement looked at the trousers. Both trouser legs were spattered with dark mud and like the overcoat, encrusted with soil clogging the weave. Opening wide the turn-ups, he saw some reddish clumps of dirt wedged in the crease. He pinched a piece, rolling it between his thumb and forefinger. It felt gritty. 'Is this the same soil as that in the field where he was found?'

Morris stepped forward and studied the pasty soil in Clement's hand. 'Can't answer that precisely. I'll ask the pathologist to run some extra tests.'

Clement placed the earth into a dish then returned to

the corpse. Neither he nor Morris spoke for several minutes.

'Could we go to where he was found?'

'Of course. It's about thirty miles from here,' Morris added.

Clement looked up. 'I'm sure you'll have turned over every stone and clod, Arthur, and I mean no disrespect by asking but I would like to see it, if you wouldn't mind.'

'Not at all. I thought we'd done a thorough search before but we didn't find the Luger. So we can't assume we've found everything the site can tell us. Perhaps another set of eyes will see things differently.'

Clement frowned. 'Is it possible the pistol has only recently been left in the field?'

'That would implicate the farmers, both of whom have been ruled out. Besides the bullet being a match, the Luger's wooden pistol grip is swollen from prolonged water damage. So I think we can eliminate that theory.'

They went upstairs to Morris's office on the first floor. It was a large room at the front of the police station overlooking St Andrew's Street. To the right was a long desk, several chairs and beneath the window was a small table. A sergeant brought in a tray with two cups and a pot of tea and set it on the table.

'Thank you, Sergeant,' Morris said. He poured the tea and waited until the man had left the room before continuing. 'Tell me your thoughts, Clement, however random.'

'Leaving aside for a moment who pulled the trigger, let's presume for now that our man wasn't a local or an itinerant farm worker but a German spy who landed at the same time as Jakobs. What troubles me about this theory, other than who actually shot him, is the absence of the parachute. What would he, or anyone else for that matter, do with it? Surely it would be buried with the deceased? So either the ground was too hard or the killer didn't have sufficient time to dig a deeper grave and so took it with him.' Clement paused. 'Do you know how long it was between when the shots were fired to when the Home Guard and police came?'

'The first responders were the Home Guard. They were on the scene within the hour. Ramsey Police didn't come until after Captain Thew from the Home Guard telephoned them from Chisholm's house. They arrived about forty minutes after that.'

'So plenty of time for the killer to leave the area and take the parachute with him.' Clement gazed at the large window. A lengthy silence ensued. 'And why are there signs of salt water on the deceased's boots?' Clement said somewhat rhetorically. He rubbed his forehead then looked again at the report. 'His stomach contents indicate that he had eaten fish. Is it possible he had only just come to Cambridgeshire? Or was he brought here to be killed and disposed of in the field? The timing aside, is there even a connection to Jakobs?'

'I'll tell you something else, Clement, that doesn't quite add up. The farmworkers who found Jakobs said they had to *wade*, their word, through the mud to get to him. The deceased was found about a hundred yards away. Ignoring the absence of a parachute, if our murdered man was another parachutist, why aren't his boots and trouser legs more caked in mud? Walking through mud would mean the whole boot, socks, trousers and all would be filled with mud. But not this man's. And, did you notice, on the corpse? There is no bruising either to the abdomen or thighs that would indicate our man had ever been wearing a parachute.'

4

Morris pulled off the main road into a narrow unsealed track to the east of the village of Wistow. They drove about a mile along a low ridge, the road twisting and descending through groves of trees and hedges before opening to a wide open space. Below them, a vast brown field stretched away in all directions. Morris slowed, and parking the car on the verge, switched off the engine. Clement stared at the scene before him. 'Is this where Jakobs landed?'

'Yes.'

'I can see why.'

In the middle distance he could see a tractor working the land about half a mile away, the soil turned and rich, ready for sowing. From where he sat in Morris's car Clement couldn't see anyone else in the fields. He opened the door and got out and breathed in the wholesome smell of farming country. Morris joined him.

'That's the copse where our man was found,' Morris said pointing to their right. Several hundred yards away to the south and adjacent to a narrow dirt track were two large oak trees surrounded by some lower growth. 'Jakobs was found just about there,' Morris said pointing to a spot in the field some hundred yards north of the copse. 'You have a look about on your own, Clement. I'll wait in the car. Take as much time as you need.'

Clement stood surveying the landscape. Turning around, he saw the low hill with the thickets of trees they had driven through. In front was a panorama of almost three hundred degrees of flat land laid to pasture or being prepared for sowing. To his left and about a mile distant, three rooftops surrounded by trees dotted the rural scene, but other than the tractor, the fields appeared deserted. Directly in front of him and some way from where Jakobs had landed was a barn. It was large and had a double door opening onto an intersection with another dirt road. The door was closed.

Clement walked down the hill, his gaze on the track beneath his feet. On a fine day, and in the warmer months, the unsealed track presented no difficulty to anyone walking but on a wet, wintery night, the dirt ground would be a slippery quagmire. No problem for a tractor but not a car. At the intersection he turned a full three hundred and sixty degrees. While the view from the hill had allowed him to see the whole area like a diorama at the museum, once on the flat land, things were not so obvious. The sound of the far-off tractor was the only noise in the pristine air. Clement turned his gaze south, to the copse, and began to walk towards it.

The barn door opened. Clement stopped. A short, robust man with a broad, weathered face and lively eyes came out and walked towards him. He wore a heavy tweed jacket and cap and his boots bore testimony to a lifetime of farming. From what Clement could tell, the man didn't seem at all surprised to see him standing in his field. At least not until the man's eyes saw the clerical collar.

'Help you with something, Vicar?' the farmer said, his darting eyes taking in the police vehicle parked on the hill.

'Mr Chisholm?' Clement asked.

'Yes. You with them?' Chisholm nodded in the direction of the parked car.

'Assisting with their enquiries.'

The farmer's eyebrows rose. 'Didn't think it would be long.'

'Do you mind going over once more what you found the day the German landed in your field?'

Chisholm shrugged. 'Found him there,' he said, pointing to the field off to his right.

'How long ago?' Clement asked.

'I'll tell you to the minute. First day of February, at exactly twenty minutes past eight in the morning. I was outside my backdoor, there,' Chisholm said, pointing towards the rooftops half a mile away and in the opposite direction from the copse. 'I was giving instructions to my three farmhands about the work for the day when we heard the shots. I got my rifle from the house and we went to investigate. Found him, bold as brass, lying on his back, his parachute over him like a blanket in the middle of my south pasture.'

'Then what?'

'I sent Ben back to call the Home Guard. I kept my rifle on him. He'd broken his ankle so he wasn't going anywhere.'

'How long before the Home Guard arrived?'

'At least an hour. Then almost another hour for Ramsey Police to come. And another for them to decide who was in charge.'

Clement stifled a smile. 'That seems a long time.'

'Yes. That's what I said at the time,' Chisholm said pursing his lips. 'But I'm just a stupid farmer so who listens to me?'

Clement heard the sarcasm and decided not to pursue that line of questioning further. 'Why do you think the second pistol wasn't found earlier?'

Chisholm looked back over the fields, as though reliving the day. 'Too far away from the blighter, I suppose.'

'You never saw it while tending your fields?'

'How could I when it was buried under mud and melting snow? Besides, I was told then they had removed everything.'

Clement nodded. He knew what had been found with the man they now knew to be Josef Jakobs. Further to what Morris had already told him, during the drive from Cambridge Clement had read both reports from the local Home Guard and Ramsey Police from the time of Jakobs's capture. They said that a German spy had landed in the field and broken his ankle. Jakobs had fired his own pistol three times into the air at first light to attract the attention of some nearby farmworkers. And, as Jakobs had been injured, he was taken immediately into custody and no further investigation of the area had been deemed necessary. Jakobs had had in his possession a Mauser automatic pistol, close to five hundred pounds in cash, a partly damaged code book, a small torch with a flashing device and maps of Upwood and Warboys airfields along with two forged identity cards, a ration book and a black bread sandwich. And, if these were not enough to convict the man, Jakobs had attempted to bury an attaché case containing a wireless transmitter under his body using a small trenching shovel later found at the scene.

'It's a mystery, though,' Chisholm said, his hands in his pockets.

'How so, Mr Chisholm?'

'Why he had two pistols. They took the one they found in his helmet. I suppose they didn't think he would have two. But it doesn't surprise me.'

'Why would that be, Mr Chisholm?' Clement asked.

'I heard four shots. I told that Captain Thew of the Home Guard at the time, but he said I was mistaken;

only three bullets missing from the chamber he kept telling me, and some nonsense about echoes in fog. I never touched the gun, of course, so I can't swear to how many were missing from the chamber. They took him away after that. I heard they shipped him off to London.'

'Did you see anything else unusual that morning?'

'By mid-morning the place was swarming with Home Guard and police trampling all over my land. If anything else happened that day, I didn't notice it.'

Clement looked away over the fields, his gaze settling on a low wooden bridge-like structure adjacent to where they were standing. It was flat, the sturdy timbers resembling railway sleepers laid sideways and sufficiently wide enough for a tractor to cross. He walked towards it. The wooden platform forded a ditch of about four to six feet in depth which extended the full length of the paddock and was half filled with water. 'Is this a natural stream?'

Chisholm shook his head. 'Drainage ditch. There's hundreds of them in this part of Cambridgeshire. This is fenland. Not from around here, are you?'

Clement smiled. 'Not highly visible, are they?'

'No. Well, if that's it?'

'Thank you, Mr Chisholm. For now.'

Chisholm grunted and turned to leave.

Clement looked up at the sky. During a full moon, the wide fields would be bathed in moonlight but the water trenches would barely be visible to anyone walking there. And with little nocturnal light, the ditches would be invisible hazards for both vehicles and anyone on foot. He glanced back to where Morris had parked the car then to Chisholm who had left him and was just opening the barn door. 'How many such channels are in these fields, Mr Chisholm?' Clement called.

Chisholm turned. 'They border every field, that's why the roads zig-zag around the pastures. Most have crossings like this one. It's how the tractor gets from one paddock to another,' he said, pointing to the wooden platform. 'But you need to know where they are. Or you'll break your leg, or worse, damage the tractor.'

'Could a car cross them?'

'If they'll take the weight of a tractor, they'll take a car. But it would be a damn-fool thing to do in winter. It would be bogged within seconds.'

'But it is possible?'

'I suppose. The driver would have to know where to cross.'

'Do you employ itinerant workers?'

'Used to. Can't get them now.' Chisholm pulled a large handkerchief from his pocket. There was something about the gesture that made Clement feel he was not only trespassing on Chisholm's land but also on his time. 'Well, thank you, Mr Chisholm.'

'Not just a stupid farmer after all, was I?' Chisholm said, his hand on the barn door handle.

Clement took the opportunity to question further. 'Thinking back to that morning, would you say there was anything different about the fourth shot?'

'As I told Captain Thew at the time, it seemed quieter

than the others.'

'Were the shots fired in succession?'

'The first three came quickly then there was a delay for the last. That's why Thew said it was an echo. Total rubbish.'

'How long between each of the shots, would you say?' Clement said ignoring the slur on Captain Thew's judgement.

'A second or two between the first three then about five to ten seconds to the fourth.'

'Could it have come from a different direction?'

Chisholm left the barn door and walked towards Clement. 'From the copse, you mean? Possibly. I just don't remember. It was four months ago.'

Clement smiled. 'Do you recall seeing any cars on the roads that day?'

Chisholm shook his head. 'Can't see the main road from here. I see the occasional lorry passing from time to time over there,' he said, pointing across the fields at least a mile distant. 'The hedges are too high to see cars. Besides, it was winter, and as I said, no one in their right mind would drive a car into these fields and expect to drive out.'

'Well, thank you again, Mr Chisholm.'

Chisholm turned and without further discussion disappeared into the barn.

Clement started walking towards the copse. The large oak trees there were already in leaf, the vibrant green of new foliage intertwined above the bushes. Once level with the copse, Clement turned back again to see Morris's car. The black police vehicle was barely discernible against the dark green foliage on the hill. He frowned. He knew, of course, that it was there but he couldn't see it that well. He paused. If the dead man had not jumped as he and Morris had speculated, but had, in fact, driven there to meet someone who did parachute down, did he know a car parked there wasn't easily visible? Had he walked to the copse to meet someone who didn't know where the car was parked? The limited amount of mud on his trousers suggested it. Did it also imply that he knew it was unwise to drive across the fields? That, surely, would suggest local knowledge. Clement stared into the ditch before him. It lay between where he stood and the copse. He lifted his gaze to the boundary hedge that separated Chisholm's land from the neighbouring farmer's land, a man named Ward.

Clement jumped the trench, scrambling up the grassy slope to the other side. In front of him was a hedge. He pushed his way through the foliage to a clear space surrounded by mature trees. It was cool. Much cooler than the open fields. Underfoot were rotting leaves and damp, decomposing branches and twigs but the space was larger than Clement had expected. He stood there, slowly turning, taking in everything. He saw the disturbed earth and shallow grave where the body had been discovered, the soil still heaped to one side. Even with the trees devoid of leaf in mid-winter, anyone in this copse would be completely unobserved. The cover of night had meant that no one had witnessed either Jakobs's descent or anyone else's. Moreover, if the fourth shot was the one that killed the man in Morris's mortuary, it stood to reason that anyone in the fields that morning would be attending to Jakobs, never suspecting that someone else was there. Clement stood beside the shallow grave and tried to imagine what had happened that morning. He knew Jakobs had had a hand shovel with him so perhaps it was standard equipment for Nazi spies. Even so, the shallow grave would have taken little time to dig in the moist soil of the copse. A man had parachuted into England and made his way to the copse to rendezvous with someone. Had that someone been the man wearing the turn-ups? Or had he gone there at first light to meet someone who'd then killed him? Clement rubbed at his furrowed brow. Surely if his death was a straightforward case of murder, the man's body would have been found by the road or in one of the ditches near the tracks, not half-buried in a copse a mile distant from the main road.

Clement turned again, his steady gaze on the copse. Under some of the hanging branches he saw a narrow track leading away from the copse. It led in the opposite direction from where he had entered. Clement pushed his way through the foliage. The path followed the boundary hedgerow on the neighbouring property's side. Taking it, Clement walked a few hundred yards, the hedge concealing him from anyone on Chisholm's land. He crossed a wooden platform then walked on to where the track rejoined the unsealed gravelled road not fifty yards from Chisholm's barn. Clement stared at Morris's car parked on the ridge above the barn. If someone had landed then killed the man sent to collect him, how did he know about the path or that a car was parked on the ridge? How did whoever jumped even know where he was in England? Clement shook his head. Perhaps car headlights had been flashed? If that were true, then another person had sat waiting in the car. So why send the man to make the rendezvous at all? Clement strode back up the hill towards Morris.

'Anything?' Morris asked as Clement closed the car door.

'Interesting.' Clement told Morris what Chisholm had said and about the ditches that criss-crossed the fields and the track on Ward's land.

Morris switched on the engine and turning the car around, headed back up the hill towards the main road. 'Chisholm said you can't see any cars on the roads from the fields because of the height of the hedges. Do you know, Arthur, while I could see this car today from the copse, I'm not so sure I would at dawn on a winter's morning, unless I knew where to look or had some binoculars or perhaps seen flashing lights. Was anyone found here waiting to collect Jakobs?'

'No. But that's not to say no one was here. If Jakobs failed to make a rendezvous with anyone sent to collect him, that person would leave the area and quickly, I would've thought. Especially if he'd seen the Home

Guard and police cars arriving.

'Was there any moonlight on the night Jakobs landed?'

'Little. Four days into the new moon.'

'Too dark to travel across farmland but not too dark to jump,' Clement said half to himself. He looked across at Morris. 'Assuming two people did land that night, and assuming Jakobs didn't know about another jumper, why did the killer wait until Jakobs fired his pistol before shooting our man? How did he even know Jakobs was still in the field and not far away? Was it purely opportunistic?'

Morris waited before responding. 'Perhaps the killer assumed Jakobs was well away. So when Jakobs fired his weapon, the killer took advantage of the situation.'

'Or did they know Jakobs was injured?' Clement suggested. 'Was Jakobs's parachute examined for sabotage?'

'I'll get that checked.'

'What do we make of all this?' Clement went on, the question rhetorical which Morris seemed to understand. 'Whoever jumped stayed in the copse till first light it being too dark and too dangerous to travel at night. I've seen those ditches. You could be seriously injured if you fell into them. Then they waited till first light to shoot the person who came to the rendezvous. Why?'

'No further need of him?'

'So our man came by car to collect him from the copse and believed he was to lead whoever landed back to the car. Instead he was shot in the copse. A one-way walk. The clothes would bear this theory out.'

'So either whoever landed knew exactly where he was and could drive himself or a third person was in the car waiting?'

Clement bit into his lip. 'But it does mean one thing, Arthur; Jakobs knew nothing about the second jumper or that someone else was there. If Jakobs had, he would never have fired his pistol into the air to attract those workers.'

'It also explains the delay between the third and fourth shots.'

Clement was deep in thought. 'Could we speak to Mr Ward?'

'Of course,' Morris said. 'It is unlikely he can add anything as he was in Ramsey the day Jakobs landed. But he may have remembered something unusual now he's had time to reflect.'

Morris drove about five miles south along the main road before turning left. Ward's house was close by. Morris drove in and switched off the engine. Within seconds a grey-haired man with deeply furrowed skin and a long flat nose came from an outbuilding at the side of the house. A spaniel dog was beside him.

'Mr Ward. Superintendent Morris.'

'I remember you. Not in uniform today?'

'I now only wear it for official duties.'

Ward's eyes shifted to Clement. 'And you?'

'Helping us with our investigations,' Morris said.

'Haven't seen any police for a while. I figured

Chisholm finding that pistol would have you all return-ing. Are you any closer to identifying that body?'

'We are pursuing inquiries, Mr Ward,' Morris told him.

'I understand you were in Ramsey the day the German landed?' Clement asked.

'That's right.'

'When did you return home?'

Ward seemed to stare into the distance. 'Around noon that day.'

'I imagine you would know most of the people here-abouts. Did you see any strangers either in town or around here?'

Ward scratched his head. 'Not that I recall. I stayed at The Angel in Ramsey then went to Miller's for the seed and produce I ordered, then I drove home. It wasn't till I got back that I heard about the Jerry landing in Chisholm's field.'

'Do you recall seeing any cars you didn't recognise on the roads on your way home?'

'I remember seeing a few police vehicles so I knew something was amiss.'

Clement paused. If Ward had been in Ramsey, there was little he could add. Morris seemed to sense there were no further questions.

'Well, thank you for your time. Should you remember anything else perhaps you would be good enough to call Cambridge Police,' Morris added.

Clement saw Morris check his watch. It was already

mid-afternoon and perhaps Morris was hungry.

'Is Ramsey the nearest town of any size, Mr Ward?' Clement asked.

'Yes.'

'Is there a public house in Wistow?'

'No. But there are several in Ramsey. *The Plough* would be best for you. You can get a meal there too.'

'Thank you, again,' Clement said.

He and Morris returned to the car and drove away. Ward stood with his dog, watching them leave.

Clement stared through the windscreen at nothing in particular. 'Why would someone who parachuted into England, kill the person who came to meet them? It doesn't make any sense.'

'Unless he already knew where he was and didn't need the contact?' Morris said glancing at Clement.

'So why send the contact to the rendezvous when he could have just remained in the car?'

Morris didn't respond.

Clement allowed the thought to flow through his mind. Was it possible the man was sent to his death? It didn't seem likely. 'So our man arrives and walks to the copse to make the rendezvous. There he is killed. The killer then buries the body, leaves the copse, with the parachute and meets a third person who is waiting in the car. Or, he drives himself away knowing where the car is parked and how to get to where he is going. You know, Arthur, given the hour of day the shots were fired, who-ever came to meet the parachutist would've needed to be already in the vicinity the night before the rendez-vous. Could we go to Ramsey before returning to Cambridge?'

'Of course.' Morris pulled onto the road and headed north.

'Let's check *The Angel* first. That way we can check on Ward's alibi at the same time,' Clement said as they drove into Ramsey. Morris parked the car in the High Street and they walked into the tiny inn that fronted directly onto the street. Once inside, Clement could see why Ward had recommended a different public house. *The Angel* was a working man's pub, the sort of inn rarely, if ever, frequented by women, with little in the way of decoration or comfort. Clement surmised that any accommodation would be similarly spartan. Morris showed the publican his warrant card and asked to see the register. Opening the book, Morris saw only one person had stayed on the night of January the thirty-first. 'Do you remember seeing any strangers in town, especially a man of medium height, in his mid-to-late forties, wearing a coat and trousers with turn-ups? The cloth had a thin blue stripe in the weave?'

The innkeeper slowly shook his head but he didn't speak.

'Did you see any unfamiliar vehicles that day?' Clement added.

Again the publican shook his head. 'No one other than my locals come here.'

'Thank you. If you remember anything unusual about

that night, please call me at Cambridge Police.' Morris left his card on the counter. Clement turned to face the patrons; all eyes were on him and Morris. No one spoke.

'Not very forthcoming were they?' Clement said quietly as they walked back to the car.

'Decidedly frosty. I'll ask Sergeant Kendall to check any black market activities in Ramsey, paying particular attention to *The Angel* and Mr Ward's visits to town.'

'At least Ward was telling the truth about being there. Where to next?'

'Are you hungry, Clement?' Morris asked opening the car door.

'I am.'

'Then it's *The Plough* next, I think,' Morris said, starting the engine. 'It's a bit late but we might be lucky.'

The Plough was at the northern end of Ramsey and stood at the end of a line of two-storey buildings that overlooked a pond of reasonable size, a Virginia creeper covering the whole façade. At the side of the inn was a narrow lane that Clement guessed led to the rear of the hotel. Stepping from the car, Clement looked around. Opposite, the road curved around a church of considerable size and beyond it and the graveyard were some very high stone walls. Set further back was an imposing but ruined gatehouse.

'The Abbey School is behind the fence,' Morris said. 'The estate used to be a twelfth-century monastery, then the home of the Lords De Ramsey until about a decade ago when it was given to the school.'

Clement opened the door to *The Plough*. Inside was dark. No one was there. Several tables and chairs occupied the front space near the window. Towards the rear was the bar and behind that a door with the word 'Private' painted on it in red. To the left was a narrow staircase that led upstairs. Morris hit the bell on the counter. A young woman of approximately twenty appeared.

'Can we get something to eat?' Morris asked.

'It's lamb stew today. I think there's enough left for you two gents.'

'That will do us nicely. And two teas, when you're ready,' Morris added. Checking his watch. 'How much?'

'That will be 2/6 each,' she said. Morris placed two half-crowns on the counter.

The girl disappeared, doubtless to place their order, then returned and scooping up the money began to clean the counter. Morris waited by the bar. 'Do you recall the German who landed in these parts a few months ago?'

'Of course! It was all the talk for weeks. And in the papers. He didn't cause any trouble though. Broke his ankle on landing. The Home Guard took him away. He was at Ramsey Police Station for a bit. You reporters?'

Morris reached for his warrant card.

'I heard about him finding that pistol,' the girl said. 'I'm guessing that's why you're here again.'

Clement looked up. Morris was frowning.

'Can I ask you about that time, Miss…?' Morris called.

'Bathgate. Cariss Bathgate.'

'Who's asking?' a man said, entering the bar. 'I'm the licensee. What do you want to know?'

'They're policemen, Dad.'

'Oh, yes.'

Morris pulled out his warrant card again. 'Do you recall seeing any unfamiliar people or vehicles around the village that day or in the days before the German landed?'

'Unfamiliar cars? I don't think so; what with the petrol rationing, you don't see many these days.'

'Yes, Dad. Remember. That swish one with the convertible top. Not like any car I've ever seen.'

'Oh, yes. Very posh. And cost a pretty penny, I'll be bound. Never seen it before or since.'

'Do you know what type it was?' Morris asked.

'No. But I would recognise it again if I saw it.'

Morris waited, the publican went on. 'Flash! Light green it was, with a convertible roof, cream coloured canvas. A good thing he only had two suitcases, because the boot wasn't big. And there was no back seat.'

'Two suitcases?' Morris asked. Clement caught his eye. Morris went on, 'Do you remember anything about the driver?'

Bathgate drew in a long breath. 'He booked a room for the night but he left early the next morning so I didn't get to talk to him. Although he wasn't exactly the chatty type.'

'What type would you say he was, Mr Bathgate?'

Clement asked, approaching the bar.

'Toff. Not from around these parts. But it's hard to tell. Once they get that public school accent, there's no telling where they're from.'

'Did he sign the register?' Morris asked.

'Must have. I'll get it,' Bathgate said and left the main bar.

A few minutes later the man returned. He placed a leather-bound book on the bar and thumbed back through the pages. 'Night of thirty-first of January.' Bathgate ran his finger down the page. 'Here it is. Gave his name as Smith. Didn't believe it. But then they usually have a girl with them when they give that name.'

'And he didn't?' Morris asked.

'No.' The publican paused, a slow frown forming. 'He did meet someone though, as I recollect. Not here. Across the way, there.' Bathgate pointed through the window at the road on the other side of the pond.

'Did they come back here?' Morris asked.

'I don't think he was that way inclined. You can always tell by the bed sheets if there's been any activity, if you know what I mean.'

'Did the man Mr Smith met also stay here?'

Bathgate shook his head.

'What address did Mr Smith give you?' Morris asked.

Bathgate looked again at the register. 'Cambridge. Not much help, is it?'

'This person Mr Smith met outside, was he local?' Clement asked.

'No.'

'You're sure about that?'

'Oh yes. I'd have known him if he was. Lived in Ramsey all my life.'

'Can you describe this other man?'

Bathgate gazed through the window as though trying to remember. 'Too long ago. I couldn't really see his face. He wasn't as tall as our Mr Smith. Ordinary, really.'

'Approximate age?'

'Hard to say. Older than Smith, but not elderly.'

'And you've never seen him before?'

'Nor since.'

'And Mr Smith stayed here that night?'

'Yes. He ate in his room and left early.'

'Where was the car?'

'Parked out back overnight. He was insistent about that. But as I said, he left early.'

'Did you see him leave?'

'No.'

'Nothing left in his room?'

Bathgate shook his head. 'But I'll tell you this; that man he met across the way there. From different ends of the social order those two and no mistake.'

'Why do you say that, Mr Bathgate?' Clement asked.

'The clothes. Regardless of the name, Smith was gentry. Flashy car, public school accent, gentleman's clothes and upper class manners; especially when it came to giving orders. That man he met, over there,' Bathgate said nodding again towards the road, 'he was no gentleman.

His clothes were old and worn, never seen a tailor. Trousers even had turn-ups.'

5

'Can you describe this Mr Smith?' Morris asked.

Bathgate leaned into the corner of the bar and gripped his chin as though thinking. 'Tall, slim build with fair hair. Cut quite short as I recall. About thirty, and like I said, well-dressed with a posh accent.'

'Anything else about him? Any distinctive marks? Anything about his manner or stance?' Morris asked.

'Anything at all, Mr Bathgate, that made him memorable – like a speech impediment or a limp?' Clement added.

Bathgate drew in his upper lip. 'He was…' Bathgate paused. 'Cocky. He had big teeth and a silly grin on his face the whole time. Made you wonder if he wasn't simple.'

'And the man he met?' Clement added.

'Like I said, he didn't stay here so I didn't get a good look at him. Nothing much comes to mind. I saw them meet. They exchanged a few words then parted.'

'The shorter man; which way did he go when he left?' Clement asked.

'Back into town. He walked quickly, with his hands in his coat pockets. Now I think about it, he wasn't a farmer.'

'What makes you say that, Mr Bathgate?' Morris said.

'Farmers walk slowly in town and with a longer stride. No, he wasn't a farmer.'

'What would you say, judging by his clothes, was his occupation?' Morris asked.

'Not a shopkeeper. Nor a clerk. A labourer of some kind would be my guess.'

'He had two suitcases. Mr Smith that is,' Cariss said on re-entering the room, a plate of hot food in each hand.

'They already know that, Cariss. Besides, they want to know what he looked like, girl, not his luggage.'

'Anything either of you can remember would be helpful,' Clement added. 'Can you recall, Miss Bathgate, if he took both his suitcases to his room?'

'Yes. I thought that was odd.'

'How so?'

'Well, why would he need two suitcases? He was hardly going to dress for dinner which he ended up having in his room on his own. Why would he want so many clothes for one night?'

'Thank you, Miss Bathgate,' Morris smiled and the

girl left them. Clement glanced at Morris. The girl's comment confirmed Clement's suspicion that the second suitcase most likely contained a wireless transmitter. He heard the swing door to the kitchen close.

Morris returned his gaze to the publican. 'About the car…'

'Caused quite a stir.'

'Oh?'

'No one hereabouts would have ever seen anything like that before. Even old Harry Hardacre came to have a look.'

'Mr Hardacre is acquainted with cars, I gather?' Morris asked.

'Has the garage in town. Said he'd read about the make but I don't remember what it was. I knew I'd never heard of it. But he'll remember. Talked about it for weeks.'

'Everyone seems to have known about the car,' Morris added.

'Small place and fancy car. Bound to bring the lads out. Although it was parked out the back. He insisted on that. Smith that is; didn't want it parked in the street.'

'Did he give a reason?' Clement asked.

'Didn't want the local kids touching it, I reckon.'

'Mr Hardacre's garage is where?' Morris asked.

'Out the door turn right and take the first on your right. Can't miss it,' Bathgate told Morris.

Finishing the meal they thanked the publican and left.

An elderly man sat in a frayed armchair in the doorway to the mechanic's garage. Beside him was an equally ancient dog.

'Mr Hardacre?' Morris asked.

'The same.'

'I am wondering if you remember a car that was here in Ramsey about four months ago? A convertible car. I understand it was green with...'

'Oh, the Lagonda. Yes, I remember it.'

'Have you seen it again since that day?'

'No. Just the once. It was parked out back of *The Plough*. My boy Robert wheeled me around to see it. Quite a machine and not a mark on it.'

'Thank you, Mr Hardacre.'

'That all?' he said, his rheumy eyes darting to Morris. 'I figured that gun found on Chisholm's place would have you returning. So the boy in the flash car is involved, is he?'

'You know the owner?'

'Not personally. Perhaps you should ask the De Ramseys. Although I hear His Lordship is with his regiment in the Far East now.' The old man closed his eyes as if to say that's all you're getting from me.

'Don't mind him,' a voice said coming towards them. The man wiped his hands on an oily cloth. 'I'm Robert Hardacre. My father grew up on the De Ramsey Estate. His Lordship isn't the most popular of men.'

Clement would liked to have known why but the old man appeared to have fallen asleep.

'Please thank your father for his help,' Morris said.

Clement and Morris walked back to where the police car was parked outside *The Plough*. Clement stood beside the car, staring at the old Abbey ruins. His gaze fixed on the spot where, so Bathgate had told them, Smith had met with another man wearing trousers with turn-ups. It was beside a level grassed area where a gravel drive led to the ruined gatehouse. Centuries old and made of stone, the gatehouse had a central arch surrounded by a twenty foot high stone wall that extended on both sides of the ancient structure. To the left the wall extended for some fifty yards before turning at right angles towards the church and an enclosed graveyard. To the right of the arch and set within the wall was a mullion window. The massive wooden double gate was closed. Clement frowned. 'Does the Abbey School have access to the gatehouse, do you know, Arthur?'

'I don't. But it's possible, given its location. The school is just behind that high wall.'

Clement stared at the twenty foot wall that extended down the right side of the gate then turned left running along the edge of the street that headed out of Ramsey.

'Is there a room behind that window?' Clement asked, his gaze fixed on the ruin. He didn't wait for Morris to respond. Crossing the road, Clement strode towards the street to the right of the gatehouse. A low narrow door-way with a small, ancient wooden door and carved pointed lintel faced directly onto the street. He tried the handle but it was locked and looked as though it had been for many years. Clement stared up. He could see the rough jagged edges of the ruined stonework but he couldn't see if a room remained within the structure.

'Care to share your thoughts, Clement?' Morris said, now beside him.

'The school is behind this wall, you say?'

Morris nodded.

'When I was at school there were always boys who seemed to know what went on outside the school grounds. They knew how to get out of the school without being seen. And get back in. They had a knack for sourcing things that other boys only dreamt about. It may yield us nothing, Arthur, but I think it's worth checking if, on the off-chance, a boy could have been here and either heard or saw Smith meet with this other man.'

They walked back to the car then took the road out of Ramsey to the east; the road that followed the curve of the massive wall. Minutes later they saw the school's wide entrance with large iron gates. They were open. Morris drove in, following the drive for some distance. Ahead was an expansive field where boys were playing cricket. Beyond was an elegant stately home. Driving up to the house, Morris parked the car at the foot of the front steps and they got out.

'A generous gift for a man who wasn't popular,' Clement said, wondering why the De Ramsey family had given the estate to the school.

'Death duties and taxes would be my guess. Sometimes things are not as altruistic as they at first seem,' Morris said and preceded Clement up the stairs. Pushing open the front door, they went inside where a sign at the foot of a handsomely carved staircase indicated the location of the school office. Following the sign, they found a woman sitting behind a desk in a small partitioned office. 'Would it be possible to see the headmaster?' Morris asked.

'Do you have an appointment?' the woman asked, her gaze shifting from Morris to Clement and lingering on his clerical collar. Morris produced his warrant card.

'One moment,' she said, lifting the telephone receiver. 'I have the police here, Headmaster. They wish to speak to you.' She waited a few seconds before replacing the receiver. 'Mr Hetherington will see you now. I'll show you the way.'

The woman led them up the elegant staircase to a wide landing where a timber panelled corridor ran the length of the building in both directions. Lining the walls were tall-backed chairs but no one sat there waiting to see the headmaster today. The woman knocked.

'Enter', a stern-voiced man replied.

'Please go in,' she said and left them.

The headmaster occupied a lavish room with a large window overlooking the vast playing field below. A man of mature years and wearing an academic gown stood from behind his desk and walked towards them.

'I understand from Miss Cook that you are policemen? Although I've never heard of a policeman in orders before. How can I help you?' Hetherington gestured towards two leather chairs before his ornate desk.

Clement smiled and showed the headmaster his security card. 'Special Duties? An even more unusual occupation for a vicar. What brings you to our door?'

'Just exploring possibilities, Headmaster. Nothing for you to worry about,' Clement replied.

'This may seem an odd request,' Morris began, 'but it is an important one; one that involves the security of our nation.'

Hetherington frowned but remained silent.

'An incident occurred outside the school fence near the old gatehouse some months ago. We are wondering if anyone, teacher or pupil, may have witnessed it?'

'What sort of incident?'

'Two men met there on the morning of the thirty-first of January.'

'Oh, yes?' Hetherington said, his stern eyes fixed on Morris.

'The day a German was discovered with a broken ankle in Mr Chisholm's field out near Wistow?'

'I remember it,' Hetherington said. 'What makes you suspect these men were witnessed?'

'It's just a theory at this stage, Headmaster.'

'I see.' Hetherington paused. 'There is a group of boys who have been reprimanded in the past for being on the wall. Generally they are no trouble but they are easily led. One boy in particular seems to exert influence. There is, of course, no guarantee that any of them were there that day.'

'Of course. Could we speak to this boy?' Morris asked.

Hetherington reached forward and grasped the telephone. 'Miss Cook, ask Michael Hasluck to come to my study immediately.' The headmaster replaced the receiver and leaned back in his chair, his gaze firmly on Clement but he remained silent.

'You have a very lovely building and grounds for your school,' Clement said. 'I understand it was a gift?'

Hetherington's startlingly blue eyes looked steadily at Clement. 'Many of our great families have been forced to endure the ignominy of divesting themselves of property or face the onerous burden of excessively harsh taxes. Our authorities should be mindful of the enormous and often unseen sacrifices our aristocratic families have made. People should know their place. However, it is the modern way, it seems. And the school has certainly benefited.'

Clement thought Hetherington was about to continue with what he evidently saw as an unnecessary and unjust breach of social protocol when a knock at the door ended the headmaster's speech.

'Enter,' Hetherington boomed.

A boy of approximately ten years of age appeared in the headmaster's study. His shoes looked scuffed and his shirt hung below his purple jacket. Clement hid a smile.

He knew the type. Not really a naughty boy, just mischievous. Such boys were often in trouble but this usually created a sharp mind and a quick tongue for evading punishment.

'Take your hands from your pockets, Hasluck. These gentlemen are from the police. They have some questions for you.'

Clement glanced at the boy. When he was ten, the headmaster telling him the police wanted to question him would have made him want to rush to the lavatory. But Hasluck was taking it all in his stride. In fact, Clement thought Hasluck would be able to entertain the whole lower school for months on this story. Hetherington remained seated, his hand inches from a leather strap that sat rolled on his desk.

Morris turned to face the lad. 'A few months ago, in late January, there was an unusual car seen in Ramsey. I was wondering if you saw it? Perhaps around the ruins?'

The boys eyes moved to the school principal.

'Tell the truth, Hasluck,' Hetherington said. 'This time your indiscretions will not be punished.'

The boy's gaze returned to Morris. 'I saw it. That was the day they got that Jerry who landed in Chisholm's field. The car was amazing. Silver-green convertible. A Lagonda.'

The boy was almost salivating; his intonation one of admiration and envy.

'You're sure that was the make?' Clement asked.

'Saw it in a magazine. Really expensive. V12 motor.

Goes like the wind.'

'Where did you see it?' Morris asked.

'Parked beside the pond.'

'Do you remember at what time of day?'

'Morning. Early.'

'You mean at dawn?' Clement asked.

'No, later. Just before morning bell.'

Hetherington's glare remained fixed on the boy. 'Bell goes at eight twenty-five, Superintendent.'

'Did you see the man driving it?' Clement asked.

The boy nodded.

'Can you describe him?'

'I can describe both of them, if you want.'

'Both?' Morris said.

'The one who drove the car got out. He threw something into the pond.'

'Do you know what?' Morris asked.

'It was large. Like a box or a suitcase. Produced ever such a splash!'

'Then what?'

'He lit a cigarette.' Hasluck glanced at the headmaster. 'I asked him for one.'

'You mean you called to him from the wall?' Clement asked.

Hasluck shook his head. 'I climb over the gate. It isn't hard. The space at the top is just wide enough for me to squeeze through. Sometimes the older boys pay me to do it and I get them things.'

Hetherington's eyes flared, but he remained silent.

'Did one of the older boys ask you to climb over that day?' Clement asked.

'No. I saw the man smoking, so I climbed over the gate and ran across the grass to where he was parked. It was really cold. It snowed later that day.'

Clement looked at the boy. 'How do you get back?'

'I climb up the jagged stones near the little door and jump from there. It's really easy.'

'The man who gave you the cigarette, can you describe him?'

'He was tall. He had really big teeth. And he smelt of expensive tobacco.'

'Anything else about him?' Morris asked.

'When he walked towards the pond, I saw him flick the cigarette into the water. He had a swagger. And his legs were sort of bowed. He was a bit ugly.'

'Was he an old man?' Clement asked.

'No. Not as old as my father but older than the senior boys here. He said I reminded him of himself when he was at school. I asked him if he went to this school. He said he didn't. He said he was a...' The boy thought for a while. 'A wickedness. I didn't know what he meant but he said it was the best school in England.'

'And the other man?' Clement asked.

'He stayed in the car. He looked at me then turned away. I thought his head looked like a ball. It was really round. His hair was flattened down so he must use hair cream. My father uses it too. He thinks it makes him look stylish but I think it's because he doesn't have much hair.'

'And this man in the car, did he also not have much hair?' Morris asked.

'No. He had hair but he uses hair cream.'

'What colour was it, fair or dark?'

'Dark. He also had a moustache and a really big chin,' Michael added, jutting out his jaw.

Clement stifled a grin. 'Could you see what he was wearing?'

'No. There was a big suitcase behind his seat though. Must have been too big for the boot because it was in sideways, with one corner poking up.'

'Did this man say anything?'

'No but he looked grumpy.'

'How do you know that?' Morris asked.

'He had a scowl on his face.'

'Then what happened?'

'That's when *Big Teeth* threw his cigarette away. Then, he got back into the car. Must have only had two puffs. What a waste.'

'Did you get the impression these men were friends?' Clement asked.

Hasluck shook his head again. 'I don't really know.' The boy grinned. 'But as he got back into the car, he smiled at me and tossed the whole cigarette packet to me. There were six left. Who does that?'

Clement looked up at Morris. 'What happened then, Michael?'

'They drove away.'

'Which way did they go?'

'The road that leads out of Ramsey, past the old gate-house.'

'Thank you, Michael. You've been most helpful. Should you remember anything else perhaps you could inform Mr Hetherington?' Morris said, looking from Michael to the school principal.

The boy nodded, his small hands going back into the pockets before glancing at the headmaster.

'Straight back to class now, Hasluck,' Hetherington barked.

The boy left the headmaster's study and Hetherington walked with Clement and Morris to the landing outside his office. 'He's not a bad boy. Just an insolent one,' Hetherington said. 'Parents are often away.'

'Thank you for allowing us to speak to him, Headmaster,' Morris said.

It was nearly six o'clock when they drove away from Ramsey. Clement stared out the window at the flat fields as they drove south, back to Cambridge.

'You know, Arthur, the more I think about it, with or without a tampered parachute, I think Jakobs was nothing more than a decoy.'

'Interesting theory.'

'I should know more after I've spoken with him.'

'When will that be?'

'Tomorrow...' Clement paused. 'I'd also like to know why someone who was so insistent that his car was parked at the rear of the inn, chose to drive such a distinctly memorable vehicle anyway?'

'Perhaps he thought no one would connect him with Jakobs. And, in fact, there isn't any proof that he is. But I have always thought there was more to this death than met the eye,' Morris said.

They drove in silence for some miles. Verdant green fields rolled away to a gentle blue sky. There was no sound of bombers today, nor the pulsating drum of enemy fighters, nor, in fact, the quick burring of friendly aircraft. Yet the tranquil scene held more secrets to be revealed. 'From young Hasluck's description, and the time of day, this other man in the car doesn't sound like our man in the mortuary. Bathgate said that Smith left early. Did he meet up with our deceased man here in Ramsey before going to Wistow or not at all? Was he even connected to Smith?'

Morris didn't respond immediately. 'We don't have any proof that the man Bathgate saw with the turn-ups actually knew Smith or even if he is the same man as seen by Bathgate. Moreover, Clement, he could merely have been asking Smith the time of day.'

Clement sighed. He needed to think. 'Perhaps I should stay overnight in Cambridge.'

'Happy to put you up, Clement.'

'Thank you, Arthur.' His thoughts returned to Smith. 'If we believe Bathgate, Smith met with a man wearing turn-ups. If he is the corpse in the mortuary, and if Smith drove him to the field at Wistow where our man was killed, that would explain the limited amount of mud on the man's clothes. Then Smith meets with a different man; the one young Hasluck witnessed in the Lagonda. Can you ask your people to check the pond and find out what Smith threw into it?'

'Already thought of that,' Morris said.

Clement continued. 'If Smith left Ramsey before dawn with our man in the mortuary, then waited at Wistow to collect this man with dark hair, why did he return to Ramsey?'

'To dispose of the suitcase young Hasluck saw most likely, containing either a radio transmitter or the parachute.'

'Is that a sufficient reason?'

'Perhaps it is as simple as that, Clement. The drainage ditches are too shallow, and the current in streams or rivers will, eventually, uncover anything submerged, so a still pond is far more preferable for permanently disposing of things.'

Clement stared at the winding, twisting road before them as they drove back to Cambridge. Was it as simple as that? Or was there another reason Smith had returned to Ramsey?

6

Friday 30th May 1941

Morris drove the car into the precinct of Cambridge Railway Station and Clement alighted. It was still early but already the railway forecourt was crammed with people. 'Thanks for the lift, Arthur. And for putting me up last night. An enjoyable evening, given the circumstances. All being well, I'll most likely be back late tonight.'

'You're welcome to stay with me again, if you wish.'

'Thank you. Most generous.' Shaking hands with the Superintendent, Clement made his way to the ticket office.

Twenty minutes later he boarded the train. The corridors were crowded with passengers, some standing while others sat on their suitcases, blocking the narrow passageways. Standing in the congested corridor, Clement leaned against the glass partition of a compartment until a young soldier inside offered him his seat. Grateful for the gesture, Clement settled himself quickly then closed his eyes, his mind alive with details and facts. The train rattled and lurched its way south, stopping frequently.

Clement pulled out his notebook and scribbled down some questions he had for Nora Ballantyne. He wanted to know if there'd been any unusual radio traffic in the Ramsey area in late January and whether there had been any SIS operations in Cambridgeshire the night Jakobs landed. The train slowed then stopped. People around him groaned but it was only temporary and the train soon moved slowly forward again. Smith's behaviour worried Clement. Why had he returned to Ramsey? Morris had thought of another possible explanation; Smith wished to use a telephone. This was certainly possible. It was reasonable to assume that Smith would want to let others know of the man's safe arrival. Clement visualised the small township of Ramsey with its still pond. He hadn't noticed any public telephone boxes but he knew a town the size of Ramsey would have some. He decided to ask Morris to check it.

His thoughts then turned to the boy, Michael Hasluck. The lad had seen the car pull up by the pond but he hadn't said from which direction it had come. Nor had the boy said that Smith had done anything other than throw something into it before leaving Ramsey. If

Morris's theory about a telephone call was correct, Smith must have made it before his encounter with Hasluck.

Clement furrowed his brow and listened to the regular rhythmic sounds of the train as his mind continued to sift facts. Three men, three suitcases: the man known as Smith had had two in the boot, one quite possibly a radio transmitter; the second man with the turn-ups was most probably the corpse in the mortuary and also the man the publican Bathgate had seen talking to Smith. The third man had dark hair and a moustache and had also had a suitcase of some size that young Hasluck had seen behind his seat in the car.

If Smith had disposed of the parachute in the pond, what did the suitcase behind the dark-haired man contain? Clement opened his eyes and stared at nothing in particular, his mind replaying events. He wondered why Smith hadn't walked to the copse? Was it just so that Smith didn't have to wade through the boggy Cambridgeshire fen? Clement stared at the windowpane, at the dirty smears formed when a moving train causes rainwater to mix with grime leaving a streaky pattern. A frown settled on his forehead. The more he thought about it, the more he thought the man with the turn-ups had been deliberately sent to his death. He could identify both Smith and the passenger that young Hasluck had also seen. Could he have been murdered for some other reason? *'Turn-up Man'*, Clement reasoned, would have known the car only held two people. Therefore, he would have expected to walk back to Ramsey. But by meeting the dark-haired man in the copse, his fate was sealed. Clement scratched his head. The truth was he had few facts, just assumptions. Other than a brief exchange witnessed by the publican, Bathgate, Smith had been careful not to associate with the man wearing turn-ups while in town. To the casual observer, there was nothing to connect them.

Was it possible that an inquisitive boy with a liking for cigarettes was the only person who had witnessed Smith and the dark-haired man together? Clement sat upright in his seat. If Smith ever learnt that he and Morris were investigating him, the boy could be in danger.

Three hours later Clement stepped from the train and hurried to the taxi rank outside King's Cross Station. Opening the door, he got in and the cab entered the bustling streets around the large station. From what Clement could see, little had changed in the nation's capital during the last few months. Sandbags were still stacked around doorways and windows were boarded up. Damaged buildings, rubble and debris were everywhere.

He alighted at the corner of Whitehall Place. Crossing the road, he strode towards the large elaborate portico and went inside. Hurrying up the stairs, he walked along the corridor to Johnny's office. The door was open but Miss Ballantyne was not at her desk. Clement knocked and a familiar voice responded.

'Come in!'

Clement pushed open the door and stepped inside.

'Clement! What a surprise! Good to see you. What brings you to London?'

Though it couldn't have been more than four months since they had last met, his old friend Captain Johnny Winthorpe looked tired and his hair was decidedly greyer. Clement sat in the chair in front of Johnny's desk and told him what had happened in Cambridgeshire.

Johnny leaned back in his plush leather chair. 'I've read the report on your visit to Corporal Hughes. But the recent developments are concerning.'

Outside, Clement heard the click-clack of high heels on the tiles.

'Would you come in please, Miss Ballantyne?' Johnny called through the open door.

Nora entered and closing the door behind her, flashed a smile at Clement.

'Major Wisdom has some requests,' Johnny said.

'Three things, if you please, Miss Ballantyne,' Clement began. 'Could you make enquiries about unusual radio traffic in Cambridgeshire on the night of the thirty-first of January possibly early morning on the first of February this year? Also, would you please telephone Superintendent Morris of Cambridge Police and ask him to arrange for a boy who attends The Abbey School, Michael Hasluck to be sent home for the remainder of the term. Morris will know what it's about. And thirdly, could you also ask Superintendent Morris to check the locations of all public telephone boxes in Ramsey especially any on the road out of Ramsey travelling east or near to the ruined gatehouse.'

Nora made some notes then turned to leave.

'What are your suspicions, Clement?' Johnny asked.

'It is possible that Jakobs was a decoy.'

'What makes you think that?'

'I think two people jumped from that aeroplane: Jakobs and another. And I think the man who was murdered was the contact, not the jumper. Whoever this second jumper is, his identity has been safeguarded from all but a select few. He is important, Johnny. Important enough that the contact who could recognise him has been murdered.'

'I understand you're meeting Jakobs this afternoon.'

Clement nodded.

'Have you any hard proof about your suspicions?'

'Not yet. What I don't understand is why, if Smith was involved in the murder of that man, would he return to Ramsey and risk being seen, especially with a high profile passenger? Could it be that disposing of the suitcase in such a manner was a signal of some kind?'

Johnny frowned as though deep in thought. 'Perhaps. Your theory about Jakobs being a decoy is interesting. As is your theory about the car. I agree it would be stupidity to use such a memorable vehicle. So, either he wanted to be seen by someone or our Mr Smith has an enormous ego and the bravado to match.' Johnny leaned back. 'More often than not, there is a simple explanation for things. It could be that the passenger, this man with the dark hair, was tired and just wanted to get to wherever they were going. And as to the use of such a vehicle, if the dark-haired man was unknown to Smith, the car may have been his way of verifying his contact once the man sent to meet him was dead. I feel it is more likely that our Mr Smith is overly confident. Why else would he engage in conversation with the boy and toss him a packet of cigarettes? We have a pretty good success rate with capturing enemy spies. He won't evade capture for long. Well done, Clement.'

'There is something else.' Clement took a deep breath. Even thinking about what had happened in Scotland four months ago made him shiver. 'Do you remember earlier this year another man with Nazi leanings was hanged at Wandsworth?'

Johnny frowned.

'You told me then that when his body was being prepared for burial, a tattoo was found under his right arm. Did anyone photograph it?'

'No need. We knew what it was. The emblem for the Hitler Youth movement. Why?'

'The body in the mortuary in Cambridge has a burn mark under his upper right arm. Morris thinks it was deliberately done.'

'To remove something, you mean?'

Clement nodded.

'Dear Lord! That could imply a network.'

'One with a Scottish connection, Johnny.'

'How sure are you about this?'

'I'm not.'

'Have you told anyone else your suspicions?'

Clement shook his head.

'I'll requisition the trial transcripts and see if there's anything there that could shed any light on a possible network. I think it unlikely, but it's worth a look.' Johnny pressed the button on his desk to summon Miss Ballantyne. The door opened within seconds.

'Nora, please obtain the transcripts for the trial you attended on our behalf earlier this year?'

Nora beamed her ever efficient smile. 'I've already heard back from Station X concerning the radio transmissions. On the night of January thirty-first this year, two encrypted messages were overheard in quick succession at twenty-one hundred hours. The following morning at exactly five o'clock another two messages were picked up. All four messages were brief. Unfortunately as all were encrypted, and our friends in Buckinghamshire haven't yet broken that code, we don't know the content.'

7

It was raining when Clement left Whitehall and walked to Waterloo Station. He took a train to Richmond, then a bus to Richmond Park. Both trips had been arduous and with the overcrowding, he'd had to stand for much of both journeys between people with wet umbrellas. By the time he alighted from the bus it was after two o'clock but at least it was no longer raining. He walked into the park, then took the path that led south. In the distance he could see the old Victorian building that was his destination. Surrounded by a solid wall, Latchmere House was where MI5 interrogated enemy agents and he wasn't looking forward to what he may find there.

He showed his pass to a guard at the gate and was then escorted to the main entrance.

'Good afternoon. My name is Major Wisdom and I'm here to see Josef Jakobs,' Clement said to a sergeant at the front door.

The sergeant checked Clement's name on the manifest then handed him a stamped card. Standing, the soldier pointed to a long, darkened corridor to the side of the entry. 'Down there, sir. At the end you'll find a door. Just knock and show the pass to the corporal there.'

Clement took the card. Following the sergeant's instruction, Clement walked along an elaborately panelled hall with old parquetry flooring. At the end he knocked and the corporal opened the door.

'Are you carrying any weapons, Major?' the corporal asked.

Clement reached down and unbuckled the scabbard that held his knife. Removing his coat, he unfastened the Welrod from its holster around his chest and handed both to the corporal.

'Please remember to collect them on leaving, sir. This way.'

Clement followed the man down a flight of stairs to a basement corridor. Every door was closed. Unlocking one on the right, the corporal ushered Clement in. In the centre of the room was a table and three chairs grouped around it. The walls had been painted grey and other than the few items of furniture and a tiny window with bars and frosted glass at ground level, the room was empty.

'Just wait here. The prisoner will be brought down to you.'

The door slammed shut.

Sitting, Clement breathed in the stale air. The room was cold and bleak. The small window provided the only natural light and no view of the outside world was visible. Ten minutes later he heard the door being opened and a tall man accompanied by a guard entered the room.

Clement stood and held the man's gaze. He wasn't sure what he'd expected but before him was a man with a narrow face, a long nose and intense, deep-set eyes, a dimpled chin and a full head of hair. Clement thought Jakobs had a proud face and was not unhandsome.

Jakobs waited while the guard locked the door, his intense gaze fastened on Clement.

'Thank you for agreeing to see me,' Clement said. 'Do you understand English?'

'Some. I don't need a priest.'

'Of course, but I'm not here to see you in that capacity. I would like to ask you some questions about the night you landed in England,' Clement said, gesturing towards a chair.

Jakobs sat in the chair with his back to the window. Pushing the chair away from the table, he then crossed his legs.

Clement sat opposite. 'You parachuted from a Heinkel 111 bomber aeroplane, I understand?'

Jakobs nodded.

'And you broke your ankle on landing.'

'No!'

'No?'

'The hatch from the Heinkel is small. I caught my foot on something as I jumped out. Landing made it worse.'

'Did anyone else jump from the aeroplane with you that night?'

'No.'

'Are you sure about that?'

Jakobs frowned. 'No one else jumped.'

'Other than the pilot and crew were you alone in the aeroplane?'

Jakobs's eyes shifted to the guard then back to Clement. He paused before answering. 'There was a man with me. He did not jump.'

'Why was he there, if he didn't jump with you?'

'To make sure I did.'

'Do you know his name?'

'No.'

'Can you describe him?'

'Enough. No more questions,' Jakobs said, standing and sounding alarmed.

Clement stood then made to leave. The guard held the key to the door and went to insert it in the lock.

Clement paused and turned to face Jakobs. 'Is your foot better now?'

'Yes,' Jakobs paused. 'Thank you.'

The barrel in the cell door lock rotated. 'Why did you come?' Clement said, genuinely concerned.

'To check on the weather.'

'So your mission was to check on British weather?

Was there another reason?'

'I have answered your questions,' Jakobs said, looking at the guard. 'No more questions now.'

'Are you sure the other man in the aeroplane didn't jump after you?' Clement persisted, his gaze firmly on Jakobs.

Jakobs sighed. 'I have already told you, he was there to make sure I jumped. If he did, then I know nothing about it.'

'Who was he?'

'I have nothing more to say. I leave now,' Jakobs said to the guard. The guard opened the door and escorted Jakobs out of the room.

Clement left the basement corridor and collecting his weapons from the corporal, returned to the sergeant on duty at the main entrance. Jakobs's answer to his last question troubled Clement. He believed that Jakobs may have known the identity of the man on the aeroplane but wouldn't say. Clement wanted to know why. 'Could I see Colonel Stephens, please, Sergeant?'

'I'll see if the commandant is available, sir.'

Twenty minutes later Clement sat in Colonel Stephens's office on the first floor. 'Thank you for allowing me to see Jakobs and for seeing me at such short notice.'

'I can hardly refuse a directive from Sir Stewart Menzies, Major. Did you find out what you wanted?'

'Not fully, thank you, Colonel,' Clement said. 'However, I have learned that there was another man on board the Heinkel the night Jakobs jumped. Jakobs has denied knowing this man's identity but I'm not convinced. I'm wondering if he's told you?'

Stephens leaned back in his chair. 'He did inform us of another man on board that night. It isn't unusual for the Abwehr to send people with their agents. Just to make sure they do jump. It may surprise you to learn, Major, that Jakobs had never parachuted prior to his jump that night.'

'What, no training?'

'None at all. Surprising, isn't it. You think he knew this other man?'

'Not personally perhaps but he may have known his identity. Why did Jakobs come to England?'

'In a word, weather. Reports for the Luftwaffe and information about our airfields.

'Do you believe him?'

'Yes. While you may think this isn't reason enough for a man to risk his life, daily reports about the weather, especially near bomber airfields, are highly prized by the Luftwaffe.'

'Did Jakobs have someone detailed to meet him on landing, do you know, Colonel?'

Stephens swallowed. He looked at the window before answering, his lips pursing. 'I've been informed of your Top Secret security clearance, Major so I will answer your question. But I need to remind you that what you are about to hear is strictly top secret.' Stephens stood and wandered over to the window and stared out. Clement could see Stephens's apprehension. He waited.

'The answer to your questions is, yes, and we knew who. A man who has been working for both us and the Abwehr.

'A double agent?'

'Yes. *Snow*, as he is called, has been giving the Abwehr fake identities including fake ration cards for some time now. The Germans give them to their agents who land in Britain. We have a list of these names and identities so it's quite easy for us to pick them up. We would have captured Jakobs easily enough anyway through *Snow*, even if he hadn't broken his ankle.'

'Did *Snow* go to meet Jakobs?'

'Yes. He said he'd intended to be there earlier but he was delayed. When he saw the Home Guard and police in attendance, he left the area.'

'Could this *Snow* have been there to meet someone else besides Jakobs?'

'Who, exactly?'

'The Abwehr man on the Heinkel. I believe he jumped after Jakobs.'

'What makes you think that?'

'The body of a man has been found in an adjacent field to where Jakobs landed. It's possible he is either this Abwehr man or someone who came to meet him. I am, however, almost sure Jakobs knows nothing about it.'

'It's possible *Snow* knew about him. I'll make some enquiries and have another chat with Jakobs.'

'He wasn't exactly forthcoming with me but perhaps

he will be with you.' Clement paused. 'I did believe Jakobs, Colonel, when he said the other man didn't jump. It could be that only now Jakobs is having doubts about it. It's also possible that Jakobs recognised this Abwehr man but is too afraid to say anything.'

'I'll let you know once I've spoken to him. Jakobs has been quite helpful to us, you know. He assisted us in getting another enemy spy to talk. That man, Karel Richter, who Jakobs knew in Germany, came to England a few days ago. Along with the usual spying paraphernalia found in his possession were a few Dutch notes and coins, five hundred and fifty-one pounds ten shillings and fourteen hundred American dollars.'

Clement's eyebrows rose involuntarily. 'Did he say why?'

'Not so much why, Major, as who. Last September we caught another German spy and he was given a choice; either work for us, or face the hangman's noose. He's been working for us for a while now. The money was for him. Richter knew him from Hamburg. As far as the Germans are concerned, this man is one of their most valuable assets and in their opinion, remains loyal to the Führer.

'Why would he need it, especially the American dollars?'

'Spying is an expensive business, Major, and *Tate*, has expensive tastes. He is a good spy, Major. One we wouldn't want to lose. It could well be that the Germans intend for him to visit our cousins across the pond at some time.'

'Do you know where he is currently?'

'He's in London.'

'Are you sure?'

'Why do you ask, Major?'

'There is a man in Cambridgeshire with expensive habits who we're very interested to speak to.'

'Not the same man, Major.'

'Can you describe this *Tate* for me, Colonel, just to be sure.'

'I can show you a photo, if that would convince you.' Stephens went to a drawer and removed a file, taking a small photograph from it. The photo showed a man in his mid-thirties, wearing glasses and smoking a cigarette. He had a thin, delicate appearance, almost effete with flowing brown hair swept over his forehead.

'Is this your man?' Stephens asked.

Clement studied the photo. The man pictured wasn't smiling so his teeth were not visible. But the hollowness of the man's cheeks and the small jaw didn't fit with the boy's description. Besides, this man wore glasses and young Hasluck, Clement believed, would have mentioned that. 'No. Thank you, Colonel...' Clement paused. 'Would it be possible for you to speak with Jakobs soon? It would be most helpful to know the identity of the Abwehr man on board the Heinkel.'

Stephens nodded. 'Where can I reach you?'

'Cambridge Police Station.'

When Clement left Latchmere House it was nearly

five o'clock. The trains from Richmond into London had been delayed and it was late evening when he boarded the train for Cambridge. He had considered staying in London overnight but the crowds, the congestion of the capital and the threat of bombing raids had convinced him to leave.

As the train rattled north, he glanced around his fellow passengers. Most were airmen returning from leave. They laughed loudly and smoked heavily. But the others, the civilians, sat mute or spoke in whispers. Clement studied their faces. There was a vacancy in their expressions, a sense of almost palpable resignation to events around them. Clement knew the war wasn't going well for the allies. It bred a mood of helplessness, even hopelessness, perhaps even defeat. The bombing had been relentless although, since the tenth when the bombing in London had been most severe, the raids appeared to have abated. Clement pondered the date; the tenth of May. A year to the day since Churchill had become Prime Minister and, more recently there had been another extraordinary event he'd read about in the newspapers. Rudolf Hess, the Deputy Führer had landed in a field in Scotland. Why had Hess done that? Clement pushed it from his mind. He had enough to think about without speculating on why the Deputy Führer flew to Scotland.

Alighting from the train, he stepped onto the platform and made his way to the station forecourt. It surprised him that Cambridge Railway Station was not more crowded. He glanced at the station clock. Nine. It would be dark soon but he wondered if Morris may still be at the police station. Crossing the street he caught a bus into town.

Entering St Andrew's Street Police Station, Clement enquired if Morris was still there. The young constable nodded. 'I'll let him know you're here.'

A moment later Clement took the stairs to the first floor. He knocked at Morris's door.

'Enter.'

Clement went inside. 'What news, Arthur?'

'We've located the car and its owner. I've also sent a message to the Abbey School to have the boy sent home for the foreseeable future. Hetherington will arrange it. How did you get on?'

Clement told Morris about his theory concerning the burn on the man in Morris's mortuary.

'Hitler Youth?'

'Could be. There was a man I met some months ago in Caithness who had a tattoo on his upper right arm. That man is now dead. Hanged for treason. The burn on our man could have been a rather harsh and perhaps hasty method of removing a similar tattoo. Also, two encrypted radio transmissions were picked up on the night of January thirty-first followed by another two at dawn the following morning. Unfortunately we don't know what either was about. What about the telephone boxes in Ramsey?'

'There are two in Ramsey. Neither are near the ruined

gatehouse but that doesn't exclude them if he used the telephone before disposing of the suitcase. There are no telephone boxes on the road east out of Ramsey. I got in touch with the telephone operator in Ramsey. She stated that she never listens to calls. I'm not so sure. But I feel certain if she had overheard a suspicious conversation, she would be the first to report it. It's more likely that Smith would know this and would use a pre-arranged coded sentence. I am still waiting to hear about the pond.'

'So, he may not have used a public telephone at all. And the car?'

'Very interesting. Apparently, these cars are custom made; for the select few and very expensive. One matching the description the boy gave us is owned by a prominent family in these parts. Of course, they don't have a criminal record so we have nothing on file.'

'Name?'

'Armstrong. Sir Hector and the Lady Helena Armstrong.'

'Gentry?'

'She is, daughter of an earl. Spends most of her time in the south of France, so I'm told. Sir Hector was knighted for services to industry. Both mix in affluent circles. Not necessarily together.'

'His profession?'

'Extremely successful businessman. Timber yards, specifically. Supplies the railways with sleepers. Needless to say, he's doing well at present.'

'Any family?'

'One son, Hugh Armstrong. Has a position in the family firm so exempt from service.'

'Age?'

'Twenty-six.'

'Have you interviewed him?'

'Not yet.'

'I'll ask London about them first. Then depending on what we learn, it may be best if I were to find digs in Cambridge for the short term. Any news yet about the soil in our man's trouser turn-ups?'

'We should have the report first thing tomorrow.'

'And Jakobs's parachute?'

'No sign of tampering. I checked it myself. Did you learn anything useful from Jakobs?'

Clement sat in the chair in front of Morris. There was a lot he couldn't tell Morris about, including the other German spies now working for MI5, but he couldn't see any reason why Morris couldn't know about the Abwehr man.

'And Jakobs is adamant this man didn't jump?' Morris asked.

'Says not, but…' Clement shook his head then ran his hand around his neck. He felt tired. 'I got the impression he may have known who the man was.'

'Did Jakobs say anything else?' Morris asked.

'He mentioned that he'd tripped and damaged his foot prior to leaving the plane. Landing just made it worse. The commandant says he will have another talk with Jakobs and telephone me here if he learns anything useful.'

'If Jakobs did recognise this man wouldn't that suggest he was someone well-known, a public figure perhaps?'

'I think that is a very real possibility,' Clement said, stifling a yawn. Outside the twilight was descending, the translucent light casting a glow over the buildings. 'Do you know, Arthur, the colonel told me that it was Jakobs's first ever jump. He'd never even done a practice drop prior to his flight to England! It begs the question; why would the Abwehr select Jakobs for the job, then give him no parachute training and send an Abwehr officer with him to make sure he went?'

'You think they expected Jakobs to be caught?' Morris paused.

'Yes.'

'Why?'

'His foot. Did Jakobs really trip on leaving the Heinkel or did the Abwehr man deliberately trip him to cause an injury?'

Morris frowned but didn't respond.

Clement went on. 'There may have been a plan to kill him on landing which they didn't need to implement. Or, they could have believed he'd be caught either there or in the vicinity. His capture would deflect any further inquiry into other events in the fields that night.' Clement realised another possibility that he didn't mention to Morris; *Snow* the double agent sent to meet Jakobs may have been ordered by his Nazi handlers to kill him.

Morris raised his eyebrows. 'They were right about that. So, not just a decoy then but also a scapegoat!' Morris leaned back in his chair. 'Someone who would be captured and, should the body in the copse ever be found, charged with murder as well as espionage. Feasible. And clever! How soon can you have the information on the Armstrongs?'

'If I call now then they should have something for us tomorrow morning. Would you mind, Arthur, if I was to sit quietly somewhere until you're ready to leave? So much has happened and there is something from the past that is troubling me about all of this. I'd just like to think it through.'

'Of course. There's a meeting room next door here. And there's a telephone there. If you need to place a call just give the number to the constable on duty.' Morris got up and opened a side door into the next room. 'I'll get Sergeant Kendall to bring you some tea and a biscuit, if we have one. Take all the time you need. You're welcome to stay with me again tonight. I'm waiting on a report from the pathologist about another case that will take about an hour, then we can leave.'

Clement smiled and went into the adjacent room, Morris closing the door behind him. It was a similar room to Morris's office in size but where Arthur had a large desk and several armchairs, this room had one long table and ten chairs neatly placed around it. On the end wall was a portrait of King George and Queen Elizabeth and beneath it a telephone on a long narrow side table. At the other end, the evening light filtered into the room from a similarly large window to the one in Morris's office.

Clement went to the window and looked down on the passers-by of Cambridge. A few minutes later he heard the soft tap on the door to the corridor and the sergeant he recognised from the duty desk entered carrying a tray with tea for one. 'Thank you. Are you Sergeant Kendall?'

'Yes, sir,' Kendall said, putting the tray on the table.

Clement smiled at the affable sergeant but already his mind was distracted. He didn't even hear Kendall leave the room. Several minutes later, Clement poured the warm tea then, walking over to the telephone, lifted the receiver and gave the constable the London number for Nora Ballantyne in Whitehall.

A woman's voice answered but Clement knew it wasn't Nora.

'Could I speak with Nora Ballantyne, please?' Clement asked. 'Major Wisdom speaking.'

'She isn't in this evening, Major Wisdom. I am acquainted with your current mission. Can I help? Joan Cunningham speaking.'

'Could you do some digging on a prominent family in Cambridgeshire?'

'Of course. Their name?'

'Sir Hector and the Lady Helena Armstrong. And their son, Hugh.'

'I'll check and get back to you, Major,' Joan said. 'Where can I reach you?'

'Cambridge Police Station. Any idea how long it will take?' Clement asked, checking his watch. It was almost dark.

'If they are known to us, I will call you back within the hour. Otherwise tomorrow at the latest.'

Thanking the woman, Clement rang off. Sitting in a chair by the window, he closed his eyes. As far as he could tell there were two lines of enquiry. The first was with Jakobs and whether or not his arrival had anything at all to do with the dead man in Morris's mortuary. The second issue had to do with the Armstrongs. Opening his eyes Clement stared at a patch of mould growing on the ceiling. He wondered if the Abwehr man had deliberately hindered Jakobs leaving the aeroplane. That, and a heavy, inexperienced landing had rendered the man immobile. Jakobs would be in pain and his attention on his injury. His capture provided the distraction needed for another to remain unobserved. And that for Clement was the sole reason Jakobs had been sent. Reporting on the British weather around the local airfields was Jakobs's cover story. Clement remembered the other captured spy, Richter. Colonel Stephens had said Jakobs knew Richter in Germany but Richter's mission was to make contact with another spy known to MI5 as Tate. Was there a connection between Tate and the Abwehr man? And why was Richter carrying so much money?

The telephone ringing startled him. He checked his

watch. Nearly ten o'clock. If it was Joan Cunningham she must have called in many favours to get a response this quickly. He crossed the room and lifted the receiver.

'Major?'

'Go ahead Miss Cunningham.'

'They are known to us so it was a fairly straightforward search. Have you ever heard of the Right Club?'

Clement frowned. He had heard of the right-wing secret society with Nazi leanings formed before the outbreak of war but he understood it hadn't lasted long. Not long enough to do any lasting damage, except, perhaps, for some of its members. The Service had swiftly infiltrated the organisation and its members had either been arrested, interned or cautioned. 'I thought it had disbanded?'

'Officially, yes. They were decidedly pro-Nazi before the war but if they are reforming, the Armstrong family and quite a few others from our own upper classes should be carefully monitored. With the war not going well for us currently, Britain would be a fertile bed for discontent.'

'But surely now, in view of Germany's failure to invade last summer, few can still hold to these beliefs?'

'People are tired of being bombed, Major. A negotiated settlement with Germany would, for many, have considerable appeal. It won't happen. The Prime Minister is adamant about that.'

Clement stared at his feet, his mind racing.

'Are you still there, Major?'

'Yes. Sorry. Could you do something else for me?'

'Of course.'

'Find me a reason to reside in one of the Cambridge Colleges; research study for something. And something else, Miss Cunningham? Could you find someone for me? I think I'm going to need some trustworthy eyes.'

Replacing the telephone receiver, he drew the chair closer to the window and sat, sipping his tea, the muted sounds of the street below the only noise. Night had descended. Clement sighed remembering former times when he used to sit with Mary in their garden in the long twilights. The memories belonged to another life, one now gone and never to return. A car horn below made his thoughts reluctantly return to the present. Hugh Armstrong, if that was Smith's true identify, had gone to a field in Cambridgeshire to collect someone, possibly the Abwehr man who had killed the man in Morris's mortuary. Why? And why had Armstrong used such a distinctive car? Was it just so a man with a moustache and dark hair would recognise his contact? Was there another reason? A moment later Clement dashed from the room. Opening the door to Morris's office without knocking, he burst in. 'Have you sent anyone to question Hugh Armstrong?'

Morris laid some papers on his desk and looked up. 'One of my detective constables is to speak to him tomorrow morning, Clement. What concerns you?'

'Find another reason for the meeting; parking infringements, noise, public nuisance, anything but do not ask why he was in Ramsey last January.'

'Your reasoning being?'

'It's a warning system, Arthur. It's how they'll know their activities have been discovered.'

8

Monday 2nd June 1941

It was just after two when Clement walked towards the wide front door of Trinity Hall College, a brown leather suitcase in his hand. The previous weekend, he'd returned to Oxford to collect some more clothing, to cancel his milk and newspaper deliveries and to inform Mrs Warrender that he wouldn't be needing her services for a few weeks. Returning to Cambridge on the Sunday, he'd spent the afternoon becoming familiar with the city and getting to know the layout of the streets and lanes. He'd also memorised the college names and locations, especially those around Trinity Hall.

Miss Cunningham, through Johnny's extensive network of contacts, had arranged for him to do research at Trinity Hall on Augustine of Hippo's writings on St Paul's Letter to The Romans and the Doctrine of Grace.

Whilst the topic was of genuine interest to Clement, he knew there would be no time for study.

Clement knocked at the porter's lodge. An elderly man, perhaps in his seventies wearing rimless glasses, with thinning hair and sallow skin was seated behind a desk. He looked up as Clement entered then removed his glasses.

'How do you do,' Clement said. 'I am Reverend Clement Wisdom. I understand you are expecting me?'

The porter checked a book on his desk then stood. 'Yes. Welcome to Trinity Hall, Reverend. I've given you a quiet room in Thorton. I thought it unlikely you'd wish to share living quarters with youngsters.' The porter collected a key from a pigeon hole behind the desk. 'Go straight through Front Court then under the arch; Hall, where you take your meals is on your left, then follow the path past the library and down to your right. Go past Gatehouse Building to Thorton and take the last staircase. Your room is on the top floor on the right. There's a nice view of the river there.'

'Thank you. That's most kind. May I know your name?' Clement said, handing over his ration book.

'William Hayward. But everyone calls me, Old Bill, on account of me being here for forty years. Just ask me if you don't know where anything is.'

Clement smiled and took the proffered key. 'I'm sure I'll be seeing you frequently then.' Bending, he picked up his suitcase. 'Are you the only porter here at Trinity Hall?'

'Oh no. There's three of us as well as two part-time assistants. We rotate the shifts so there's always someone here.'

Clement smiled and left the lodge. He breathed in the summer air, the colour of the grass in Front Court like emeralds in the afternoon sun. The centuries-old stone buildings surrounded him. It seemed to Clement that once inside the old university buildings, the war ceased to exist. Staying on the path, he crossed the courtyard, noticing the chapel on his left before finally finding Thorton. His staircase was near the river and beside a gardener's store.

Climbing the stairs, Clement opened the door to his room. It was small with whitewashed walls and the smallest of gas heaters wedged into a pre-existing fireplace. To one side of it was a faded, red velvet upholstered Victorian armchair and above the mantelpiece hung a mirror. In the corner of the room was the bed and beside it a table and chair. A wardrobe stood to his left. Lifting the suitcase onto the bed, he unpacked his few clothes and placed a Bible on the table along with a notebook and pen. Checking the stairwell again, he glanced at the door opposite wondering if anyone was there. He knocked but no one opened it. Returning to his room, he closed his door to the stairwell and locked it. Standing in the middle of the room, he scanned the walls and floor, his gaze resting on the fireplace. Kneeling in front of it, he manoeuvred the gas heater out of the fireplace then ran his fingers along the inside edge of the mantelpiece, feeling for the brick ledge. It was narrow but he hoped sufficiently wide enough to hide his pistol. Taking his Welrod and ammunition from his suitcase, he placed them into the holster and secreted both on the brick ledge before replacing the heater. Closing the door to his room, he then placed a thread over the lintel. With his gun concealed in the fireplace, he left the building.

Standing on the Memorial Terrace he gazed at the river. To his right was the gardener's shed and behind it a bridge crossed the Cam River. In the other direction, the river curved around to the next college. In front of him and across the steady-flowing river was the large grassy area known as *The Backs*. Below him, a short flight of stone steps descended from the terrace into the river. Clement turned and walked back along the path. He stopped by a large tree, his gaze on the Gatehouse arch. Clement guessed it accessed the lane behind the college. He walked towards it. At the rear of the arch were two gates; a large one for vehicles, a smaller one for pedestrians. Both were locked. Clement returned to the path, walking back towards the main entrance. Passing the porter's lodge, he waved to Bill Hayward.

Hayward called after him. 'Reverend! Don't be late for Hall. Students must be seated by seven, the Fellows arrive after that and once they're seated you won't get in.'

'Thank you, I'll make sure I'm there on time,' Clement said.

Leaving the main entry, he turned left and walked down Trinity Lane towards the river. At the rear of Gatehouse were three doorways, all shut. Two were the gates he'd seen from the other side but there was a third, a little distance away and closer to the river, set into the red brick wall. All were locked. Walking on, he crossed the bridge and walked for some way along a path then returned to *The Backs* and sat watching the passers-by and the river traffic. He checked his watch. Heeding Old Bill's warning, he headed back to college.

Clement ate quickly. Not because he was hungry but he wanted to chat with Bill Hayward while most of the students were still in Hall. Making his excuses to the young man sitting beside him, Clement hurried to the porter's lodge.

'Mind if I come in?' Clement asked, poking his head around the lodge door.

'Reverend Wisdom? Everything alright for you? Had a nice afternoon?'

'Yes. Thank you. While out, I saw some doors in the Gatehouse building. I think they lead out to the lane. Are they in use?'

Bill shook his head. 'Haven't been in years. And strictly off limits for students.' Hayward stood. 'I'm about to make myself a cup of tea. Would you like one?'

'That's most kind,' Clement smiled.

Hayward filled a kettle and placed it on a single gas jet set into a bench under the window. The lodge telephone rang.

'Trinity Hall, Hayward speaking.'

Clement waited.

'He's at supper currently,' Bill said. 'Do you want him to return your call? And the number?' A minute late Bill replaced the telephone receiver and made an entry into a large book that was open on his desk.

By the time Hall had emptied, Clement had learned about Bill's fellow porters: Paul Edwards and Ted McBryde. Both were of mature age, married and resided in Cambridge. The two assistant porters also lived off-site. Bill, although more advanced in years than any of the other porters was a bachelor and lived in college. Because of his years of faithful service to Trinity Hall, Hayward occupied a set of rooms on the first floor formerly reserved for visiting Fellows.

'That's quite a privilege, isn't it?'

'Indeed it is!'

'Have you been there long?'

'Not long. Just this year in fact,' Bill said, standing. He returned the cups to a tray on a bench beside the gas burner.

'You must have seen many things over the years?' Clement asked.

'Oh, yes, indeed. I know all the comings and goings. We've had our share of future leaders as well as misfits and delinquents. Most are from good families keen to see their sons advance and contribute to the nation in politics and...' Bill suddenly stopped.

Clement looked up.

Hayward was standing at the window almost transfixed.

'Are you alright?' Clement asked.

Hayward stared through the window. Clement followed his gaze but he didn't see anything.

'What? Yes, I'm fine. I must get on Reverend Wisdom. Loose talk. Discouraged and all that.'

Clement stood, wondering why the elderly man had so suddenly stopped speaking. 'Well, thank you for the tea. As it's a lovely evening, I may explore Cambridge further before I retire.'

'Yes. You do that, Reverend Wisdom,' Hayward said, but Clement could see the man was distracted.

Clement walked out of the lodge as a group of raucous students were coming in. He smiled and stood aside as the young men streamed into the porter's lodge. Old Bill's attention would be on them. Clement stood at the main entry but, checking that Hayward was occupied, he returned to Front Court and began to stroll towards a bench on the path in the corner of the courtyard. Passing the porter's lodge windows, he bent to tie his shoelace. He glanced up. Through an upper floor window of the building opposite, he saw two young men. They were completely stationary, like statues, with blank expressions staring out into the courtyard. Clement finished tying his shoelaces and stood. Without looking back at the two men in the window, he walked back to the front door and leaving the college, wandered into town.

9

Tuesday 3rd June 1941

Clement locked his room and walked to the porter's lodge. He'd spent the morning in the library and had requested some ancient books to be made available for further research. He hoped it would satisfy any interested person of his purpose in being at the college. Now he needed two things: to find out if the college priest conducted a daily service and to buy a pipe. Not that he'd taken up smoking but holding the pipe was the signal he and Morris had devised to make contact with each other.

'Morning, Bill,' Clement said on entering the lodge.

Bill looked up but Clement didn't see any of the bonhomie he'd experienced earlier. 'Can you tell me when the college priest conducts Evensong?'

'Nine,' Bill replied.

'May I know his name?'

'Father Rathbourne.' Bill walked to the rear of the lodge and opened a drawer in the filing cabinet, his back to Clement.

'Thank you,' Clement said but Hayward didn't respond.

Hayward's behaviour perplexed Clement. He could see that the old porter was perturbed. Something had rattled the man. Clement had hoped that between the porters and the priest, he would be able to learn more about the inside life at Trinity Hall. But since Hayward's odd reaction and the presence of the two young men in the upper floor window who appeared to be watching him, Bill's manner had changed and Clement didn't know why. Leaving the college, he strolled along Trinity Lane and joined the crowds of people on the Parade.

The day was sunny and bright. Finding a tobacconist on the Parade he purchased the pipe and some tobacco then placed it all into his coat pocket. He'd suggested to Morris that he would take a walk every afternoon at three past the police station, where it would be arranged that the duty sergeant Clement recognised, Sergeant Kendall, would be standing at the front of the building. If Morris wanted Clement to make contact, Kendall would be smoking a pipe. If Clement wanted to contact Morris, Clement would be smoking a pipe as he passed. They would then meet an hour later on the first floor of the old university bookshop at the corner of Trinity and St Mary's Streets.

Purchasing the pipe, Clement returned to the college library. Bill Hayward was attending to the post when Clement passed the lodge. Collecting the ancient tomes from the librarian, he sat by a window in the library, reading. He'd hoped to see either of the two young men he'd seen in the upper floor window but neither had entered nor passed the library. Clement returned to his room. The cleaner had been in during the morning so Clement checked the fireplace. The Welrod was still on the ledge. Leaving it there, he left his room, replacing the thread over the lintel and went straight to the porter's lodge. As he entered the porters domain, he glanced at the upper floor window but no one was there. Ted McBryde was on the desk.

'I had a look around the college yesterday after I arrived. It's lovely, isn't it? Can you tell me what rooms surround this courtyard?' he asked, pointing towards the building opposite.

'Not for students,' Ted said. 'Fellows rooms and Father Rathbourne's lodgings.'

Clement smiled. Gaining access to the upper floors had suddenly become easier. Thanking McBryde, he walked into town.

Just on three o'clock, Clement strolled along St Andrew's Street towards the police station. Kendall was standing at the door, the smoke from his pipe rising on the breeze. Clement checked his watch. Four minutes past three. Taking the long way back into the centre of town, he made his way to the Parade, entering the bookshop just after four. Morris was sitting in a leather chair in a corner of the upper floor.

'What happened with young Armstrong?' Clement asked, taking a book on existentialism from the shelf.

'Sergeant Kendall gave him a talking to he may never forget. Told Armstrong that numerous elderly ladies had complained about his fast driving around the streets of Cambridge. He was given a warning and told not to misbehave again.'

Clement smiled. 'Where is Armstrong now?'

'His parents own a farm just north of Cambridge on the Waterbeach Road called Hitcham Hall. But when in town, he is the guest of the Master of Caius.'

Clement raised his eyebrows. 'Do you think he suspected anything?'

Morris shook his head. 'Kendall confirmed young Hasluck's description of him though. Tall, about six feet, with close-cropped blond hair, clean shaven, prominent teeth. And quite an attitude about him apparently. Kendall said that while young Armstrong was most apologetic for offending elderly ladies, Kendall thought it all bluff. Young upstart, I think were the words Kendall used. But I have something else that will interest you. The pathology report about the soil is in.' Morris's eyebrows raised, his lips pursed together. 'Something neither of us expected, I'm sure.'

Morris handed Clement the report, open at the appropriate page.

Clement ran his gaze down the page until his eye settled on the pathologist's findings. He read it silently. The predominant soil, the report stated, was alluvial, commonly found in floodplains and the fenland of Cambridgeshire. However the turn-ups had contained fragments of Old Red Sandstone, commonly used in construction and for monuments. This type of stone was not found in Cambridgeshire but was quarried in Scotland as well as parts of Orkney, Shetland and Norway. Clement closed the report.

An icy shiver coursed through him. Any reminder of his former mission to Caithness always had the same effect. He looked up at Morris unable to speak, his mind numb. There was a long silence. He felt his heart pounding in his chest. He swallowed, telling himself that a reference to Scotland didn't make for a conclusive Caithness connection. But it didn't change how he felt. There were unresolved issues from that mission and any reminder for Clement was like a cobweb shroud; the invisible tendrils still clinging to his skin.

Morris was staring at him. 'Something you want to tell me, Clement?'

'Sorry Arthur. I can't talk about it.'

Morris frowned. 'Something else you should know, Clement. I've had the Lagonda under surveillance. It's garaged in Tenison Road, adjacent to the railway station. No one has been near it in days.' Morris stood and placed his hat back on his head. 'See you later then.' He walked towards the stairs and without waiting for a reply, left the bookshop.

Clement gazed out of the adjacent window, the front door to Gonville and Caius College in the centre of his view. Below, he watched Morris exit the building, turning left into St Mary's Street. Morris hadn't looked back.

People hurried along the streets below: students, shoppers, business people. And murderers. Clement sat for some time in the leather chair in the corner, his mind on the report. Old Red Sandstone. Clement blinked several times, wondering if the deceased man was Scottish? If he were, and if he'd had any connection to the traitors in Caithness, why was he in Cambridgeshire? Small wonder no one had claimed the body. And what of Hugh Armstrong? Clement glanced at his watch. He needed to be elsewhere.

Leaving the bookshop he made his way through the evening crowds and down Trinity Lane, crossing the river to *The Backs* and the grassy meadow opposite King's College he'd explored earlier. Sitting on a bench under a sprawling oak he checked his watch again; a few minutes before six o'clock. At exactly six, a man wearing a long overcoat and hat and carrying a pack over his shoulder approached, coming from the town end and walking slowly along the riverbank.

Clement beamed and stared into the face of a man he had known for years. 'How are you, Reg? You've lost weight, I think.'

'This is about the last place I expected to see you, Clement. What's happening?'

Reg Naylor had lived in Fearnley Maughton and was the only person Clement currently knew from his prewar life. He gestured to the bench and Reg sat down, pulling his overcoat around him.

'It's still a bit cool, but not as cold as some places,' Clement said, thinking of Scotland and the last time he and Reg had worked together.

'Unlike you, Clement, I never left there. Not until three days ago.'

Clement turned to face his old friend. 'What? Why?'

'After that business in Caithness, they sent me to another location in the north.' Reg laughed. 'I used to think you spoke in riddles about the 'Cloak and Dagger Brigade' but now...'

'Reg?'

'Can't say where I was. They must have thought I was useful in a fight. Anyway, I've learned quite a bit more, courtesy of the Ministry of Dirty Tricks. I've met some brave lads. And lasses.' Reg shook his head. 'No job for a girl. But they are fearless. They'll need to be.'

Clement frowned. He didn't think much would unnerve Reg but he sensed a degree of reservation about his old friend that he'd never previously seen.

'What's the job, Clement?'

Clement smiled. Whilst he sensed some restraint in his former neighbour, the old pragmatic Reg wasn't too far beneath the surface. 'Look-out, at present. See if you can find a job in one of the pubs along the Parade. You should hear some local gossip there. Make up some cover story for being in Cambridge; looking for a former flame, that sort of thing should do. I need any information about the Armstrong family, especially the son, Hugh Armstrong. Morris tells me his parents own a place called Hitcham Hall on the Waterbeach Road but while in town he stays at Caius.'

'Anything else?'

'Any information about Armstrong's car, a Lagonda. These vehicles are for the very wealthy so your source will most likely be well-heeled.' Clement shot a glance around the area before continuing. 'Also any reference to Scotland.'

Reg raised his eyebrows.

'Just a theory at present, Reg, but keep your eyes and ears open.'

Reg nodded and Clement told Reg what he learned since he'd met Morris in Godstow.

'So, some Abwehr man arrived in England, killed the unknown man in the mortuary and is still here.'

'That's about it,' Clement said.

'And the dead man came from somewhere in the north and was sent to meet Herr Abwehr. So all we need to do is take the young Mr Hugh Armstrong and find out who he met and where he took him. Easy!'

'Unfortunately, it's not quite that simple.' Clement told Reg his theories on the Lagonda's use. 'If we brought young Armstrong in, any others in the network would be warned of our interest and they would most likely disappear.'

'Network?'

'Yes. I think so. One that extends from Cambridge-shire to Scotland. Possibly further.'

'So you need to infiltrate the group?'

'That could be the best.'

'How?'

'As young Armstrong lives in Caius when in Cambridge, I need to find someone who will introduce us. Perhaps the priest at Trinity Hall will know his counterpart at Caius. But while I do this, dig up anything you can find on the Armstrong family and, if possible, where young Armstrong goes and who he meets. You know the drill.'

'Got it! Where do we meet?'

'Until you find a job, come here every night at six o'clock. If you have nothing to tell me, walk straight past me, otherwise exactly as you are now.'

'Bring any weapons with you, Clement?'

'I'm wearing my knife. And I have a Welrod pistol with me. It's secreted on a ledge in the fireplace of my room. You?'

'Knife and Sten. And a few other small things,' Reg said and standing, continued walking along the bank. Clement watched him take the bridge over the River Cam adjacent to Trinity Hall and head back into town.

Clement sat a further ten minutes, his eye on the swift flowing stream which wound its way north towards King's Lynn and The Wash many miles distant. Leaving *The Backs* he made his way back to Trinity Hall.

Returning to college he hurried to Hall and found a seat, his eye searching for the two young men. They were not there. Neither was the college priest, Father Rathbourne. When Clement enquired about the evening service, he was informed that Evensong had been cancelled. No reason was given.

10

Wednesday 4th June 1941

Reg was sitting on the grassy bank when Clement approached at six o'clock.

'I've got a job in a pub,' Reg said, not moving from his reclining position by the river. 'I wait tables and pull beers.'

Clement smiled. 'Where?'

'*The Eagle*. In Bene't Street just off the Parade. Good view of who's coming and going from Caius College. There's a rear lane behind the pub, too.'

'I'll eat lunch at *The Eagle* every day.'

'Got it,' Reg rolled onto his side then stood slowly. He sauntered away.

Clement waited until Reg was some distance from him before walking back to the college. He climbed the stairs to his room and, letting himself in, slumped in the faded red chair, his mind sifting what he knew. He closed his eyes and rubbed his hand over his face. Why was a manual labourer sent to meet the Abwehr man and then killed? There was no answer and Clement felt the frustration. He glanced at his watch. It was just before seven. He hoped the priest would be at supper tonight.

As Clement walked into Hall, he saw a man wearing a clerical collar. He walked straight towards the priest and stood behind the next chair as the Fellows entered. Rathbourne was a tall man although now hunched. He had a long, serious visage and deep-set eyes. The Latin prayer was said and with a scraping of wooden chairs on ancient floors, they took their seats and supper commenced.

'Father Rathbourne?' Clement enquired.

'Yes,' Rathbourne snapped.

The abrupt response surprised Clement. 'How do you do. I'm Reverend Clement Wisdom.'

'The visiting vicar studying St Augustine. The Master told me you had a parish in East Sussex?' Rathbourne said, without making any eye contact with Clement.

'Yes. That's correct. In Fearnley Maughton, it's a small village just east of Lewes.'

'Nice part of the country. So why did you move?'

'My wife died.'

'This war is responsible for a great many unnecessary deaths.'

'She died from pneumonia, actually.'

'We shouldn't be in it. It's all a senseless waste of life.

They are our cousins, for goodness sake.' Rathbourne turned to stare at him, the munching continuing. Clement noted that Rathbourne's intense eyes were almost black. He had a full head of near-black hair, and strong prominent eyebrows with a large, angular nose. Clement wondered if Rathbourne had French or Spanish ancestors. Small beads of saliva were collecting at the corners of his mouth and a crumb had lodged in the fold where his lips joined. Rathbourne grabbed a napkin and wiped his mouth. An awkward pause ensued.

Clement changed the subject. 'I am wondering if you would like me to assist you with anything? You must be very busy and I could take Matins or Evensong on occasions for you, if you'd like?'

Rathbourne sniffed loudly then turned again to face Clement. 'I'll think about it,' Rathbourne said, shovelling another fork-load of food into his mouth. 'What's your view on this war?'

Clement made a quick assessment. 'I am, like a great many, tired of the bombing. So much destruction and sad loss of innocent life.' Clement waited hoping that Rathbourne would continue to talk.

'Warmongers. Self-serving warmongers. And Churchill is the worst of them. He and his Jewish friends.'

Clement watched the priest reach for a plate of bread and rip a handful of dough from it. 'You don't support the Prime Minister then?' Clement ventured.

Rathbourne spun around in his chair. 'Needless. The

whole thing. What have the Poles ever done for us? I ask you?'

Clement picked up his knife and fork. 'I so agree with you,' he lied.

Rathbourne grunted but continued to eat. Clement thought it wisest not to pursue the topic further. Nothing more was said. Rathbourne continued to eat and drink with the ferocity of a farmyard animal. Clement wondered what had called a man like Rathbourne to the priesthood. As much as he would have liked to have asked, Clement thought better of it. Rathbourne pushed his empty plate away and stood to leave, throwing his napkin onto the plate. He turned to face Clement. 'Come to chapel this evening. Nine o'clock, Father Wisdom. Then afterwards, I'll show you where the vestments are kept.'

'I prefer the title Reverend...' but Rathbourne had already left the table. Clement stared after the elderly man. He wasn't sure if Rathbourne was hard of hearing or had been deliberately ill-mannered. During the whole course of the meal, Rathbourne hadn't spoken to a soul other than himself. Clement watched the man leave Hall. Ill-mannered or deaf, it mattered little to Clement and Rathbourne's religious proclivities were of no relevance to his current situation. However, the man's political opinions were another matter entirely. And he hadn't seen either of the two young men.

Clement wandered back across the courtyard towards his room on the upper floor. It was still light, the sun picking out the shapes of leaves on the trees in *The Backs* and making the river sparkle. He stood on the memorial terrace for a few minutes staring at the water below. His gaze settled on the stone steps that descended from the side of the terrace to the Cam River. A small rowboat was tied up there.

He left the terrace and took the stairs to his room. Standing on the landing outside his door, he ran his hand along the upper edge and retrieved the thread from the lintel. Opening the door wide, his eyes scanned the room. Nothing that he could see had been disturbed. Not that he expected trouble. The actions were purely precautionary. He closed the door and locked it, placing the thread on the inside lintel. Why had Bill Hayward allocated him a room at the far end of the college? Clement hadn't thought about it before, believing the room was permanently given to older students, but now he was beginning to wonder if perhaps it had been Bill's intention to give him a room close to the river. Was it just a kindly gesture? Or was he there because it was as far away from Father Rathbourne's rooms as possible? Was it even significant?

Just before nine, he heard the chapel bell. Closing the door to his room, he replaced the thread over his door and headed downstairs. Despite the summoning bell, only two people sat in the pews. Rathbourne started the service never once making eye contact with any of his small congregation. For clerics like Rathbourne, Clement decided, it almost didn't matter that few attended; it was the observance of ritual that was important. An hour later the service concluded. As the two people in front of him stood, he recognised the two young men from the window. At the door Rathbourne grasped his shoulder. 'You can take the Eucharist this Sunday. After I've shown you where things are kept you may care to come to my study. You can meet some other people who think as we do.'

'Thank you. When?'

'As soon as we've finished here.'

'I'd like that,' Clement said. 'Where are your rooms?'

'Here. First floor, staircase next to the chapel.'

Clement waited while Rathbourne disrobed. The vestments were exactly where Clement expected them to be, in the vestry. But Rathbourne appeared intent on showing him how everything was folded and stored. It seemed straightforward to Clement but he didn't say so. From Rathbourne's manner, Clement was in no doubt that the priest saw everything in the vestry as his personal property and that anyone other than himself handling the items was in some way sacrilegious. Half an hour later, they left the chapel and walked to the priest's nearby rooms.

Rathbourne opened his door and Clement stepped into the room. Before him, seated on either side of a large stone fireplace, were the two young men. Standing beside them was a tall young man with blond hair and prominent teeth.

Rathbourne closed the door behind him. Clement

heard the key being inserted into the lock, the barrel sliding into place.

'This is Father Wisdom. He's visiting from East Sussex. Father Wisdom, may I introduce Gus Hutchinson, reading theology, Bertie Hawkins, mathematics and Hugh Armstrong, the son of a friend of mine.'

'What's a priest from East Sussex doing in Cambridge?' Armstrong asked, a smirk forming on his face.

'Running away,' Clement answered.

'From?'

'Ghosts.'

'Father Wisdom is a widower, Hugh,' Rathbourne said.

'A victim of the Luftwaffe, presumably,' Hugh said.

'No.'

'Will you have a whisky, Father Wisdom?' Rathbourne asked, pouring five whiskies.

'Why not?'

'Why not indeed.' Rathbourne passed the tray to Hugh who handed the drinks around.

'A toast,' Hugh interrupted. 'To leadership!' Armstrong swallowed the whisky in one gulp.

'To absent friends and other martyrs,' Rathbourne said. 'Won't you sit down, Father Wisdom?' Rathbourne indicated the window seat. 'But, first things first, Hugh. You see, Father Wisdom, we must be careful. These are strange times. A country divided. It's important to know who is a friend and who is not.'

Clement glanced around the faces, a sense of unease

131

growing rapidly. 'I'm not really sure what you're talking about Father Rathbourne.' Clement placed the glass on a nearby table.

'Not drinking, Father?' Hugh asked, the young man's eyes fixed on him.

'We all like to mix with those of similar beliefs. It's human nature, don't you think?' Rathbourne went on. The two expressionless young men by the fireplace hadn't moved.

'I've never really thought about it. But perhaps that is not a Christian sentiment, Father Rathbourne. After all, we are all instructed to love our neighbour, as well as our enemies.'

'So you are sympathetic to the Germans?' Rathbourne pressed.

Clement's gaze shifted from Rathbourne to Armstrong and the two young men who, Clement decided, resembled carved stone dogs now standing on either side of the fireplace. He looked again at Rathbourne. The priest's black eyes were fixed on him. He saw determination and something else; manipulative cunning. Clement glanced at Armstrong. There Clement saw wide-eyed, maniacal fanaticism. The two young men seemed impassive to everything. Clement thought quickly before speaking. 'I have nothing against the individual. It's the government who has deceived.'

'I couldn't have put it better myself!' Rathbourne said, walking towards Clement but not looking at him. In fact,

Clement thought Rathbourne was looking out the window.

Clement reached for the whisky. Rathbourne, Clement decided, not Armstrong was in charge. But what relationship existed between them? Clement flicked a glance at the two young men who remained impassive beside the fireplace, like a pair of andirons. Clement was in no doubt that they would do whatever Rathbourne instructed without a moment's hesitation.

Rathbourne turned, his gaze shifting from the window back to the room. 'Perhaps you should come to lunch? And you can meet others who share our opinions?'

Clement saw Armstrong flick a wide-eyed glare at Rathbourne.

Clement stood. 'As I'm new here in Cambridge, I'd be most honoured to be included in your group.'

Rathbourne smiled. 'Tomorrow then? We meet at Caius. Shall we say noon?'

Clement walked towards the door. 'Thank you. And thank you for the whisky.'

'Hugh, see our guest out.'

Armstrong unlocked the door and held it wide. As Clement stepped into the stairwell he felt a sense of utter relief to be away. What had been Rathbourne's purpose in inviting him? Clement didn't know but it wasn't to share opinions of any kind. Clement walked towards the porter's lodge by the front door to the college. He flicked a glance up to the window of Rathbourne's rooms. The curtains hadn't been drawn and he could see Rathbourne and the others talking. He guessed he was the topic of their conversation. As he approached the porter's lodge, he nodded to Old Bill. 'I need to go out for half an hour. I won't be late.'

'A moment if you will. May I offer a word of advice?' Bill Hayward said almost in a whisper.

'Of course.'

'I've been here a long time, Reverend Wisdom.' Hayward hesitated, his eyes flicking around. 'Whatever it is you're up to, just be careful. The walls here have eyes as well as ears.'

Clement smiled and left the lodge, closing the heavy main door behind him. He hurried away. It had been a strange evening, and now Bill Hayward had thought it necessary to warn him about something.

Clement pulled his coat around him. Trinity Lane was dark now, the high stone walls on either side towering over him. A chill breeze wrapped around him, his footsteps echoing on the cobbles. Or were there more than just his footsteps? Turning, he saw he was alone in the lane. He stopped and listened. 'You're imagining things,' he whispered to himself. Despite this, he hurried on, turning right at the top into King's Parade. A cool, cloudless night had descended and a half moon now illuminated King's College Chapel. Before turning left into Bene't Street, he waited in a doorway. Bill Hayward's words of warning were ringing in his ears. Why had it so unnerved him? Clement shook his head; imagined ghosts where there are none. A few minutes later Clement went to the side door of *The Eagle* where Reg had told him he had a room and taking the stairs to the upper floor, knocked on Reg's door.

'Clement! What's happened?'

'I'm not sure, Reg. Something's not right. Rathbourne is definitely involved and guess who I met this evening?' Clement didn't wait for Reg to answer. 'Hugh Armstrong.'

'So what's the game?'

'Unsure. But Rathbourne appears to be in charge. Even Old Bill the college porter told me the walls there have eyes and ears, so he knows more than he's letting on. Depending on his leanings, he could be a good source, if needed. But...' Clement paused. He scratched his head. 'Hayward's frightened. It's more than just the old members of the Right Club socialising. Something's happening.'

'Any ideas?'

'None. Armstrong referred to leadership. If it was just an old network getting together over drinks, why the enigmatic conversations? And why would they try to involve me?'

'Do you think they suspect you?'

'I've given them no cause to.'

'Perhaps you should move out, Clement.'

'Not yet. I'll have lunch with them tomorrow at Caius

and let you know. Perhaps we should meet more frequently.'

'Come to *The Eagle* after the lunch. We'll work out a
plan then. But I'll keep an eye out for you anyway. I have
a few new skills not even you know about.'

Clement left by the rear access to the lane and took
byways to get back to college. He tried the front door
and found it locked as he'd expected. Taking his set of
keys from his coat pocket, he opened the door, entered
and relocked it. As he passed the porter's lodge, he could
see Old Bill hunched at his desk.

11

Thursday 5th June 1941

He'd overslept. Checking the time, he dressed quickly and hurried towards Hall hopeful of making it in time for breakfast. The college was a frenzy of activity. Huddles of students clustered in hushed conversation. Clement walked past a group with intense expressions and pale complexions. He quickened his stride. Staring at each student as he passed, he saw wide-eyed incredulity, or was it fear on their faces? Beyond Hall, across Front Court and standing by the main entrance to college was a police constable. Standing outside the porter's lodge, Clement could see a group of men standing around the main door. The Master was there, speaking to Sergeant Kendall. Ahead, Clement saw Morris talking to the police pathologist Clement recognised from the police station. Clement hung back a little, not wanting to make eye contact with Morris or Kendall. Behind them, Clement could see a body was lying on a stretcher covered with a shroud.

'What's happened?' Clement whispered to Paul Edwards, the porter on duty.

Paul was ashen-faced. 'Nothing like this has ever happened before. Bill's been here for over forty years! He's been killed! Shot in the chest! Point-blank! Who would do such a thing?'

'This is dreadful news! What have the police said?'

'They think it could have been an attempted burglary. It can't be. Nothing appears to be out of place. Nothing's taken that I can see.' Edwards shook his head. 'Apparently his wallet is still in his pocket, so it can't have been theft, can it? Who would want to hurt Old Bill?'

Clement and Edwards stood to one side as the pathologist left with the body of Bill Hayward which was being trolleyed out by the two mortuary attendants from the police station.

Clement glanced across at Morris. In view of Bill's warning, for Clement, it wasn't so much who had killed Hayward as why. He left Edwards and walked towards Morris. 'Excuse me, Inspector. Can you tell me what has happened?'

'You are?' Morris asked.

'Reverend Clement Wisdom, I'm doing some research here at college,' he said, relieved that Morris was keeping up the pretence.

'And it's Superintendent Morris, not Inspector. I understand you are recently arrived here at college, Reverend Wisdom?'

'Yes, that's correct.'

Morris checked a notebook. 'You had drinks in Father Rathbourne's rooms last night, after Evensong, I understand, around ten o'clock? What time did you return to your own accommodation?'

'About half past ten.'

'Can anyone confirm that?'

'As I saw no one after leaving Father Rathbourne's rooms, I suppose not.'

'My pathologist says Mr Hayward was killed between ten and midnight. Without an alibi, I'll need to speak to you further. Noon. At the police station. And, Reverend Wisdom, don't leave Cambridge.'

'Of course. But after I left Father Rathbourne's rooms, I saw no one.'

'That doesn't bode well for you then, does it?'

Clement watched Morris go about the routine questions. He stood in the covered walkway outside the lodge. The crowd that had gathered there gradually dispersed. He wanted to check the lodge himself but he knew that would have to wait until Edwards was alone. Clement thought about Morris knowing he had been in Rathbourne's rooms last night. Rathbourne must have told Morris as Clement felt sure Hugh Armstrong would not have come forward. Clement's mind returned to the old porter. Was his death connected to the warning? If so, his remarks had been overheard. Or was it as Edwards had said; an attempted burglary that had gone horribly wrong? Clement turned at the sound of approaching footsteps. The Master was walking briskly towards Edwards. 'I have telephoned McBryde and asked him to come in, Edwards. In view of your friendship with the deceased, I think it would be best for you to go home for the remainder of today.'

'Thank you, Master. I'd be grateful,' Edwards replied.

'Excuse me, Master,' Clement interrupted. 'As I am a clergyman and currently residing here at Trinity Hall, perhaps I could stand in until Mr McBryde arrives?'

'That is most generous. Thank you Reverend Wisdom.'

'Just happy to help, Master.'

By late morning, Clement was finally alone and able to close the lodge door. He stared into the room as though seeing it for the first time. If it had been an attempted burglary, the thief hadn't disturbed much. Did that mean the burglar had broken into the lodge for something specific? Had whatever it was been found? If not, would he return? But why kill Bill Hayward? Clement wanted to see the body but until midday, all he could do was conjecture. His eyes scanned the room tracing every ledge and shelf. There was no evidence of a struggle. In Clement's opinion, Hayward's death had all the elements of an assassination. Swift and calculated, Hayward had been shot at his desk with no time to stand or protest before his killer fired the weapon. Clement thought back to the previous night. He had spoken to Hayward around ten, then gone out, returning around eleven. He'd seen Hayward hunched over the desk on his return. He hadn't thought twice about it, believing Hayward was writing up the daily log or perhaps had fallen asleep. Was it possible the man was already dead by the time Clement returned to college; killed in the hour after he left and before he returned? Or was it later? If anyone had witnessed Clement leaving the college by the front gate, he knew he would be the prime suspect. He thought again about Rathbourne. The priest had told Morris about the drinks, but not that he'd seen Clement leave college. Did that mean Rathbourne had not seen his departure?

Clement checked his watch, the meeting with Morris still forty minutes away and McBryde due momentarily. He realised his meeting with Morris would preclude him attending the lunch at Caius. He pondered Rathbourne's invitation but he couldn't draw any conclusions. At least none that made any sense to him.

With Fellows and students at tutorials and lectures, the lodge became eerily quiet. Clement went to the door and looked out. The front door was open and he could see the constable standing outside, his feet astride. Clement turned and stared again at the murder scene.

Was there anything that didn't look as it should? He walked towards Bill's desk, stepping over the police rope and staring at the thick pool of blood on the blotter. While the stain extended over everything on the desk, most of it had flowed down the front and side of where Bill had been sitting. A pool of congealed viscous fluid lay on the rug beneath the desk. Although Clement hadn't seen the body, he surmised Bill's trousers and shirt would be soaked in blood. Clement lifted his gaze. If Bill had been shot in the chest as Edwards had said, surely there would be blood splatter on the shelves of books and files behind him? Clement walked to the shelves, his eyes squinting, searching for a bullet lodged in the books that lined the wall behind the desk. That there was no blood splatter anywhere made Clement shudder. No exit wound. Clement had seen it before but if the bullet had been subsonic, this altered everything. Subsonic bullets were not available to just anyone and that included the police.

He stood by the fireplace, his gaze still on the desk blotter. Why was it not a head shot? Assassins, as he understood it, preferred head shots. Usually two. So why had Hayward been shot once in the chest?

'What's happened?' McBryde said, walking into the lodge.

Clement looked up at the porter, McBryde's sudden entrance surprising him. 'Mr Hayward has been shot. I'm sorry, but I know nothing more than this.'

'Why are you here? Where's Edwards?'

'The Master sent him home and asked me to man the fort until you arrived,' Clement answered. 'But I'll leave now you're here.'

Clement hurried away, his appointment with Morris

in ten minutes. Hayward's murder played on his mind. Had the man been shot in the chest rather than the head to conceal the wound so that anyone passing the lodge would think Hayward was asleep at his desk? Was this to buy time for the murderer to get away? Until Clement knew more about the man's injuries there would be no answers. It troubled him that Hayward's warning to him may have been overheard. Clement quickened his step. Why had Hayward thought it necessary to make the comment? Surely, if it had been overheard, it didn't warrant his death?

Clement weaved his way through a line of students coming along Trinity Lane. On the Parade, the streets were crowded but he almost didn't see them as he wound his way towards St Andrew's Street. His thoughts went to the other cold-blooded death; the man in Morris's mortuary. The same impassive kill of an assassination and both shots to the chest, not the head. Was it the same killer? Hayward's death had so few similarities to the man in Morris's mortuary. No one knew the dead man from the copse but everyone knew Old Bill. Clement hurried on through the jostling crowds. He wanted to know what Morris had learned and to see if Hayward had suffered any other injuries prior to death that would indicate interrogation. Clement rounded the corner into St Andrew's Street, the police station only minutes away.

He entered the imposing building. People sat in chairs around a waiting area. None were people he recognised.

He smiled at Sergeant Kendall at the duty desk.

'Please go straight up, sir. Superintendent Morris is expecting you.'

Clement nodded and took the stairs to Morris's office. He knocked lightly at the door.

'Come in,' Morris called. Clement opened the door. 'Ah! Clement. Please, sit down. Quite a morning.'

'What can you tell me, Arthur?'

'Close range shot. Bullet to the chest.'

'Silenced?'

'And subsonic.'

Clement winced. 'I thought it had to have been. The Master sent Edwards home so I was able to have a quick look around the lodge before McBryde arrived.'

'Did you find anything?'

'No. I should tell you that I wasn't completely honest with you earlier. I did leave college last night after drinks with Father Rathbourne. It was just after ten. I returned to my room an hour later.'

'Why?'

'I went to see a friend.'

Morris eyebrows rose. 'I'm sure you'll tell me about it when you can.'

Clement smiled. 'Thank you. However, I can tell you this. When I returned to college, I saw Hayward sitting at the porter's desk. He didn't look up. I thought he hadn't heard me but it's possible he was already dead.' Clement told Morris what Bill had said to him.

'Could they have known Mr Hayward had warned

you?'

'Only if I'd been followed and we'd been overheard. But why would it warrant his death?'

'Perhaps he told his killer about it,' Morris added.

'Surely if that were the case his body would have been on the floor; shot while standing talking to his killer in the lodge. In my opinion, Arthur, if Hayward was seated at the time he was shot, he didn't have time to either defend himself or shout out anything before he was killed. Further, I cannot see any similarities between the two deaths except that both were killed with shots to the chest. It just doesn't make any sense. Were there any other injuries to Hayward's body?'

'None.'

'I've asked myself if, perhaps, I'd been seen leaving college and Hayward's death was timed to implicate me. If that were true, why has no one stepped forward to tell you this?'

Morris leaned back in his chair. 'Is there even the remotest possibility, Clement, that someone knows your real purpose in being in Cambridge?'

Clement shook his head. 'No. There are only four people, other than yourself, who know I am here; three are in the Service and the fourth works for me. And I trust him above anyone.'

'Your friend in Cambridge?'

'Yes. I was supposed to have lunch with Rathbourne and Armstrong today at Caius but in view of what's happened, there's no point in me trying to infiltrate this group now.'

'That's as well, Clement. Because until I have some-one else, you're my prime suspect.'

12

Friday 6th June 1941

Clement heard the key rotate in the cell door lock. He stood up from where he was sitting on the bunk. It had been a long cold night in the police cell.

Morris entered, carrying Clement's Fairbairn-Sykes dagger. He handed it to Clement. 'We've searched your room. You may be interested to know, Clement, that we found a Luger under your mattress. There are no prints, of course. But we are telling the college that you have been taken into custody. 'Did you bring any other weapons with you to Cambridge?'

'You didn't find the pistol I have secreted in the fireplace in my room?'

'No. I'm sorry about this, Clement, but I actually think a prison cell is the safest place for you right now.'

'I agree, Arthur. And for the record, I didn't kill Bill Hayward.'

'I never thought you did but things must look right. I'll get Sergeant Kendall to get the pistol, if it's still there.'

'No need, my friend can get it. I missed the rendez-vous with him last night so I'll need to get a message to him anyway. He's working at *The Eagle*.'

'Of course. You can use the telephone in the inter-view room at the end. You won't be overheard there.'

Clement followed Morris out of the police cells and along the unadorned corridor to the furthest room from the front door of the police station. 'Take a seat, Clem-ent. While you make your phone call, I'll arrange something for you to eat.'

There was a knock on the open door and Kendall en-tered. 'Sorry, sir. There's a man at the front desk asking to see the prisoner.'

'Name?'

'Says his name is Fearnley Maughton.'

Clement smiled, replacing the telephone receiver. 'He said he'd be looking out for me.'

'Escort the man here, would you Sergeant. And bring some tea and something for Reverend Wisdom to eat.'

Morris closed the door. 'Who is he?'

'My man in the shadows, Reg Naylor. You've met him. Last year in Fearnley Maughton,' Clement said, sit-ting down.

A few minutes later the door opened and Reg came in. 'You alright, Clement?'

'Yes, thank you, Reg. You remember Superintendent Arthur Morris?'

'Yes. The chief inspector from Lewes, isn't it?'

'The same. You involved with Clement currently?' Morris asked.

Reg nodded. 'What are you doing here, Clement?'

'Last night, one of the porters at Trinity Hall was murdered. It happened around the same time that I came to see you.'

'And you think Clement did this?' Reg said to Morris.

'Of course not. But until I find out who did, prison provides Clement some degree of safety and oddly, some freedom of movement to come and go unobserved whenever he wishes.'

'Reg, I need you to get my Welrod from my room.'

'Done, Clement,' Reg said, taking the weapon from his coat pocket and placing it on the desk. 'When you didn't show up I knew something was wrong.'

Clement wrapped the underarm holster around his chest and inserted the Welrod.

'Now to bring you up to speed with what we are doing, Clement,' Morris began. 'I've got Trinity Hall under constant surveillance. So far only students and the occasional Fellow seem to use the front. No one suspicious at this stage.'

'You won't find your man or men using the front door, Morris,' Reg said. 'If you want to see who comes and goes, you have to be in *The Backs*. If there are steps to anywhere, someone is using them. And there are steps from Trinity Hall College to the river. I'll tell you something else. They are in use. By promiscuous students mostly but also others. Students use them from midnight to around three. Others, a lot older than students, use them in the early hours, just before dawn.'

'I saw a dinghy tied up there yesterday. Any ideas who's using them, Reg?' Clement asked.

'From your description, I'd say your young Mr Armstrong. I've been watching for three nights. Tuesday night, well, early Wednesday morning in fact, a rowboat left from the steps at the rear of the college at five in the morning. Same routine Thursday morning and again this morning. I got the sense that it wasn't unusual.'

'How?' Clement asked.

'Oarsman knows Armstrong. Even though nothing was said, there was a familiarity between them. Even their actions, how he got into the boat, everything seemed to be familiar ground and as I said, there was no conversation as to where to sit or where to go. Then it returned about three hours later. But not with young Armstrong. Just the oarsman who ties it up and disappears up the college steps. Then this morning, right on cue at five, Armstrong and the oarsman leave together from the college steps again but as yet the boat hasn't returned.'

'So where does Armstrong go?' Morris asked.

A knock at the door halted conversation. Kendall poked his head around. Entering, he placed a tray on the table with some tea and sandwiches. 'Something you

150

should know, sir.'

'What is it, Kendall?'

'We've just received a telephone call from Ramsey, sir. The Abbey School has had a break-in. In the early hours of this morning, a cleaner saw a torch light through the headmaster's office window. They went immediately to the principal's residence to alert him but by the time they got back to his study, the intruders had vanished.'

'What happened?' Morris asked.

'Ransacked the principal's office. Emptied filing cabinets and spread the contents all over the floor. Will I tell the headmaster you'll be out to see them later, sir?'

Morris turned to face Clement. 'With your permission, Clement, it could be a good idea if Sergeant Kendall knows what's going on.'

Clement looked at the sergeant then at Morris.

Morris must have seen his hesitation. 'Sergeant Kendall has been my bagman since I arrived in Cambridge. You can trust him, Clement.'

'If you think it advisable.'

Morris looked up at Kendall. 'Close the door, Sergeant. You recognise Reverend Wisdom, of course, but I think it could be a good idea if you were a little more involved. These men, Kendall, are members of our Secret Intelligence Service. Reverend Wisdom is here only to provide him with a safe place. While I want the community to think he is detained here, he is here for his protection and ease of movement. If he wishes to leave

151

at any time, you will not hinder his going or coming back for that matter. The same applies to this man, Mr Naylor. In fact, you are to give them every assistance. One more thing, Kendall; you are not to mention this to anyone. Anyone, is that clear? Lives depend on it. Tell the head-master I will be there this afternoon.'

The door closed.

Clement leaned back in the chair and glanced at the clock on the wall. 'Why did they leave it till midday to telephone you?'

'Good question,' Morris said. 'I'll ask them.'

'We must now assume that whoever these people are, they have learned where the boy lives.' Clement told Reg about Michael Hasluck.

'I'll visit the school then go to the boy's home,' Morris said.

'What do you want me to do, Clement?' Reg asked.

'Catch a few hours' sleep, Reg. Then meet me here in the police car park out the back at midnight. I want to see if the Lagonda is still in the garage in Tenison Street. Then I want another look at the porter's lodge at Trinity Hall. Something's there.' Clement shook his head. 'Ar-thur, can you take your constable off the front door to Trinity Hall tonight?'

Morris nodded. 'Of course. What do you suspect?'

'I don't believe Hayward was killed because of what he said to me. He's been there such a long time, his loy-alty wouldn't be in question.' Clement looked away, his mind sifting facts. 'There was no indication of a struggle in the porter's lodge. Does that mean Hayward was threatened and when he didn't comply instantly, he was shot? Or was it because he knew something or had just learned something that the killer didn't want passed on?'

'A callous act whichever way you look at it,' Morris added.

Clement pondered Hugh Armstrong, a man who Clement believed would do whatever was required. As would either of Rathbourne's watchdogs. 'After we've checked the car, we'll pay the lodge a visit. Then Reg and I will check *The Backs* around five tomorrow morning.'

Reg stood to leave. 'See you at midnight, Clement.'

It was late afternoon when Clement heard the key in the cell door. Morris entered. 'Just back from Ramsey. No real damage at the school. Hetherington is treating it as just naughty boys which is why he didn't telephone us earlier. Apparently the Deputy Head was insistent the police should be called in. Hetherington is conducting his own investigations within the school.'

'Do you believe it?'

'Hetherington's a quiet man. Doesn't give much away. But I'm inclined to think he may be correct. If it were a burglary, something would surely have been taken. Remember they were undisturbed for some time before the headmaster arrived. And Hetherington says that despite the mess, nothing has been stolen. If, on the other hand, it was someone interested in young Michael's whereabouts, nothing would be out of place because they wouldn't want anyone knowing they'd been there.'

'And what of the boy?' Clement asked.

'More interesting. Lives at a place called Wilstock House near Lode. I've been there before. Six or more months ago, about a burglary. It's a large house. The boy is the only son of Sir Cedric and Lady Ellen Hasluck. According to the butler at Wilstock, the family is in Portugal. The boy was at the house only one night before his uncle came and took him away. The butler doesn't know where.'

Clement leaned back, his head resting on the wall. 'Do we even know if the boy has an uncle?'

'If it's genuine, the boy is fine,' Morris said. 'If not, kidnapping is a police matter anyway, not SIS. I'll check on it.' Morris left him but Clement noted the door wasn't locked.

The boy's whereabouts worried Clement but other than a chance encounter with Armstrong in Ramsey, there was nothing to connect young Hasluck to Armstrong. Clement hoped he was worrying needlessly.

Clement sat alone in the police interview room and closed his eyes. He tried to push everything from his mind, to allow his subconscious to sift what he knew. He visualised his garden in Oxford; the oak tree and the sound of the sparrows at sunset. But Michael Hasluck refused to be ignored. For the first time in days, he prayed. Mostly for the boy's safety but also for his current mission. Old Bill Hayward's death puzzled and disturbed him. So callous, so cold-blooded. Was it even connected to the dead, unidentified man found in the Cambridgeshire fenland? Clement's mind drifted to Hugh Armstrong, Rathbourne and his two watchdogs. He felt the icy chill of conspiracy. But something about it worried him. If the deaths were connected then whatever this was, it had tentacles that traversed miles, counties even and crossed social barriers. He felt sure it was something more complex than the resurgence of the far-right group. Or was it a network of Nazi spies? He thought of Jakobs and the other German spies at Latchmere House. What if there were other spies that hadn't been caught? Both Jakobs and the other man, Richter had been carrying large sums of money. What was that really used for? He had no way of knowing. He pondered the corpse in Morris's mortuary and the discovery of Old Red Sandstone found in the turn-ups. Did a type of rock found only in Scotland's north make for a Scottish connection? The thought sent shivers through his body. Yet, despite all that had happened and all his conjecture, it was still just that. There was no hard proof of any connection between the boy and Armstrong or between Armstrong and the man in the mortuary, or to the murder of Bill Hayward. Regardless, *C* needed to be kept abreast of developments and that meant a call to Nora Ballantyne.

At midnight Kendall led Clement along the corridor, turned off the lights and unlocked the rear door to the police station.

Clement shook hands with the sergeant. 'Could you

hold this for a while, Sergeant Kendall?' Clement pulled his clerical collar from his throat. 'Don't know when I'll need it again.'

Stepping outside, Clement heard the rear door to the police station close behind him. He breathed in the fresh night air, invigorating after the stale police cell. Within seconds Reg appeared out of the darkness. He carried a rucksack.

'What's in the bag?' Clement asked.

'Extra ammunition, a couple of grenades and some new surprises.'

Running across the police station yard, they disappeared into the night. Fifteen minutes later they entered Tenison Street. Clement went straight to the garage, his hand reaching for the door handle. Inserting the lock-picks, he rotated the lock easily. Checking the street again, Reg pulled the right-hand side door open just enough for them to slip inside. Closing it again, Clement flicked on the torch. The Lagonda was there. He placed his hand on the engine; cold. Reg picked the door lock in seconds. Checking the interior, Clement found some road maps in the glove box; one was of London, the next of Buckinghamshire, the third of Hampshire. He unfolded the maps carefully and checked each. There were no marks on any of them drawing attention to anywhere in particular. Replacing them, he closed the glove box. Coming around the car he shone the torch onto the boot latch then along the edges. Two small threads had been stuck to the right side of the boot. Reg pulled some tweezers from his rucksack and lifted the threads, placing them carefully into a white handkerchief then folding it in two. Clement sprang the latch.

Inside were two suitcases. He stared at them. Both were of elegant leather with reinforced leather edges. Checking for any wires or threads first, he sprang the catches and looked inside each. He had expected to see a wireless and a parachute. What he found were neatly folded gentleman's clothing, each item expertly wrapped in tissue paper. Clement withdrew his knife and using the tip, carefully lifted the edge of each packet. From what he could tell without tearing the wrapping, the suitcase contained a coat, trousers and dress shirt of a gentleman's evening apparel complete with gold studs and cufflinks, bow tie, patent pumps and a pair of silk socks with suspenders. He unlatched the other suitcase. It held the same apparel, but the shoes were several sizes larger.

Reg's bewildered expression mirrored his own. Why were clothes so important that threads had been used to indicate any tampering?

'Trojan horse?' Reg mouthed.

Clement raised his eyebrows as he lifted the suitcases and ran his hand over the boot's felt lining, his fingers searching every crevice for anything hidden within the compartment. He found nothing. Even the side pockets were empty. Quietly, he closed the boot and replaced the threads with a smear of Vaseline from Reg's pack. Lifting the torch, he shone the beam onto the walls across the ceiling and along the floor. Nothing. Except for the car, the garage was completely empty.

'Would you know if anything was amiss under the car?' Clement whispered.

Reg nodded and, lying on the floor, wriggled his way beneath the vehicle. A minute later he pulled himself out. 'Nothing. Not under the car and no concealed mechanic's pit beneath the vehicle. And what's more, Clement, there isn't a speck of dust under there anywhere. What do you make of it?'

'I have no idea.' He took a final look around the space. It made little sense to him.

Relocking the garage, they left Tenison Street, returning to King's Parade just on two o'clock.

The Parade was deserted. Clement gazed up to the heavens. The night was clear and the waxing moon cast its bright light over the street and fenced grounds. Clement checked his watch. McBryde would be on duty in the porter's lodge. He slowed.

'Clement?'

'Just thinking. Why kill Hayward?' He knew his question was rhetorical. 'There has to be something there; something I've missed.'

'Looking for anything in particular?'

'Something he wouldn't leave in his rooms. Something that he didn't want anyone else to see. Something valuable.'

158

'You're the boss, Clement.'

Hunching, they ran into the darkness of Trinity Lane, their footsteps tapping on the cobblestones, finally stopping at the corner, the main door to Trinity Hall just across from them and not twenty feet away.

They crouched at the corner, the high stone walls of Gonville and Caius College at their backs. Clement stared at the front door to Trinity Hall. He couldn't quite grasp what worried him. He turned to Reg. 'Is it reasonable to assume that Hayward's death was not a senseless act of cold-blooded murder, but the result of a threat of some kind?'

'To make him give up something? Something he was prepared to die for rather than give it up?'

Clement stared at his old friend. 'Was it something he had or something he knew?' Clement frowned. 'What do college porters see on a regular basis?' he whispered, but he was thinking aloud.

'You're asking me? I never went to university, Clement, so I've no idea. But I imagine they see the post. But how would he read other people's mail if the letters are sealed?'

'So a postcard, then?' Clement said, following Reg's line of thought.

'What else do these porters do?' Reg asked.

Clement tried to remember Bill's movements on the two occasions he'd been in the lodge. 'They take messages. There's a telephone log.'

'They log all incoming telephone calls? Can they over-hear these calls?'

'I suppose it's possible. The telephone rang when I was there. He recorded it in a log.'

'Is it possible Hayward was blackmailing someone?'

'Also a possibility.' Clement stared at his feet as he often did when thinking. 'What would a man of Hayward's years of tenure be blackmailing someone at the college about? Something that has been going on for some time. But if that's the case, why kill him now?'

Reg shrugged.

Clement looked up at Trinity Hall's front door. It would be locked now. He stared at it, closed, silent, secretive. It said, you can't come in. You're not one of us. Clement felt it. Not that he was envious. Quite the reverse in fact. Something was going on there. Something that was deadly serious.

They crossed the twenty feet in silence. Reg took his lock-picks from his pack and rotated the lock, the barrel sliding back. Clement reached down and withdrew his knife. Turning the handle, they slipped inside and closed Trinity Hall's front door. The door to the porter's lodge was just off to the right. Clement peered around the window. McBryde was sitting at a desk off to one side, his back to the door.

'Reg, knock on the porter's door and engage McBryde in conversation. Get him to come out of the office. Say you were in a student's room and got locked into college and now you want to leave,' Clement whispered.

Reg nodded. 'How long do you need?'

'As long as you can. Cough twice then sneeze when you think he's about to return.'

'Got it.'

Clement tiptoed past the lodge and disappeared into Front Court and stood beneath the lodge windows. His gaze flashed to the windows of Rathbourne's rooms. No one stood there. Not surprising, given the hour. Within a minute Reg was pounding on the porter's door. Through the side windows, Clement saw McBryde stand, then open the door to the covered walkway adjacent to the main entry. Reg was speaking loudly as though drunk. With McBryde's back to him, Clement slipped the window lock and pulled himself over the ledge and into the lodge.

He went straight to the call log sitting on the shelf behind the porter's desk. Keeping his eye on the door, Clement flipped through the pages for all incoming calls for the evening of Wednesday the fourth of June. His gaze scanned the entries. At half past ten that Wednesday evening, the same night he'd had drinks with Father Rathbourne, one incoming call had been logged and no recipient noted. Clement's gaze scanned the other pages. All entries included the date and time of the call along with the name of the caller and the recipient. But not the call on Wednesday evening. The only comment placed beside the time of the call were the initials *W.C.* Clement turned around, his eye falling on the student records. Opening the drawers in turn, he checked both *W* and *C* in the student files but nothing stood out. Neither was there any reference to a call being received. Although Clement knew young Armstrong stayed as a guest at Caius, he checked under *A*. No Armstrong was listed. Then he checked for a file on Rathbourne. His ears strained for the sneeze, but Reg was keeping McBryde's attention. Clement scanned Rathbourne's file and read that Sir Hector Armstrong paid the fees for the priest's accommodation. But this information wasn't a secret and was freely available for all the porters. As Clement closed the drawer, his gaze fell on the small fireplace. It wasn't lit. Clement knelt before it and ran his hand along the under surface of the chimney, feeling for the narrow ledge. His fingers felt a small metal box. Withdrawing it he opened the lid. Inside was a large roll of cash, all five-pound notes.

Outside, Clement heard the signal. Returning the box to the fireplace, he quickly stood, went to the open window and pulled himself over the sill, falling forward, dropping onto the path. Quietly he closed the window as McBryde re-entered the room.

Two minutes later, he rejoined Reg outside and together they left the college and hurried down Trinity Lane, crossing the River Cam to *The Backs*. Below them, a small rowboat was tied up at Trinity Hall steps.

13

Waxing moonlight cast shadows around them. Clement gazed up. The moon would be full in two days. Despite the season, a cool breeze enveloped them while above, occasional clouds flickered stark, grey-blue light over the river. Clement spread his coat on the damp ground and lay down, his elbows supporting his grip on the binoculars. Reg squatted beside him. If Reg was correct about the frequent usage of the small boat tied up there, they didn't have long to wait before someone arrived.

'Did you find anything in the porter's lodge?' Reg whispered.

'Money. Quite a bit and all in five-pound notes.'

Reg allowed a half-exhaled whistle to escape his mouth. 'What did you do with it?'

'Put it back. Morris can watch to see if the lodge is broken into again. If it was about money, then someone will try again soon.'

'You don't believe it was theft, do you?'

'No.'

'It's possible that the money didn't belong to Hayward. He may not even have known it was there,' Reg said.

'Perhaps.'

'Did you find anything else?'

Clement told Reg about the telephone call received at half past ten on Wednesday night.

'The initials are hardly likely to be those of Winston Churchill. Why would the Prime Minister call Rathbourne, a man who you know to be antagonistic to our fearless leader. You know, Clement, it's much more likely to be the initials of the college gardener, or the cleaner. Maybe they're not supposed to receive calls and that's why the old boy only used initials.'

'You are probably correct, Reg. More than likely a simple explanation,' Clement added, but he wasn't convinced. He didn't like loose ends any more than he did coincidences and this case had too many of both. In his opinion, when it came to murder, it almost invariably was never simply explained. Besides which, Clement thought it highly unlikely Hayward would choose death to protect the identity of the gardener or cleaner. Surely if one was prepared to put one's life on the line, it had to be for either a cause or person of national importance or to protect someone held dear. Was it possible the gardener or cleaner was an undercover alias, much like Corporal Hughes for the head of SIS? The fact was that Clement just didn't know. He thought on Reg's earlier remark about blackmail. If Hayward was blackmailing someone, that person held a very big secret, given the amount of money stashed away. Clement frowned. Was it the other way around? Was Bill receiving hush money? If that was so, then Hayward had been receiving payments for some time. So why kill him now?

Clement thought back over his own movements that night. Had the killer also used the window to escape from the lodge?

'I've been a fool!' he said, looking across at Reg who was now lying on the grass, his eyes closed. 'I've made it so easy for them. By returning to college through the front door, I walked straight past Hayward's killer and he saw me. All they had to do was plant the Luger and I would be suspect number one. What better way to be rid of me than to see me arrested for murder? Hanged or not, I would be in gaol for months. Certainly sufficient time for them to do whatever they intend.'

'Does that mean they know you are a threat to them?' Reg asked.

'I don't believe so. More likely I was an opportune scapegoat.'

'Is it possible they know about your connection with Morris?' Reg asked.

Clement stared at the river, black and fast flowing.

'How could they?' But he was beginning to have doubts. Was he just an opportune scapegoat for Hayward's murder? If that was so, what about the break-in at the school? Was that coincidence too? It worried Clement. More than a week had passed since young Michael had been taken from the school. By speaking to the lad, Clement believed he had put the boy in danger. He cast his mind back. Morris had said the uncle had taken him away the day after Michael was sent home. That made it the Saturday, the last day of May. And, a week ago. This uncle was a Fellow living at Caius. So did Hugh Armstrong when in town. Had Michael told his uncle about the day Clement and Morris had come to the school? Had the uncle then told Armstrong? Was Michael in even more danger now?

Half past four. Clement shivered under his coat. If the previous routine was still to be followed, they didn't have long to wait. The moon was higher now and he could see some stars glistening above him. He rolled over, rubbing his hips, his gaze falling on Reg's pack. 'What's in the bag, Reg?'

Reg stood and reached for his pack. 'The usuals as well as three little gems, and my personal favourites. In fact, Clement, you should have one.' Reg reached into the bag and withdrew what Clement thought was a notebook. 'This is a pocket incendiary,' Reg said, grinning. He ran his finger along the edge of the device. 'There's a coloured rod here, at the side. Remove it to uncover a slot. It covers the time pencil key. Red for thirty minutes, white for two hours, green for six, yellow for twelve and blue for twenty-four. To activate, remove the rod then run the edge of a coin along the groove.' Clement took the weapon and studied it then put it in his jacket pocket.

Footsteps. Several. They both heard them.

Clement reached for his binoculars as three dark forms then a smaller fourth descended the steps to the river. No one spoke. Within seconds, one stood in the middle of the dinghy before sitting. Then the distinctive sounds of oars being placed in rowlocks.

Clement rolled onto his belly to steady the binoculars. In the boat Clement saw a man sitting on the middle seat, his hands already on the oars. Another man then descended the steps and stepped into the boat, sitting aft. This man wore a cap and the collar of his coat was pulled up making it impossible to see his face. Another descended the five steps to the boat. Clement knew immediately that it was the stooped figure of Father Rathbourne. Beside him was the small frame of a child. Clement's heart sank. The boy's hands were bound and a gag was tied over his mouth. The oarsman reached up, took the lad and sat him beside the unknown man. Rathbourne stayed on the steps. Clement steadied the binoculars on the boy.

'And be careful!' Rathbourne's whisper to the oarsman carried through the still night. 'Let nothing happen to either of them. Your life on it!' With that Rathbourne climbed back up the steps and waited in the shadows.

Clement watched, his anxiety and anger increasing.

167

Young Hasluck was struggling to free his hands but the man sitting beside him lashed out, catching the side of the boy's head. Michael whimpered under the gag then sat subdued. Clement stared at the child. Michael had been such a confident boy, leader of the lower fourth. Now he sat cowering and complicit. Clement felt sick with guilt for involving the lad in the first place. Surely kidnapping the child would raise alarm? Attention would be drawn; something these conspirators wouldn't want. Clement refocused the binoculars but their faces were shrouded. By their size and stature, Clement didn't believe the men now in the boat to be Rathbourne's henchmen; Gus Hutchinson and Bertie Hawkins. The oarsman was sturdy, the other tall and of slim build. Rathbourne remained on the steps, standing in the shadows. Clement studied the priest, the only one facing the river and whose face Clement could see. What was it about Rathbourne's expression? There was something almost obsequious about Rathbourne's demeanour. It wasn't directed towards the oarsman to whom Rathbourne clearly gave orders but was it directed towards the tall man or the child?

'What are you thinking, Clement?' Reg signed.

The dinghy moved slowly past them, the sound of the oars in their rowlocks the only noise. Clement waited until they could no longer hear the oars dipping in and out of the water or the rhythmic sound of the oars rotating in the rowlocks. The dinghy now was but a shadow of black on the flickering river.

'Speculating about the boy,' Clement whispered. 'The uncle aside, why are his parents in Portugal?' He knew his question was rhetorical. 'Reg, follow the boat. Watch where it goes. Then wait and watch to see who returns and when. Then come to the police station.'

'Got it! Where will you be?'

'Police station.'

Reg nodded and disappeared into the pre-dawn gloom, the sack slung over his right shoulder.

Clement hurried away. Morning's light was beginning to settle and even though still early, he had no wish to encounter any stray Trinity Hall students who may recognise him. He walked along the grassy verge, then crossed the bridge adjacent to Trinity Hall. Hurrying along the narrow dark walkway, he passed the three locked doors from the lane into Gatehouse, his footsteps just audible on the street.

A crisp breeze slid through the narrow passageways. Grey morning shadows dipped into the lane. He stopped. Was it footsteps? He turned. A man stood in the shadow-filled lane some twenty feet behind and facing him. He remained completely still. Clement waited, his attention on the man. The man was staring at him.

The blow was heavy. Clement reeled sideways, the shock confounding. He held his hands to his head and blinked, one hand reaching out for the wall to steady himself as he backed away.

The pain was intense, like an explosion in his brain. The blow had come from behind and now blood was running down the side of his head. He struggled to see. No random attack this, nor common thief. Beside him was a large man dressed in black. Clement struggled to stand upright, to see his attacker. Nothing about the man was familiar. All he could make out was the shape of a large man with a bald head. Clement had no idea who the person was. 'Who are...?'

'If you call out, you will die. Instantly,' a male voice said into his ear from behind him. A hood was pulled over Clement's head.

Clement struggled but his head was pounding, his brain spinning and his body reeling. Behind him, two strong arms grabbed him, dragging his arms backwards. Someone bound them, then grasping his upper arms, propelled him forward. A strong hand pushed him on, his feet stumbling and tripping as he struggled to remain upright. He blundered into the cold stone wall beside him. Staggering, he lunged forward trying to break free of the formidable grip. But whoever held him captive instantly released his tight hold and Clement fell forward onto the pavement, his head hitting the hard stones. He rolled sideways, a low agonized groan his only response. He felt sick and light-headed. Nausea welled up. He couldn't see. He felt as though his head had been crushed. Warm blood began to trickle down the side of his face and into his mouth. His head throbbed, his brain ricocheting within his skull. He gasped for air, trying to stop himself from fainting or vomiting. In that instant, the heel of a booted foot came down on his right shin.

Even though in intense pain, Clement knew if he moved, his leg would be crushed. He lay still, his breathing exaggerated. He gulped air, desperately trying to stay conscious. A voice whispered into his left ear. It was male with a heavy Glaswegian accent.

'Stand. Quietly. Or you die. Your choice.'

Clement blinked and sat up. Rolling onto his side, he struggled to stand, his ears straining for anything to help him get his bearings. His attacker's hands ran over his coat, the hand removing his Welrod then, feeling down his trousered legs, settled on the scabbard of his knife. Clement kicked out. The butt of a weapon crashed down again on his right shoulder and this time he felt searing pain shoot through his neck and arm. He fell backwards onto cold cobblestones, groaning, the pain increasing. His breath now was short and rapid and he believed he was close to death. The man's boot was on his chest, the pressure strong and determined. Clement knew what it meant. He also knew there were at least two if not three men hovering around him. Despite the pain, and the fluctuating levels of unconsciousness, he remained absolutely still. He felt his muscles relax, accepting that death was only seconds away. One man unstrapped the scabbard of his Fairbairn-Sykes knife and dragged him to his feet. Suspended between two men, they walked him for some time. He tried to remember the direction as they turned first right then left. Then left again. He heard a knock. The man pushed him forward and he stumbled over a doorstep, a door closing behind him.

There was no sound, except the shuffling of feet. The surface under his tread seemed smoother but he knew he wasn't inside a building. Then another door and again he was pushed forward. Now he felt soft ground beneath his feet, a lawn or garden perhaps. They pushed him on. They crossed a path of no more than six feet in width before the ground felt soft again. Then some steps. He counted five. His footsteps seemed to echo and he surmised he was in a closed corridor of some kind. Then another door.

'He was wearing these,' the Scot said.

'Interesting. Take him downstairs,' an educated voice said.

Clement knew he had not heard the voice before. It was an older man's voice, cultured and commanding.

'Lock the door. He's of no harm to us now.'

A man grasped Clement's arm and pushed him along a stone-floored corridor. The air was cool. A damp subterranean smell wafted up, the aroma a mix of mould and perpetual dampness. He stood completely still and braced himself for whatever his captor had in mind for him. As the door behind slammed shut, a hand pulled the hood from his head.

Darkness. His head was pounding and he could no longer feel his right shoulder but his numb hands were free. Feeling for the wall beside him, he inched his foot forward and felt the edge of a step. Gradually he descended ten steps, hoping that his eyes would soon become accustomed to the gloom. Minutes passed but there was no light. Running his hand down a stone wall, he slid down the rough surface and sat on the damp floor. Breathing deeply he struggled to suppress the pain. He needed to think. He closed his eyes and took long regulated breaths. How had they known where he was?

14

Clement lay on the damp floor. All he wanted was sleep. It was the body's response to trauma but while his body needed the panacea of unconsciousness, his mind struggled to understand what had happened. Had he and Reg been followed? Despite Morris putting it about that he had been detained for the murder of Bill Hayward, someone knew otherwise. Clement reached for his handkerchief and, spitting into it, dabbed his brow. He licked his dry lips and tasted blood. It had congealed down the side of his face and he could feel that his left eye was cut above his eyebrow. It was beginning to swell and would be badly bruised. By tomorrow it would be so swollen he may not be able to see. At least, he told himself, he was alive. He moved his right arm. While a searing pain shot through his muscles, he knew nothing was broken. He sat up. Then standing, he inched his way along the wall, feeling every surface.

Shelves lined two of the four walls and he guessed he was in a cellar or coal store. He prayed for a coal chute of some kind but he felt nothing other than the cold, hard stone walls. He closed his eyes and thought back, trying to remember how he'd come to this cellar. What he did know was that he couldn't be too far from where he'd been attacked in Trinity Lane. Inching his way along the fourth wall, he found the steps again. Climbing them he tried the door.

It was locked.

There was no escape. Either they intended him to die there or he would be moved at some time. Descending the steps, he inched his way around the room again, then slid onto the floor and sat opposite the steps in the dark.

His mind went in and out of lucidity. 'Start at the beginning,' he said aloud, trying to concentrate. There had been a third person present the night Josef Jakobs had landed. Someone important. Important enough for Jakobs to have been callously sacrificed, and for the unidentified man in Morris's mortuary to have been shot at point-blank range. Was Bill Hayward another? Then there was Michael Hasluck. Other than providing tangible proof of a connection between himself and Morris, why had the lad been abducted? Clement shivered. He felt the weight of guilt and fear for the boy's welfare. If it hadn't been for young Hasluck's chance encounter with Armstrong and the Lagonda, Clement would still be unaware of the dark-haired man's existence. He visualised the tall man in the dinghy, trying to recall if there was anything familiar about him. He hadn't seen the man's face so, whilst it seemed likely, he had no way of telling if it was the Abwehr man or someone else entirely.

Clement swallowed hard. Innocent people entangled by fate. Wickedness. Clement felt himself frown. He flinched and put his hand to his face as the raw shooting pain flashed down his cheek and neck. That word; wickedness. Michael Hasluck had used it. He'd said Armstrong went to a school that sounded like wickedness. Clement sat up. The clothes in the boot of the car. The map of Hampshire. 'Not wickedness. Wykehamist,' he said aloud. Somehow his discovery helped alleviate his exploding headache and he found himself smiling.

Clement wriggled his left foot, the action unconscious; his Fairbairn-Sykes knife no longer attached to his lower left leg. Then, he remembered Reg's new device. The Scot had searched for weapons, running his hands over Clement's torso and arms but the pocket notebook had been overlooked. His fingers felt its smooth metal surface. It's presence gave him hope.

Time passed. In the cold hours that followed his cheek had swollen such that his eye felt like a slit in his face and his shoulder ached in the bitter cold of the underground cellar. He forced himself to concentrate, to keep his mind busy recalling everything he had heard and what he knew. But there were so many loose ends. He let his head fall back on the cold wall. The cold. It always triggered his memories of Caithness and he shivered at the recollection. Scotland. He thought of the traitor hanged for treason following his mission to the far northern county. That man had had a Hitler Youth tattoo under his upper right arm. Did that connect him to the dead man currently in Morris's mortuary? Were there other connections between this mission and his last? Clement stood and marched around the cellar, his mind on the past. He heard his stomach groan. He felt hungry but he guessed eating would be denied him. In the darkness, he found the steps to the door again and sat down on them, his thoughts returning to Caithness. His mind began to list the connections with his current situation to Scotland: his recent attacker with the strong Glaswegian accent, a convicted traitor who'd once lived in Glasgow, the Hitler Youth tattoos on both the traitor and the dead man in Morris's mortuary, and Old Red Sandstone. Clement drew in a long breath and exhaled slowly then rested his head in his palms and forced himself to think. 'Glasgow,' he said aloud. Was the man in Morris's mortuary Scottish? Or from further north where Old Red Sandstone was quarried: Orkney, or even Shetland or Norway? Clement stared into the darkened space in front of him. He remembered Father Rathbourne's toast to absent friends and martyrs. Did that include the Caithness traitor? Wrapping his arms around his chest, he took a long deep breath. *In the shadow of Thy wings, I will make my refuge, until these calamities are passed*, he said aloud, quoting Psalm Fifty-Seven. Then he recalled something he'd earlier dismissed.

15

Clement stared into the dark empty space. Why had Rudolf Hess flown into Scotland? Clement tried to remember what he'd read in the newspapers. Hess, apparently, had come to negotiate a peace deal believing that certain members of the British aristocracy would support his endeavours. The Duke of Hamilton had been mentioned in the newspapers but his involvement with the Deputy Führer had been denied in the House of Commons, and the duke was currently serving as an Air Commodore with the Royal Air Force. Clement rubbed at his aching forehead. He couldn't remember if others had been mentioned. Was a misguided belief the only reason Rudolf Hess had come to Britain? Surely the Deputy Führer wouldn't make such an audacious trip without certainty of his reception? Clement recalled the date; the tenth of May and just less than a month ago. The newspapers had reported Hess had been taken into custody immediately. The duke had denied any collusion with Hess and even Hitler himself had described Hess's mystery flight as delusional. Clement held his hands around his neck hoping what little heat they provided would soothe the incessant ache. He allowed his head to drop forward, timing his breathing with every wave of persistent pain. Each time he inhaled, the stench of his own urine and centuries of damp filled his nostrils. 'Endurance is the key,' he said aloud. He knew it was how his enemy worked; isolation eroded courage, clouded the mind and broke the spirit. They would leave him there just long enough to believe he was defeated. Compliant. Someone would come, eventually, he told himself. Even if only to check if he were dead. He felt sleepy, the adrenaline that had surged previously now left him feeling exhausted. He fought the cold and the pain, regulating his breathing and walking in circles around his cell to keep his body warm and his mind active.

Facts and suppositions blurred. He had been over it all before. He knew that. It couldn't all be supposition. He needed something concrete to work on. He searched his memory for something, anything he'd overlooked; a tiny fact, a shred of evidence he'd dismissed as unimportant. Even a different way of thinking about it may give him some insight. But nothing new or different came to mind. Of one thing, however, he was certain; these people were ruthless even to kidnap and cold-blooded murder. He also believed he would not be permitted to live beyond his usefulness. Whatever that was, it explained why he was not already dead. It gave him a glimmer of hope and if they moved him, a chance at escape. The sound of the door above crashed in on his thoughts. Light flooded in and down the staircase. He shielded his eyes.

'Stand up, Reverend Wisdom. You are leaving us.'

Clement heard the educated voice and footsteps descend.

'Who are you?' Clement demanded, shielding his eyes from the glare.

An older man of considerable stature with a serious face and white hair stood before him, sniffing the pungent air. A slow smile spread over his face but he made no comment. He turned, the light from above suddenly highlighting the man's facial features. Prominent teeth was evidently a dominant gene in the Armstrong family. Clement guessed he was Hugh's father, Sir Hector Armstrong.

'You will not be returning, Reverend Wisdom. Myself and others have worked too hard to achieve this. All the players are in place and now it's just a matter of days.'

A figure appeared in the doorway above them and Hugh Armstrong ran down the stairs.

'Let me deal with him, Pa.'

'All in good time, Hugh. Bring the other one!'

Young Armstrong ran up the steps and disappeared through the light-filled doorway.

'Could I have some water and something to eat?' Clement asked, his gaze fixed on Sir Hector Armstrong.

'Soon. After you, Reverend,' Armstrong said, indicating the stairs.

Clement climbed the steps. They led into a darkened covered walkway that connected one building to another. Beyond, in both directions, he saw tended gardens and manicured lawns. On the air, he heard the sound of a bell ringing, short and sharp. A few minutes later another peel, again short and abrupt. Voices now, loud and raucous came from somewhere around him. A few feet away a light, strong and bright, glowed in another corridor. No one walked there. There was an evening light to the air but it wasn't yet dark. He realised he must have been underground for almost the entire day. At least Morris and Reg would know by now he was missing. Clement prayed they were looking for him.

'So you are young Armstrong's father, Hector Armstrong?' Clement said in the hope that someone would see or hear him there.

'Sir Hector, to you. You are going on a journey, Reverend.' Hector Armstrong turned abruptly, his eyes almost glowering with disdain. 'For you, it will be a long one. And I can guarantee, they will never discover your body.'

Clement heard the threat, the attempt at intimidation. Whatever Armstrong had in mind for him, his death was a certainty. Footsteps behind him. He turned. A short man, completely bald and with a stern, almost expressionless face stood before him. The man held a dark-coloured cloth in his hands and Clement suspected he was the Scot.

'You said I could have something to eat and drink,' he said, turning back to Armstrong.

'And I said soon.'

'Is that really necessary now?' Clement asked, nodding at the hood in the henchman's grip.

'Yes,' Hector Armstrong said. 'I do not intend for you to escape, Reverend. You see, I know of your skills. You killed a brave man, a patriot and another man died because of you. I have kept your weapons as mementoes.'

Clement swallowed, his mouth dry. The threat was sincere. He stared at Hector Armstrong but didn't respond. He knew Armstrong's words were not bluff. But how had Armstrong learned of his current involvement, much less his previous mission to Scotland? Armstrong's steady gaze had not shifted. Suddenly Clement's arms were pulled back. He winced as a wave of pain spread over him but his mind was on Armstrong and Caithness. He swallowed several times trying to lubricate his dry mouth.

The strong arm gripped his wounded shoulder, the hood instantly was over his head. He was pushed along the covered corridor, the sound of his boots creating a slight echo in the covered passage. Above him he heard the voices again, loud. Then sudden quiet. Then the scraping of chairs on wooden floors. College. Mealtime.

He knew he wasn't in Trinity Hall. It had to be Caius. And if Caius mealtimes were the same as Trinity Hall then it was just before half-past seven in the evening.

A minute later, he felt a cool balmy evening breeze on his skin. A path was beneath his feet but there were no steps. He guessed it was a rear access into Caius. The strong grip pushed him forward until he no longer felt the solid path under his boots. Then the unmistakable crunch of gravel beneath his tread. He heard a sharp metallic click. He took a quick breath in, his heart pounding and swung around. Was he walking to his execution?

'Get in!' the Scottish voice said.

'Into what?' Clement said.

'Untie his hands,' Sir Hector said. 'But keep a hand on his injured shoulder. If he tries anything, break it.'

Someone untied the rope and pulled the hood back slightly. Clement stood completely still. He could see the gravel now beneath his feet and off to one side, a set of large tyres, the sort used on lorries. He then heard several sets of feet approaching from behind.

'Sit on the lorry tray and swing your legs in,' the Scot said into his ear and pushed him forward. Clement felt the metal edge of the lowered tray. Turning around and with his palms on the edge of the tray, he pulled himself into a lorry, then swinging his legs up, rolled over, knelt and stood. He heard someone, he guessed the Scot, climb in beside him. He had hoped for an opportunity to run but with so many around him, it would be futile and may mean he was never left alone again. Or worse, shot where he stood. The Scot turned him around and retied his hands, the hood once more pulled down hard on his head.

'Sit!' the Scot said.

Inching back, Clement's heel hit the edge of something metal. Slowly he lowered himself onto a long hard seat. A bottle was pushed into his hands. Lifting it under the edge of his hood, he put the bottle to his lips and swallowed the thirst-quenching water.

'Where are you taking me?' Clement asked.

There was no answer but he sensed he was not alone.

'Where are you taking me?' Clement repeated, his voice raised.

'Be quiet!' the Scot said, his guttural voice constrained. Clement presumed his voice was low so as not to be overheard by others around the college. He knew he was surrounded by people but would any of them hear him if he called out for help? Students at supper. It was unlikely any noise he managed to make would even be heard. He felt someone sit beside him. Then the harsh breath on his ear. 'Remain seated. Keep quiet. Or your shins will feel my boot!'

Clement waited. The lorry rocked slightly as someone jumped from the lorry to the gravel. He remembered Armstrong had instructed his son to bring another. He felt the lorry move again. Someone got in but no one spoke. Then he heard approaching footsteps, several coming across the gravel. Whoever it was, was resisting hard. The lorry rocked more violently this time and

Clement surmised the person was both an adult and he suspected, male. He could hear the muted mutterings of protestation and guessed that whoever it was, was gagged. He prayed it wasn't Reg.

The tray at the rear of the lorry slammed shut. A minute later he heard the roar of the engine. He sat back, pondering the other occupants in the lorry. Himself, the Scot, perhaps a driver, and either one or two others. He leaned his head against a metal strut behind him as the lorry drove away.

They drove for about half an hour, always on a hard surface. He listened for any familiar sounds; air raid sirens, rail crossings, people, crowds, even the sound of animals or aircraft but nothing came to him. Eventually, the vehicle slowed. He heard the crunching of another gravelled surface. The vehicle stopped and a door opened. Then the lorry drove forward then stopped again. The door slammed shut. A gate, he reasoned. Then something soft hit the side of the lorry; bushes or tree branches perhaps but the vehicle didn't stop. When it finally did, he heard a door open, then footsteps to the rear of the lorry and the hard click of the tray being lowered.

'Stand,' the man said.

Clement stood, his feet spread wide to keep his balance. The Scot was behind him again, the strong grip edging him forward, towards the rear of the lorry. 'Sit! Swing your legs over the edge and get out!'

Clement sat down on the vehicle floor as instructed

and, edging forward, wriggled his way to the edge of the tray and jumped down. He felt the gravel under his feet. His captor was behind him, pushing him forward. They walked no further than twenty yards. He heard a door creak open. Then the rope that tied his hands was removed. In that instant, two strong arms gripped his body from behind, pinning his arms. He felt a hand in the middle of his back. Then, in one swift action, the hand punched him forward. A second later a clattering door closed behind him.

He fell forward and lay still, listening, expecting a blow. Nothing happened. Beneath him he smelt straw. He waited, not moving. Still he heard nothing. Was someone standing over him? Rolling over, he slowly removed the hood, his hands immediately covering his head. He had expected to see someone. The Scot or perhaps the other unknown occupant from the lorry. Even with his eye now hideously painful and swollen, he could just see. No one stood over him.

16

Clement sat up. He was in a large barn, two stories in height with high beams. He turned around, his ears straining. There was no sound; neither human nor animal. 'Is anyone there?' he asked quietly. No one responded. He stood, the barn's lofty roof high above him. He was completely alone. Whoever had shared the lorry ride with him had not accompanied him. By the diminishing light in the building, he guessed it was between nine and ten at night. The barn was an ancient building, large and made of stone. Farm machinery of various kinds were on one side. Above him, suspended from the overhead rafters was a block and chain. He had seen such things before but he didn't really know what they were used for. A large metal hook hung from the block. He stared at it feeling uneasy.

Clement slowly turned around, staring at the walls. There were no windows and soon the whole barn would be in darkness. Only the large double entry doors afforded a chance at escape. He walked towards them and pulled the handle. Locked, and a heavy wooden beam bolted the door from the outside.

Reaching into his pocket, he withdrew Reg's innocuous device, feeling it between his fingers. It was the only weapon he had. From the time taken in the lorry to leave Cambridge and to arrive at the barn, he knew he was still in Cambridgeshire. Once he left the county, there may not be another opportunity to escape. He looked at the device and thought back. To activate it, Reg had said to remove the rod, select the colour for the time delay then run a coin along the groove. He rummaged in his pocket until he found a shilling. Red for thirty minutes. It was the shortest time available. Removing the rod, he ran the coin along the groove, then placed the device directly below the right-hand side of the door and covered it with straw. Noting the time on his watch, he took refuge behind the tractor.

He waited. Fifteen minutes passed. Then the sound of someone lifting the beam over the door. He peered around the edge of a tyre. The door opened and a girl of approximately sixteen with a frightened expression entered carrying a tray.

Clement stood but he didn't walk towards her. The girl approached him, her mouth open, her timid eyes wide.

'I apologise, I must look quite a fright,' he said, hoping to draw the girl a little further away from the door.

The girl nodded and put the tray on a straw bale on the ground near to where Clement stood. 'I was told to bring you this. It's not much.'

He watched her. While she appeared scared, from her comment, he thought she seemed concerned for him.

'Thank you. May I know your name?'

'I'm not supposed to talk to you.'

'Surely it can't hurt if you tell me your name?'

'Isabel.'

'Do you live here, Isabel?' Clement persisted.

'No. In the village.'

'Which village is that?'

'I told you not to speak to him!' Hector Armstrong's voice bellowed from the doorway.

The girl jumped in fright. Curtsying, she turned and scurried past Armstrong who stood in the barn door less than two feet away from the concealed explosive.

Clement stepped forward hoping that Armstrong would stay where he was. Hector Armstrong was staring at him. There were so many questions Clement wanted to ask. Even if he'd had hours available, he knew Armstrong was unlikely to answer them. He held Armstrong's glare hoping to keep the man where he stood for a few more minutes. 'Why am I here?' Clement demanded.

'Our plans are now close to fruition. Not even Menzies himself could stop it now.'

'Who?'

A slow smile spread over Armstrong's face revealing

his large teeth. 'You really must think we are stupid, *Hope.*'

Clement heard the word. His head spun. His eye twitched as a hundred memories flooded back. *Hope* had been his cover name in Caithness. He could feel himself swaying. He stepped back, trying to steady himself, to control his reactions. Armstrong smiled, a mocking sneer curling his lips.

'I told you. You are responsible for the deaths of two important people. I will not allow you to kill any more. Besides, now we have you, we're not likely to let you go anywhere. You'll be taken to an island far away, where you will die and your body will be taken out to sea where it will never be found.'

'Shetland?'

Armstrong's eyes narrowed. Clement saw the reaction and knew his guess had been correct. He flicked a glance at his watch. Armstrong saw the move and frowned.

Clement threw himself sideways behind the wheels of the tractor as an explosion ripped the barn door from its hinges sending it spinning into the air. Armstrong disappeared in a haze of smoke and flame as timber splinters like daggers flew in every direction. A loud groan-like scream pierced the haze. A second later, Clement rushed forward through the smoke and leapt over Armstrong's prostrate body. He didn't know if the man was dead or just badly injured and he didn't wait to find out. He ran across the yard. Light rain was falling. He saw the lorry parked nearby. He ran on. Jumping a low stone fence, he ran into a field and through some long grass.

He knew within seconds that any others in the house would be on the scene. Minutes later, the front of the house was lit up by the fire that was taking hold in the straw-filled barn. He heard the sound of barking dogs. He stopped and turning, listened, his breathing short and exaggerated, his heart pounding. Torch lights now flashed around the barn and highlighted the house beyond. It was two storey and covered with creeper. A large porch covered the main entry. Lights flashed again panning across the fields. Clement threw himself onto the ground, his gaze on the house. In the side glare of a torch light, Clement could see the Scot. He had two large black dogs with him both straining at the leash.

Clement stood, his eyes as wide as possible. Somewhere there had to be a ditch or channel. He needed the safety of water. Holding his aching shoulder he ran on, his breathing audible, his mouth dry, the ground beneath his feet now damp. The dogs were barking. If the Scot let them off the leash, Clement believed he would be torn to pieces.

He ran fast across the open fields and hurled himself into the darkness. His ankle twisted in the furrowed, slippery ground and he fell. Scrambling to his feet, he got up quickly and kept running. Crossing a field of low crops, his foot went from under him again and he fell down a slope, rolling over and over and landing in the shin-deep water. It was ice cold. Picking himself up, he waded along the ditch for twenty yards then climbed the opposite bank and ran along the edge before sliding back into the water again. On his third climb out of the ditch, he saw a light in the distance, far off to his right and away from the barn. It was only for a second. Then again. He frowned and crouched in the furrowed field, a trickle of water running down his face. People were shouting. But not from the direction of the far-off flashing light. He stayed low and peered into the darkness. Not far ahead, he saw the looming silhouette of a two-storey dwelling. He froze, his eyes wide. He had run in a circle. The cross ditch had returned him to the house. He continued to stare. The dogs were still in the fields, some distance away. Off to his right, and several hundred yards away, the flashing light started again. He noted that the people in the yard paid it no attention. They remained huddled around what was left of the barn door, and the body of Hector Armstrong.

Clement waited. For the first time he thought about the lights. Visible lights at night were strictly forbidden yet these people showed scant regard for attracting Nazi bombers.

The front door of the house opened and a woman came out. She ran towards Hugh Armstrong who was kneeling beside his father's prostrate body. Within minutes three others came out of the house. Clement saw the familiar hunched shape of Father Rathbourne and the two impassive young men who never seemed to be too far away from the priest. They all huddled around

Hector Armstrong, lifting his body. Suddenly Hugh stood up, and looked out across the fields, his voice raised, 'Find him! I want him alive! After I'm finished with him, he'll beg for death.'

'They're out looking for him. He won't get far,' Rathbourne said.

Clement waited until the body of Hector Armstrong was taken inside. The door closed. The dogs barked. It was dark now.

Staying low, Clement circled the front yard, the lorry not twenty feet from him. Then the front door opened again. Clement fell to the ground and inched his way under a nearby shrub. Another man came out and standing on the porch, lit a cigarette. Clement didn't recognise him. He reached for his binoculars. This man had thinning grey hair, a high forehead and an indifferent, almost haughty expression. Was this the man Michael had seen in the Lagonda? Clement searched the face but this man had grey hair and his jawline was not obviously prominent, neither did he have a moustache. The sound of dogs barking carried on the night air. Clement kept his gaze on the man smoking who, it appeared, was in no hurry to join the search. The door opened again, the light from the hallway inside illuminating the porch. The man smoking turned, the light from the house highlighting his face. Another man stepped outside. Clement froze.

17

He lay in the shrubs, his head buried in the decomposing leaves. He felt numb. How could he have missed it? Lifting the binoculars again he watched the faces. As astounded as he felt at seeing Walter Bainbridge, Clement needed to hear their conversation. Quietly, he crawled forward through the shrubs and lay flat in the garden beside the front porch, the two men above him.

'Is he dead?' the grey-haired man asked Bainbridge.

'Yes.'

Clement saw the man's hand stub out his cigarette on the post beside him.

'What happens now?' Bainbridge's voice.

'We wait. It must go ahead.'

'How! With Haushofer arrested and Sir Hector dead. That imbecile son of his can't run it.'

'I'm well aware of that! Teddy will be here soon. And

we can't leave Hess languishing in Latchmere House, or wherever they've got him now, for much longer.'

'If only Haushofer hadn't gone back.'

'There's no point in dwelling on that. Besides he had to return to assist Hess. We couldn't have foreseen Hitler's reaction. Nor that the Gestapo would arrest him. It can't be helped.' The man shook his head. 'It doesn't matter now anyway.'

'It's an ill omen,' Bainbridge added.

'Nonsense! You just keep Hugh under control until everyone arrives.'

'When will that be?'

'Any day. Just as soon as the weather is right.'

Clement waited in the bushes until they returned inside the house and the door closed. He stood slowly and stared at the barn where some nearby farmworkers were attempting to extinguish the flames. People were running everywhere.

Clement's mind raced. Whoever this grey-haired man was, he moved in influential circles. Clement didn't know who Haushofer was but he evidently was connected to Rudolf Hess. Perhaps the Abwehr man on the Heinkel had been this Haushofer and he'd somehow since returned to Germany. Clement stared at his feet, his mind on the grey-haired man. Hector Armstrong's death appeared to be nothing more to him than an inconvenience but the presence of Walter Bainbridge, the Oxford school archivist, told Clement much. He pursed his lips. Learning that Armstrong had known about his

Caithness mission confirmed his suspicions about the Scottish connection but he felt betrayed by Bainbridge. Clement stared at the ground beneath his feet. His position at St Edward's School had been arranged by the Service. Had SIS known about Bainbridge? Clement couldn't think about any of it now. Despite all he'd overheard, his first priority was to get away.

Leaving his position by the front porch and hunching low, he ran along the side of the house. He felt the crushing realisation of what he had always known; he was just as expendable to the Service as Hugh Armstrong was to his cause. Working with SIS made one so. Death and danger went with the job.

He squatted beneath a window at the side of the house. He needed to contact Reg and Morris. Standing, he ran to the rear of the house and crouching there, waited. Hugh Armstrong would be pre-occupied with the death of his father for now, but very soon that emotion would be replaced with rage and revenge. In the darkness Clement heard a door open. The girl, Isabel, walked out. He wondered about the girl's loyalty to Armstrong. What Clement had witnessed in the barn told him that Isabel was afraid of Hector Armstrong. Did that fear extend to the son? Hugh's volatile temper convinced Clement that it would. Wise girl, he thought. In the light from the doorway, he watched her. She wore a heavy overcoat and carried a bag over her shoulder. He watched her walk away from the house. The door closed and darkness returned. She hadn't looked back.

He waited until she had almost disappeared into the gloom, her form just discernible in what was left of the twilight and the rising three-quarter moon. He ran forward, then stopped near a shed. He could hear the dogs, their intense yapping clear on the night air. They seemed further away now. Hurrying through a gate he could see the girl in front of him. Then, away to his right, he saw the flashing light again. He stopped and crouched in the field, his stare on the intermittent light. It was still some distance away across the meadows. The girl halted and turned slightly.

Clement breathed a sigh of relief. The light was a signal for Isabel to find her way home in the dark. Keeping back, Clement cut across the fields, heading slightly east of Isabel and her destination. Ten minutes later he pushed his way through a narrow strip of woodland then up a steep embankment before jumping over a low stone wall to a road beyond. Waiting there, he saw her higher up the street opening a gate to a cottage where a curtain had been lifted showing a sliver of light. She went inside. The curtain fell into place. It was dark again.

Clement looked back over the fields he had just crossed. He couldn't see the house now and the fire had evidently been extinguished. He listened to the sounds on the night air but no man-made noise came to him. A little further along the road he saw the outline of several larger dwellings clustered together. Hurrying towards the buildings he looked up at the sign above an inn door; *The Bridge*.

He went in, the welcome warmth radiating towards him. Inside was a small front room with an L-shaped bar. Men filled the cramped space, by their clothes, farm-workers. The conversation ceased as Clement approached.

'You don't look so good. You been in a fight?' the barman said.

Clement shook his head. 'Got lost and fell into a ditch,' he said, indicating his sodden clothes.

'If you'd like a drink, you'll need to be quick. I was about to close up.'

'I'd be grateful.'

'I've got a room if you need it? Where have you come from?' the barman asked, pulling a beer and placing it on the counter.

'I don't know this pub,' Clement said, putting some coins on the bar.

'Then you don't know Waterbeach,' the barman said. 'We are the only pub this side of the river for miles.'

Clement turned around. Everyone was staring at him. All, Clement decided, were farmers. They wore the heavy warm clothes of an outdoor life and had the florid skin of years spent working out of doors in all weathers. Several dogs lay beside the hearth, too tired to even stir as he entered the room.

'The barman asked you a question?' a large man said, stepping forward. A dog's head lifted.

Clement held the man's stare. In his opinion, no one in the room gave the impression of supporting a far-right political conspiracy. Neither had they thought it necessary to assist with a burning barn about a mile away but he wasn't taking any chances. 'I'm a guest at a house further up river,' Clement said. 'I went out for a walk and I've become hopelessly lost. And now it's raining. As you see, I've fallen a few times,' Clement said, 'They're probably looking for me now. If I could use your telephone?'

'In the hall. Local calls only, sorry,' the barman said, nodding in the direction of a door.

Clement downed the drink and left the bar. He guessed he had somewhere between five and ten minutes before his whereabouts would become known. Standing in the hall, he dialled Morris's home telephone number.

'Superintendent Morris speaking?'

Clement hung up. He checked his watch. He'd already been at *The Bridge* too long. Any minute now he expected the Scot and his dogs to burst into the place. He returned to the bar. 'They're on their way,' he said to the barman. 'Thanks for the drink. Hopefully the rain has abated. I'll wait outside. And thanks for the use of the telephone.'

'Where did you say you'd come from?' the publican asked.

Clement turned. 'A house on the river just outside Cambridge.'

'Which side of the lock?'

'Cambridge side,' he gambled. Clement watched the faces. He didn't know about a lock so he hoped he sounded convincing. He looked around the faces. While he thought it unlikely these men were involved with Armstrong, he wasn't in any doubt that for the price of a drink they would tell anyone who asked about him. 'It doesn't have a name,' he said, then added, 'I'm a guest of the Master of Caius.' Clement watched for a reaction but he didn't see any. He reached for the door handle.

Closing the door on the pub, he listened for the dogs. He could hear the barking but they were some distance away. He breathed in the cool night air. His eye was painful and his shoulder numb. Rubbing his aching arm, he walked towards the stone wall and sat on it in case anyone in the pub was watching. He waited a further two minutes then turned, his gaze on the pub entrance. The curtains over the front windows were still drawn and no one from the pub had followed him outside. Swinging his legs over the wall, he jumped down and ran back across the road, skirting the inn. Crossing the grass, he headed towards the river.

The Bridge, so Clement had learned from Morris, was about eight miles downstream from Cambridge. Morris had told him to take a rowboat from the jetty and row upstream to Horningsea on the other side of The Cam where he would meet him within the hour. Clement crouched under a low hedge by the river. The riverbank was low and in the strong moonlight he could see several rowboats were tied up to a small platform at the edge of the water. Choosing the smallest, he crept onto the jetty and untied the dinghy then stepped aboard. Using an oar, he pushed the boat away from the bank then sitting, quietly placed the oars into the rowlocks. He pulled on the oars, wincing with the pain in his shoulder.

The river wasn't especially fast flowing but with his recent injuries, every stroke sent a stab of pain through his neck and shoulder. As he rounded a bend under Clayhithe Bridge, *The Bridge* disappeared from his view. No one had come after him.

He dipped the oars into the silent waters. Everything about his current mission disturbed him. Loose ends. Things from the past and the astounding things he'd overheard. At least he now knew how his adversaries had always been a step ahead of him. If he had not seen Bainbridge with his own eyes he would never have believed the man capable of such treachery.

Bainbridge had evidently been watching Clement's every move since he arrived in Oxford. Clement thought of the notes he'd left for him saying when and for how long he'd be away. Clement recalled the day of Morris's call. Bainbridge had been absent that morning. Clement shook his head in disbelief. Bainbridge must have alerted someone local to keep him under surveillance. He thought of the people on the bus: women with shopping baskets and children, airmen and an elderly academic. While Bainbridge's involvement astonished him, it was nothing in comparison to Hector Armstrong. There was a truly evil man who thought nothing of manipulating others to commit murder and kidnap and who knew what else. Clement shivered. Hector Armstrong was chilling but his words were more so and Clement's fears about a connection with his mission in Caithness had been vindicated, even to a knowledge of Clement's former cover name. That small detail had been passed on to others in the network and it told Clement that his movements had been watched for months.

The realisation made him feel sick and naive. Old Red Sandstone. Without that discovery he would still be stumbling around. The police pathologist had said the stone was used for buildings and monuments. Monuments like headstones for graves, perhaps? Glasgow both then and now still held secrets. And he needed to know the answers.

He listened to the night and the rhythmic sound of the oars in their rowlocks, breathing out with each stroke, trying to build up some momentum against the current. His head throbbed. He pushed the pain from his thoughts, his mind dwelling on the conversation he'd overheard. Something was imminent and he'd overheard the names of two of the most infamous men of the Nazi regime along with another German; a man named Haushofer who had been arrested by the Gestapo. Did that fact make him friend or foe? Clement didn't know. He wanted to speak with Colonel Stephens and hear what he'd learned from Jakobs. If Jakobs was proving uncooperative, perhaps mentioning Haushofer's name would elicit a response. A long breath escaped his lips as he rowed, his mind distracted from the throbbing pain in his head and shoulder.

He leaned into the rowing, the moonlight casting its intense glow over black waters. With every stroke, Clement felt the tangle of conspiracy; overwhelming and far-reaching. This was more than embedding a few spies or the resurgence of a far-right group. This had taken years to establish and involved every echelon of society. From Shetland to Cambridgeshire and Oxford and who knew where else. And, it included the enemy, and not just any low-ranking official but the two highest ranking officers of the Third Reich. Clement's mind dwelt on the man smoking on Armstrong's front porch. He didn't know who this man was but he was convinced this was not the same man Michael had seen in the Lagonda. His English was that of a native speaker, and a well-educated one at that. And his hair was grey not dark. If this grey-haired man was someone else, was Herr Abwehr this Haushofer?

A light wind wrapped around his body and he began to shiver. He felt chilled to the core from wet clothes and realised deception. He took a deep breath and kept his mind focused on the rhythmic action of the oars. In the moonlight he saw the spire, black, pointing like a dagger against the night sky. At the river's edge he saw Morris's silhouette standing on a jetty. Standing with him was a familiar figure.

18

Sunday 8th June 1941

'God's teeth, Clement! What's happened to you?'
Reg asked, helping him from the dinghy.

'Long story. I hope you came by car, Arthur?'

'I'll get you to a doctor.'

'Thank you, but not yet. No one in this area can see me.' Clement turned to Reg. 'Destroy that dinghy, would you, Reg. No explosives, just put a hole in it. A big one.'

'Got it!'

Reg reached for his pack, then swinging it onto his shoulder left Clement and Morris standing by the jetty. In the moonlight Clement saw Reg pull the dinghy from the water. Using his Fairbairn-Sykes knife, Reg sliced along the dinghy's timbers, prising the wooden beams apart until a large gap appeared between the planks. Returning the craft to the water, Reg placed two large stones from the riverbank into the hull and pushed the boat out into the stream, waiting for gravity to take effect.

The dinghy sank slowly into the river. Leaving the bank, Clement and Morris walked silently up a gently sloping hill towards the church. It stood out against the night sky, its spire towering above them. As they passed it, Clement read the name; St Peter's Horningsea. Made of flint with an old wooden door and porch at one side it was a large church for a rural village. The path meandered around the church and into a small adjoining graveyard with numerous large trees. In front and over a high stone fence was a two-storey dwelling that Clement guessed was the rectory. To the right of this was another, smaller building. Parked not far away Clement saw the police car.

In silence they walked past the headstones to the vehicle. Morris opened the boot, retrieving a blanket and a cardboard box with a red cross on the side. 'Wrap this around you, Clement, and sit on the back seat,' Morris whispered. 'I'll put a compress on your eye for now but it will need stitches.'

'What's that building?' Clement replied, nodding towards the nearest dwelling.

'*Crown and Punchbowl Inn*,' Morris said. 'Best we leave here soon so as not to arouse the publican or anyone else.'

Clement pulled the blanket round him. He stared at the riverside scene in the intermittent moonlight, his gaze fixed on the path from the river, waiting for Reg to return. Within minutes he saw his old friend running back up the hill, his pack over his broad shoulders. By God's hand and men like Morris and Reg, Clement believed he had been saved from certain death. With his safe deliverance, he finally allowed the weariness to seep into his bones. He felt utterly exhausted.

Morris closed the car door. A minute later Reg tossed his pack into the boot then sat in the front beside Morris. 'No one will be using that boat again.'

'I'll drive you back to Oxford, Clement. Try and get some sleep.'

'Not there either, thank you, Arthur.' Clement explained why as Morris started the engine and drove slowly along the gravel path to the main road south.

'Bloody hell! But that would mean whoever these people are, they've been watching you since Caithness,' Reg said.

'So it would appear,' Clement said. 'Did the boat return to Trinity Hall steps, Reg?'

'Yes. Only the oarsman was on board. What I don't understand, Clement, is if these people wanted you dead and knew where you lived, why haven't they tried anything sooner?'

'Good question...' Clement paused. 'In view of what Hector Armstrong said, it's possible my activities have been used as a warning system for any SIS interest. One thing I do know; they didn't want my body found.'

'Why do you say that?'

'Armstrong said as much.' He told them his theory about Shetland.

'One big explosion would send them all to kingdom come! We could still do it. While they're all together,' Reg said, twisting in his seat to look at Clement.

'Thank you, Reg,' Clement answered. 'As enticing as that sounds, we cannot do it for the simple reason that they aren't all together. They're waiting for someone or some people to arrive. We have to get them all. If we don't, they will abort and so would any chance we have of capturing them.' Clement leaned his head back. In his mind he saw the image of Hugh Armstrong shouting across the fields, the threatening words a salient reminder to Clement that his current safety was temporary. 'It's possible this organisation is bigger than any of us imagined. It's hierarchical, like a private army. Men at the top, educated men of influence, like Hector Armstrong, and lower ranks, like the Scot. We just have to make sure nothing happens to any more of them. For now.'

'So who'll replace Hector Armstrong? His son?'

'I think that unlikely, Reg,' Clement said, but he believed he already knew. The man was already in the country, albeit at Latchmere House. Now, it was just a matter of time.

Silence settled in the car again as Morris drove south through the village of Fen Ditton, heading towards Cambridge.

Reg reached into his coat pocket. 'Have you got any weapons on you, Clement?'

'Both taken. And I used the notebook.'

Reg flipped his coat collar and removed a miniature Fairbairn-Sykes commando knife from within the folds of the lapel and handed it to Clement.

'Thank you, Reg. Another notebook would be helpful, if you have one?'

Reg grinned. Rummaging in his pack, he passed one to Clement. As much as his head and neck ached, Clement smiled.

'You may like to have this too,' Reg said, passing Clement a large-barrelled Welrod.

In the rear-view mirror Clement saw Morris flick a glance back to him but Morris made no comment. 'It may interest you to know, Clement,' Morris began, 'that the money you found secreted in the fireplace in the porter's lodge at Trinity Hall was a considerable amount. Over five hundred pounds, in fact. And, as you said, all in five-pound notes. Both Mr McBryde and Mr Edwards deny any knowledge of the cash box and by their reactions I'm inclined to believe them. So, I must ask myself; why would Mr Hayward have such an amount and why would he keep it secreted in the porter's lodge and not in a bank or in his rooms?'

'Clement and I talked about that,' Reg said, and told Morris about the telephone call and the initials *W.C.*

Morris raised his eyebrows but didn't say anything. 'Do you suspect anyone in particular?'

'No. And despite the initials, it's hardly likely to be our Prime Minister.'

'So, hush money, then. Given the amount, Hayward obviously kept the secret, so why kill him?' Morris added.

Clement sat up. 'Unless it was a single payment,' Clement paused. 'Perhaps they always intended to kill Hayward then retrieve the money, so the amount was immaterial. We'll soon know. Whatever they're planning Hayward wasn't part of it. But he knew something and he died because of it. Do you know the farms around Waterbeach, Arthur?'

Morris nodded. 'Armstrong has a place in the neighbourhood, Hitcham Hall. Most likely it's where they took you.'

'And the money. Where is it now?'

'We put it back. Like to see who comes looking for it. McBryde said he'd check it daily.'

'Can he be trusted?' Reg asked.

'He's a former prison guard,' Morris said. 'So I'm sure he can be relied upon to inform us.' Morris turned the car onto the main road south.

Clement rested his head against the smooth leather of the seat back and stared through the car window at nothing in particular. 'Although I haven't seen young Michael, I think it likely he's at Hitcham Hall. Did you learn anything about the boy's family, Arthur?'

'Yes. And no. He does have an uncle, his mother's brother. John Laughton was a member of the Right Club and is currently a Fellow at Cambridge.'

'Which college?' Clement asked.

'Caius.'

A shiver coursed through Clement's body.

'I asked to see Michael when I went to the house, if you recall. The butler told me that the uncle took him away the day after he'd been sent home from school.'

'Is the uncle involved?' Reg asked.

Clement thought back to the night he and Reg had seen the boy in the dinghy. 'Quite possibly. If he is, it could have been him in the dinghy with the lad.' Clement frowned, remembering that night. Would an uncle slap his nephew the way that man had hit Michael? But if not Michael's uncle then who had been the man with him in the dinghy? Clement realised it had probably been the grey-haired man he'd seen talking to Bainbridge at Hitcham Hall. He began to wonder if the uncle had also been kidnapped and was the unknown passenger with him in the lorry? For now, there were no answers.

'You're positive it was Michael Hasluck you saw?' Morris asked.

Clement paused, his gaze distant. 'Yes. Although, I couldn't swear to it. It was dark.'

Morris drove into the rear of the police station. It was just before one o'clock in the morning. The weather had turned much cooler and it was raining again. Clement shivered in his damp clothes. They went upstairs to Morris's office. 'Would you mind if I use a telephone, Arthur? I need to make an out-of-area call.'

'Of course, just give the number to the constable, he'll connect the call.' Morris showed Clement into the meeting room then left him alone. Clement walked over to the telephone and gave the operator the emergency number for late-night calls to SIS.

'Captain Winthorpe, please.'

After some minutes Johnny answered.

'Johnny, I need the telephone number for Latchmere House. It's urgent.'

'What's going on, Clement?'

'I need to speak with Colonel Stephens. I'll call you later, Johnny.'

Clement scribbled the number on a notebook then asked the constable to connect him. 'Colonel Stephens, please. It's urgent. Major Wisdom speaking.'

'You do know what time it is?' the operator at Latchmere said.

'I do and this is urgent.'

'Very well, but he won't be pleased.'

Clement waited, the exhaustion flooding through his aching body. His eye was so sore now he could hardly think. But this call could not wait.

'Stephens here. This better be an emergency, Major.'

'It is. Do you know a German named Haushofer?'

Clement heard the intake of breath. When the colonel did speak, his voice was subdued. 'I know the name. Go on.'

'I understand he was arrested recently. By the Gestapo. Is he one of yours?'

'You're well informed, Major. But not that well informed. The answer is no. Albrecht Haushofer is an advisor to the Nazi Party and a personal friend of Rudolf Hess. His arrest was the day after Hess arrived in Britain. Hitler, it appears, is distancing himself from the Deputy Führer and his associates. It may be a political move on Hitler's part, so it may be temporary. We just don't know yet.'

'Would you have a picture of Haushofer?'

'We'll have one somewhere.'

'Show it to Jakobs and ask him if this was the Abwehr man with him on the aeroplane? If Jakobs proves truculent, remind him that it was this man who injured his foot on leaving the aeroplane and that I believe it was done deliberately.'

'I'll get back to you when I have something. And by the way, *Snow* says he had no knowledge of another jumper that night.'

Clement sat in the chair facing the telephone. He didn't expect to hear from Stephens for a day or so. He closed his eyes. He wondered about *Snow* and whether the double agent really had known about the Abwehr man. It no longer mattered. Clement did, however, wonder if Hitler had known of Hess's mission? Was it even the Führer's initiative? Either way, Rudolf Hess was in Latchmere House and Hitler had turned his back on his Deputy Führer and his supporters. Did that mean whatever Hector Armstrong was planning wouldn't now go ahead? Armstrong had said nothing would stop it, not even *C*. Was it possible that Hitler didn't know about Armstrong and his group? So what part did this Haushofer play? Clement rested his head in his palm. He needed sleep and medical attention.

Reg came into the meeting room and sat beside him. 'You look exhausted, Clement. You have to get out of those wet clothes and you need rest. Can't function for too long without it.'

Clement smiled. 'Thank you, Reg. I feel badly that I haven't asked you about Geraldine.'

'I had a letter recently. Post takes a long time to come from Australia. You may remember, Clement, I sent her there when our house in East Sussex was compulsorily acquired. She's with our son Charles.'

'He worked on a sheep station there, as I recall. How's she managing?'

'Not too well. In fact, Charles left the property in outback New South Wales because she found it all too different. Too remote. They live in Sydney now in a suburb called Gladesville. Charles works in a small munitions factory and they live in a house on the Parramatta River. She seems to like it there. Closer to shops and other women. I'd like to see it myself one day. You look tired, Clement. I'll stop my prattling.'

'I'm exhausted, if truth be told, Reg. I'm pleased Geraldine is happier there and I like hearing about normal things. I have so few of them in my life now.'

Morris entered the room. 'I've arranged for the police doctor to come first thing. You are welcome to stay with me again, Clement, but I feel for your safety; it may be best if you were to sleep in one of the cells downstairs. Sergeant Kendall is arranging some dry clothes for you.'

Clement was too weary to protest.

'And we're locking you in. Just a precaution.'

'Reg, can you do something for me?'

'Just name it, Clement?'

'Watch Hitcham Hall. Who comes, who goes.'

'Where will you be?' Reg asked.

'I need some answers to a question that has been plaguing me for some time. I'll be as quick as I can.' He glanced at Morris. 'And I hope I will learn the identity of the man in the mortuary.' Clement checked his watch. 'I'll be away a few days. If I haven't returned in the meantime, I'll join you outside Hitcham Hall in four days.'

'Friday then. When?'

'Midnight.'

'Right.'

'In the meantime, if you have anything to report, telephone Nora Ballantyne.'

'Is there anyone in particular you want to know about, Clement?'

'There's a man with them. He's in charge; at least for now. He's well educated; high forehead, thinning grey hair and the arrogance of the privileged. And I'd like to know if the boy is there.'

'This grey-haired man, is he German or English?'

'I don't know for certain, most likely English. But he is the key to everything.'

19

Despite the relative safety of the police cell, and his total exhaustion, Clement had not slept well. The past, his past, had kept him awake. That Armstrong had known his cover name for his mission to Caithness haunted him. No one outside the SIS had known this. Or so Clement had thought. In the seven hours he'd hoped to sleep before the doctor's arrival at nine, Clement relived every detail of his last mission. He thought of everything he knew about the man convicted of espionage and since executed. That man had had a Hitler Youth tattoo and had once lived in Glasgow. He'd been involved in the murder of another man in Glasgow whose body had been found in Sighthill Cemetery. Clement recalled the murdered man's name from his report following the Caithness mission: John William Nicholson. While the traitor Clement had exposed in Caithness had not been convicted of killing Nicholson, Clement had always believed he was in some way complicit in the man's death. As far as Clement knew, that crime remained unsolved and with the coming of war, it was a case unlikely to ever be reopened; especially now that the prime suspect was dead. But something nagged him about it. Was it personal for Clement? Or was there a connection between an executed traitor, the murder of John William Nicholson, Hector Armstrong and a murdered man found in the Cambridgeshire fenland?

The knock on his cell door roused him. Sergeant Kendall entered carrying a tray. Clement couldn't believe it when he saw the eggs.

'How on earth?' Clement said, wondering how Kendall had enough coupons for him to have two eggs.

'Mrs Kendall keeps a few chickens. We won't miss them and it will do you good, sir.'

Clement sat on the cell bunk and ate the delicious breakfast but his mind was on the identity of three men: the grey-haired man at Hitcham Hall, the unknown man in the lorry, who was possibly Michael's uncle, and the man in Morris's mortuary. He hoped that Glasgow would hold the key to the identity of at least one of these men. While he didn't know what the group were about to do, he knew he was getting closer. All around him people were preparing for something. Something that included not only manual labourers but also well-educated and successful Englishmen and high-ranking Germans.

Whatever their intentions, Clement knew it was treason. And treason, especially in wartime, was a hanging offence. The cell door opened and Kendall came in with another man.

'This is Doctor Bell, Major,' Kendall said.

The doctor put his bag on a table and commenced cleaning the cut over Clement's eye. Thirty minutes later, Clement had three stitches and was wearing an eye patch.

'Superintendent Morris has asked you to join him upstairs, sir, when you've finished with Doctor Bell,' Kendall said. 'After I've seen the Doctor out, I'll bring you a bowl of warm water and a towel.' Kendall leaned towards Clement and in a quiet voice added, 'And I've some soap too. Mrs Kendall has cleaned and dried your clothes as best she can.'

'That is most kind of you, Sergeant, and your wife. Please thank her for me. You've been so very kind.'

Doctor Bell packed up his instruments. 'I'll take the stitches out in five days.'

'Thank you,' Clement said, but he thought it unlikely. Kendall escorted the doctor out and closed the cell door. Changing into his dry clothes, Clement folded the prison garments and left them on the cell bunk. Taking the stairs to Morris's office, he knocked at the door, then entered.

'I hope you got a few hours' sleep, Clement,' Morris said, standing. 'How's the eye?'

'I'll be alright. Sergeant Kendall has been looking after me like a prince. Would you mind if I were to use the telephone again, Arthur?'

'You know where it is. But before you do, I have a message for you. You are to call a Colonel Stephens. I understand you know his number.'

Clement nodded and using the internal door let himself into the meeting room. He lifted the receiver.

The telephone rang twice before Clement heard the colonel's gruff voice.

'Went as white as a sheet when I showed Jakobs the photo,' Stephens told Clement. 'And when I said you believed he had been deliberately injured, he became quite helpful. So I think we can say that your Abwehr man was indeed Haushofer. Question is, Major, if he landed in Britain in late January, how is it he's in a Gestapo Prison in Germany?' Stephens paused but Clement didn't respond. 'One other thing, Major, that may be of interest to you. *Tate* has received a very large amount of money from a surprising source. A Japanese man, on behalf of the Abwehr, has delivered over twenty thousand pounds to *Tate* with the instructions that the funds are to be made available for Sir Hector Armstrong. Of course, he won't be getting it but interesting nonetheless.'

Thanking Stephens, Clement replaced the receiver and sat in the chair by the telephone. Twenty thousand pounds was an enormous sum of money. He stared at the dark blue carpet, his mind sifting thoughts; known facts, suppositions, speculations but they always led him to the same conclusion. While he had no idea how Haushofer had left Britain, he believed he now knew what the group were planning. His hand reached for the telephone receiver.

'Captain Winthorpe, please.' Clement waited. *C* had told him to keep Nora Ballantyne informed but what he needed to tell Johnny warranted a higher security clearance than Nora, and perhaps even himself, held.

'How's the investigation coming, Clement?' Johnny asked. He listened as Clement told him about Albrecht Haushofer.'

'Good Lord! Twenty thousand pounds!'

'And, it was Haushofer in the aeroplane with Jakobs. So how is it he's now in Germany?'

Clement waited but Johnny didn't respond.

'And what's more important, Johnny; why did Rudolf Hess fly into Scotland?'

'It remains a quandary.'

Clement thought for a moment before speaking. 'I think they are planning a coup d'état. If they can't invade us by force from without, they'll attempt to take control of the government from within with the assistance of some highly influential Englishmen. This group is more than just a few people, Johnny. It's large, extensive and well-established. And, I believe it is about far more than a negotiated peace deal with Hitler. That may be the cover they are telling others, but this is more insidious; they intend for the Nazi's to take control of Britain. To them it doesn't matter that Hess is in Latchmere House. As soon as they control Westminster, Hess will be released. He's just biding his time. And there are layers to this organisation, Johnny, like a private army. Some are from the working classes; manual labourers, blue collar workers and the like but others are from a small but esteemed group of our own people. Important people, people of affluence and privilege. Then there's the enemy. I don't believe Haushofer and Hess are the only Germans involved. There will be others. And who are they waiting for before they attempt this coup? My question is, Johnny; are foolish but well-meaning people being manipulated by thugs and murderers? Or are they knowingly committing treason and willingly assisting in insurrection?'

'But for this to be successful, there must be thousands involved.'

'Yes, and it may even include schoolchildren.'

'What?'

'Hitler Youth, Johnny. I know from the former headmaster's speeches at St Edward's that boys from Germany came on exchange programmes to Britain. Were they used by their masters to collect information to be passed on to men like Bainbridge for transmission to Germany? The one thing in our favour, Johnny, is that once the ring leaders are exposed and removed, the masses will, hopefully, lose interest. But they must be removed before the coup takes place or it really will be unstoppable.'

'I'll telephone *C*. He must be informed.'

'I have to go to Glasgow, Johnny. If I'm wrong and the murder of the man found dead in Cambridgeshire is nothing more than a straightforward police investigation, then Morris can deal with that. But if I'm right, then this dead man was involved in something much bigger, and we need to move quickly.'

'Why Glasgow?'

Clement swallowed. He wasn't completely sure that his trip to Glasgow wasn't, in some part, personally motivated. His nemesis from Caithness had laughed at him, calling him *Hopeless*. That had stung. Regardless, there was a genuine Glasgow connection in the death of John William Nicholson. 'It may not only be Glasgow, Johnny. There could be hundreds of cells of insurrectionists in every large town in the country but I already know that there are people in Glasgow, or from Glasgow, who have a connection to this organisation and the recent past. *My* recent past. I've been watched, Johnny. SIS should be looking into where they place operatives. I would never have suspected Bainbridge because SIS found me that position. I have to ask, is there a mole in SIS? Or was Bainbridge targeted because of me and turned?'

'Let's hope the latter, Clement. Either way, we'll be reassessing all our safe houses and contacts now. I'll clear it with *C*. You go to Glasgow. How long do you intend to be there?'

'I'll come to London tonight and stay with the Guards

at St James's then leave for Glasgow first thing tomorrow. I told Sergeant Naylor I'd meet him midnight Friday at the latest.'

'One more thing, Clement. If these people have been watching you for months, they may still be, so be careful.'

20

Monday 9th June 1941

I t was late afternoon when Clement arrived in Glasgow. The trip north had been slow and arduous. Delays of all kinds had meant a full day of changing trains and crowded stations. Bomb damage and track repair was a never-ending problem especially in the Midlands and albeit that it was given top priority, travel was slow.

Striding along the platform, Clement glanced at the clock at the far end. Just after six. What should have taken around six hours had been extended to ten. Clement weaved his way between the departing passengers, always checking the people around him in case anyone was watching him. Reaching into his pocket he found his ticket and passed it to the ticket collector at the end of the platform. Once clear of the barrier, he waited by a newsstand until all the passengers from his train had dispersed. Buying a newspaper, he clutched his battered suitcase then approached a station attendant.

'Do you know of a reasonable guest house in this vicinity?' Clement asked.

The man's eye roved over his crushed and stained clothes. 'There's one over the way, there. Not posh, but I'm guessing it will suit you.'

'Thank you.' Clement strode through the terminus, his gaze constantly searching the crowds around him.

Outside it was still light. Clement checked his watch. In the northern city, sunset was not due for another few hours. Further along the street, he saw a long queue waiting by a bus stop. Despite being June, it was cool. People huddled like birds against a chill wind. Suitcases were everywhere, clogging the footpaths. Clement stood watching them as light rain began to fall. Umbrellas were raised by the patiently waiting passengers. Clement pulled up his collar and crossed the street.

The buildings opposite, while stylish in architecture, had seen better days. Four storeys in height, there were two gaps in the old stone façade courtesy of the Luftwaffe's devastating raids last March. Piles of rubble still lay heaped over the sites and random stacks of timber lay in jagged piles beside the footpaths. Of the remaining buildings, all the windows were boarded up and those that weren't had the distinctive criss-cross taping. He knew the Germans had targeted the shipbuilding industries along the River Clyde but the carnage in one of the main streets of Glasgow was an ever-present reminder that life may be short and the enemy never far away. Opposite, he saw a dimly back-lit, glass-panelled sign, *The Caledonian Palace Hotel and Boarding House.*

Crossing the street, he climbed five worn stone steps and opened the door to the inappropriately named guest house.

'How many nights?' a gravel-voiced woman said, her gaze on his eye patch.

'Just the one. And a room at the front, please,' Clement said.

'You a heavy sleeper?' she asked.

'Always have been,' he lied.

Noise no longer mattered to him. Besides, even if his time in the Scottish city extended beyond one night, until the conspirators were caught, he could only ever be one night in any one place.

'I'll need your ration card, if you're having breakfast,' the woman said.

Clement produced the card and paid his two shillings. The woman placed a key with a large wooden tag attached to it on the desk. 'No lights without the blackout curtains drawn. No women in the room. And a shilling for the gas meter.'

Clement handed over the extra shilling and took the key. At one time he would have been horrified by the woman's suggestion of impropriety. He couldn't blame her. Despite not wearing his clerical collar, he knew he looked dishevelled; more like a vagrant than a man of

God.

Upstairs he found room nine. It was small and grimy with a window that had been nailed closed and taped against blast damage but it had what he needed, a view of the street. He stood just back from the sill and stared out. The light rain had increased and it was wetting the streets and pavements. A few cars passed. A bus had evidently collected the queue of people. Others with umbrellas were hurrying to or from the station. Several bicycles pedalled past, their riders hunched against the rain. His gaze lingered over the entrance to the railway station opposite. No one seemed to be loitering about watching the boarding house. He checked the street in both directions, then scrutinised every doorway or niche he could see. While people perpetually came and went from the railway station entrance, no one stood watching the boarding house.

Clement drew the blackout curtains then lit the gas lamp and checked the room. There were no homely touches at *The Caledonian Palace and Boarding House*. Clement wondered if there ever had been. The room contained a single metal bed with a pillow, sheet and an old army blanket folded on a worn ticking mattress. On the opposite wall was a small washstand with jug and bowl. A coat stand and chair were the only other pieces of furniture in the room. On one wall, paint was peeling from the top corner and not a single picture graced any of the walls. The radiator was on the wall beneath the window. He turned it on then checked the lock on the door. It wasn't strong. Tearing a thread from his coat, he placed it on top of the doorjamb, then drawing the chair up to the window, took a sandwich and a small cake he'd bought from a station cafe at some unknown railway station during one of the many stops en route, and placed the food on the window sill. He ate the meagre meal and then undressed, folding his clothes over the back of the chair and placing it beside the radiator. Adrenaline had kept him going throughout the day but now exhaustion was taking hold and his eye ached. Making up the bed, he put the Welrod and knife under the pillow. Pushing the explosive notebook into his left sock, he climbed into bed.

He woke with a start. Reaching for his watch, he threw back the blanket and rose to draw the curtains. The room was cold, the shilling in the meter having run out sometime during the night. Wrapping his overcoat around himself, he stood by the window and gazed out. It surprised him that it was already eight o'clock. Outside, rain still fell and a strong wind was turning umbrellas inside out. Despite his spartan surroundings, he'd slept well. Even his eye and shoulder felt a little better. Turning, he reached for his clothes, hurriedly pulling on his vest before fastening the holster on over his shirt. Securing his knife to his shin and the Welrod in its holster, he dressed quickly then adjusted the eye patch into place. Five minutes later he retrieved the thread from the door and left the room.

The boarding house reception was unattended when

he descended the stairs. He placed the key on the desk, then retrieved his ration book from behind the counter. He could hear the woman's gravel-edged voice in an adjacent room, doubtless serving the meal. For a second he wondered what she'd be preparing for them. Porridge. He wrinkled his nose at the thought of it. He'd never liked it. He hadn't intended to have breakfast at the hotel, but he'd complied with the woman's request about the ration book so as not to raise suspicion. Placing the book into his coat, he left.

Outside, the wind tore at his coat. Standing a moment at the front door to the hotel, he pulled up his coat collar while checking the railway station entrance opposite. Despite being a weekday, few people walked the streets and those that did hunched against the wind, their umbrellas struggling to keep their shape. He checked the doorways and newsstands. No one seemed interested in him. Pulling his overcoat tight around him, he crossed the road and entered the station again. To his right was the cloakroom. Leaving the suitcase with the attendant there, he pocketed the ticket and returned to the street, turning right and walking north. At the first corner he asked a stranger for directions to Sighthill Cemetery.

Thirty-five minutes later he stepped from the bus. On his left was St Kevin's Catholic Church, in front of him and across the road were the gates to the cemetery. It seemed a bleak place; the wet windy day keeping all but mourners indoors. He crossed the road and entered the cemetery. A little distance away was a monument to the fallen of the last war. He walked towards it, its red colour an instant reminder of why he was here. To his right, he saw a small gathering of people dressed in black. They were walking away from a recently dug grave. Some walked alone, others huddled around the bereaved. Beside the grave, a man in workman's clothes stood, a shovel in his hand. Clement watched him for a while. The man waited for the mourners to leave before pushing the shovel into a pile of soil.

Clement crossed the path and approached him. 'Morning.'

The gravedigger looked up.

Clement saw the fleeting reaction to his two-day-old beard, the eye patch and his dishevelled appearance.

'Morning,' came a wary reply but the man didn't stop his work. Clement wasn't sure if it was his appearance or his English accent that had caused the man's cautious response.

'Do you know where I might find the stonemasons who make the monuments and headstones?'

The man stopped shovelling and stared at him before speaking. 'Buchanan's do most of the work here. They're on the canal in Port Dundas.'

'Is it far?'

'Not far.' The man turned and pointed back towards the cemetery entrance. 'Take Fountainwell Road there, then right onto Pinkston Road. Once you cross over the railway, you'll see the yard.'

'Thank you,' Clement said. He paused. 'Have you

worked here long?' he asked, hoping the question would yield something.

'All my working life.'

'Do you remember a murder that took place here, in the cemetery some years ago?'

The man's eyes narrowed. 'Aye, but then there have been more than one death here over the years. Derelicts mostly,' he said, his eyes again roaming over Clement's clothes.

'They said this man was killed by his wife,' Clement said, hoping it would trigger the man's memory.

'Aye, I remember.'

'Do you recall his name?' Clement asked. Clement already knew the name, but he needed to be sure they were talking about the same murder.

'Bill Nicolson. That's N-I-C-O-L-S-O-N. No 'H'.'

Clement frowned. 'That's an unusual spelling. No wonder I'm having trouble locating his family.'

The gravedigger ran his tongue around his lips before speaking. 'What's your interest in him?'

'I'm trying to find if Mr John William Nicholson had any family. There's an inheritance which I'm sure his family would appreciate having.' Clement bit his tongue. He didn't like lying.

'He had a wife. But then you know that. She vanished the same night he died. I'm guessing you know that too.'

'Any other family?'

The man put the shovel down on the dirt and shot a quick glance around him. Clement did likewise but the mourners had gone and there were no others in the cemetery.

'He had a brother,' the man said. 'And a sister too, as I recall.'

'His brother, did he also work here?'

'Not here. He worked for a time at Buchanan's. They'll most likely know where he is now.'

'Do you remember his name?'

'John something. But then they both were. They do that double name thing. It's a tradition apparently. Probably after their father.'

'And the sister?'

'You ask a lot of questions.'

'Well, it's a considerable sum, so I'm keen to find his relatives.'

The man sniffed loudly but didn't respond.

'Well, thank you. You've been most helpful,' Clement replied. He wrapped his coat around himself and walked away. He hoped he hadn't asked too many questions making the man suspicious. But a description of a man wearing an eye patch wouldn't necessarily lead to him. The eye patch had been useful and he decided to keep it even after he no longer needed it. He hurried on, staring at his feet as he walked. Buchanan's. He swallowed, the cold wind making even his good eye water.

Following the man's directions, Clement headed for Port Dundas and the hoped for Buchanan's. Twenty minutes later he saw the slabs of marble, granite and red sandstone leaning against a high side fence. He walked into the yard and approached a man sitting outside a small wooden hut. He was warming his hands on a struggling fire in an old cut-down forty-four-gallon drum.

'Good morning. I'm wondering if you can help me. I'm looking for a John Nicolson who worked here?'

'Aren't we all!' the man said, his Glaswegian accent thick. 'Left here a month ago saying his old father was sick and we haven't seen him since.'

'Do you mean John William or his brother?'

The man eyed him, the strong brow creased and fixed. 'Bill Nicolson's dead. Murdered by his wife, or so it's said. I'm talking about his brother John.'

'I understand both John William and his brother were named John. Do you know if Bill's brother had a second name?'

'Never asked.'

'Where does the father live?'

'Levenwick. Shetland.'

Clement felt the shiver course through him. 'Can you tell me where he lived here in Glasgow?'

'You with the police?'

'I am. I'm Superintendent Morris, Cambridgeshire Police. I think your Mr John Nicolson is the man I have lying on a slab in my mortuary.' Clement bit his tongue hoping the man wouldn't ask to see a warrant card.

'Is that so? Aye, well that would explain it. Although, I can't imagine what he would be doing there. You should speak to his sister.'

'Would you know her name and address?'

'I'll have something in the files. Accidents happen in this line of work so we usually ask for a next-of-kin. She was in domestic service as I recall. Ailsa something.' Standing, the man walked into the small kiosk. Clement waited by the door. He could see the man scribbling something on a slip of paper from a file.

'Here you are. For his sake I hope you're wrong about him being dead. Good worker. Strong.'

'Did you know him well?'

'A bit. He was different to his brother. Bill, well, I don't wish to speak ill of the dead, especially as he was murdered, but he was a bully. When he'd had a skinful, he'd hit almost anyone or anything.'

'And his brother wasn't a violent man?'

'Not a bit of it. He was a thinker, stored things up, you know, mulled things over in his head. Much good it did him.'

'Strange that all of them were in Glasgow?'

'Aye, well siblings, so I suppose it's natural. Although John was the odd man out among them. Bill and Ailsa were ardent for the workers' rights. Surprised me when he joined such a group.'

'Bill or John was it who joined this group?'

'John. Went to the meetings every Thursday night. Regular as clockwork. They were all in it, except the woman, of course. She couldn't go.'

'She didn't attend?'

The man stared at him. 'You ever heard of a woman at Lodge? That'll be the day!'

21

Tuesday 10th June 1941

Clement walked away. He could feel the man's eyes on him as he left. He looked at the note: Ailsa Hazelton, Twenty-Five Devonshire Gardens. At the cemetery gates he asked some passers-by about directions. Nearly two hours later he stood on the Great Western Road. Twenty-Five Devonshire Gardens was one of an elegant line of Georgian terraced houses for the well-heeled of Glasgow. Clement looked along the line of grand homes. He wondered if he should knock at the tradesman's entrance. In any household, it was always either the housekeeper or the butler who knew what was going on above and below stairs. He knocked at the front door. Within minutes an ancient-looking butler opened the door, a scowl on his face.

Clement reached for his SIS warrant card. 'Does an

Ailsa Hazelton work here?'

The butler frowned, then scrutinised Clement's face. 'No, she does not. She left of her own accord about a year ago.'

'Would you have a forwarding address for her?'

'It isn't my habit to keep the forwarding addresses of low-ranking domestic servants.'

'Did she leave with a reference?'

'She did not. In fact, she left in the middle of the night without a word to anyone. And we've not seen or heard from her since.'

'Would another member of your staff still be in contact with her?'

'I think that unlikely.'

'Could you ask. It is important.'

'I'll ask. Wait here.' The door closed, denying Clement entry.

Clement pulled the collar of his overcoat up around his head while he waited for the butler to return.

The door opened and the man reappeared. 'No one knows where she is now.'

Clement wondered if, in fact the butler had even bothered to ask. He decided to walk around to the rear of the house. Waiting by a fence in the rear lane, Clement watched the back door of Twenty-Five Devonshire Gardens. It wasn't long before a woman of mature years came out with a bucket of kitchen scraps.

Clement walked over to the fence and called to her. 'Is Ailsa in?'

The woman looked up. 'Now there's a name I've not heard in a while.'

'I haven't been in Glasgow for a while myself,' Clement said.

'Then you've had a wasted journey.'

'Really? Why's that?'

'She hasn't worked here for, let me see, at least a year.'

'Do you know where she is now?'

'Down south, I think. Told me she was hopeful of a plum job working for some toff in Cambridge, I think it was. Not sure I believed her. But she did get a letter. She was very happy about that. She went that night. Just ups and leaves. And not a word to anyone.'

Clement smiled. 'I hope it's all she hoped for then. Her brother must miss her.'

'You knew her brother?'

'Yes. That is John not Bill.'

'Oh Bill! Had a temper on him and no mistake. Didn't surprise me when his wife took a knife to him. John, though, he was different. He used to visit his dad regularly.'

'Shetland, wasn't it?'

'Yes, that's right.'

Clement saw the figure in an upper floor window. The butler stood watching him.

'I'd better let you get on. Thank you for your time.'

Clement hurried away, hoping the woman wouldn't be in too much trouble for speaking to him. Taking the return bus into the city, he went straight to the railway station. *The Caledonian Palace Hotel and Boarding House* looked unchanged as he entered the terminus. He glanced up to his room on the upper level. Even the curtains were in the same position as he had left them. He wondered if the woman had even discovered he'd gone.

He walked towards the cloakroom and retrieved his suitcase then joined a queue to purchase his train ticket. Staying on the forecourt, he found the station cafe and bought some food for the journey. Mingling with the crowds, he sat with small groups, changing seats regularly, never sitting alone. As soon as the London train platform was announced, he went directly to the ticket barrier and walked onto the platform amid the other passengers.

Weaving his way through the crowds on the platform, he checked the people around him. People stood, huddled in small groups, embracing their loved ones. He moved around them, always checking behind him for anyone following. Others, mostly men in uniform, found their compartments and climbed aboard. Locating the nearest third class carriage, he found a seat. He checked his watch. He'd decided not to stay another night in Glasgow but take the late train and sleep through the night. All being well, he would be in London first thing in the morning. The compartment began to fill. Three Naval ratings with blank expressions and two soldiers joined him, their large packs taking over the racks above their heads. Other than the most fleeting of glances, none showed the slightest interest in him. Clement looked through the window as the train pulled away from the platform.

The train crawled through the suburbs of Glasgow. From his window he could see the bomb damage from the two devastating raids of mid-March. Street urchins were scrounging through the endless rubble for whatever they could find. Leaning his head on the window, he closed his eyes.

The trip to Glasgow had yielded answers. He felt sure he now knew the identity of the dead man in Morris's mortuary. Clement wondered about John Nicolson. From other people's observations, John Nicolson was a decent man, unlike his brother Bill. Was John unconnected to the people in Caithness? Clement recalled the woman's comments about the man; John returned to Shetland regularly to see his father. Was that true or was it an excuse? Either way, the man was now dead. And the reference to Freemasonry had told Clement how they all communicated with each other. Clement knew nothing about Freemasonry and he didn't choose to but he did know of its entrenched secrecy and covert ways of identifying each other. It was an established organisation, with a hierarchy of power that wielded considerable influence among its members in every level of society.

Clement thought of Nicolson's sister who had left Glasgow for Cambridge, Ailsa Hazelton. Clement frowned. A.H. Why did so many of these people have names with the A.H. initials: Ailsa Hazelton, Albrecht

Haushofer, even the name Rudolf Hess had initially given to authorities when he'd first landed in Scotland was Alfred Horn. Was it just coincidence? Clement thought of Rathbourne's two watchdogs: Gus Hutchinson and Bertie Hawkins whose full names would surely be Augustus Hutchinson and Albert Hawkins. Clement felt a sinister shiver course through his body. Even Hector Armstrong's initials and his son's were a variation of A.H. Was it purely coincidence?

It was just on dawn when the train pulled into Euston Station. Wednesday. So much had happened he had to remind himself of the day of the week. Clement strode across the forecourt grateful he was within walking distance of King's Cross Station. He'd been away two full days. People thronged the platforms, a constant swirl of activity. Clement checked the departure board and found the platform number for the train to Cambridge. It said the train would leave within the hour but timetables were often inaccurate and delays could be long. While he was tired, he had slept a little on the train. He no longer felt the soreness in his eye. The swelling had reduced slightly and the eye patch had been useful. It had an effect on people. Whenever he wore his clerical collar, he felt conspicuous and people would chat to him in public places, but the patch turned people away and right now, he was grateful for it.

Clement stood in the corridor of the train for what he hoped would be a short journey to Cambridge. While he now believed he knew the identities of two of the three previously unknown men, he didn't understand why John Nicolson had been killed. Neither could he see the motive for Bill Hayward's death. Clement rubbed his hand along his bearded face. 'Of course,' Clement said half under his breath. Hayward must have known about the boy. He may even have brought meals for the lad and attended to his laundry. And the money had bought Old Bill's silence. Clement began to believe Hayward had been killed because he was no longer needed. But it didn't explain why they had the boy? Every time Clement visualised young Michael, he felt sick. Clement thought back, trying to form a chronology of events. They had moved Michael last Saturday, three days after Bill Hayward's death. Clement frowned, trying to recollect when the break-in at the Abbey School had been. It had happened during the night on Thursday the twenty-ninth. He had asked Nora to telephone Morris to have the boy sent home on the Friday. Michael's uncle had taken him to Caius on the Saturday, and a week later, Clement had seen Michael in the dinghy at five on the Saturday morning with, he speculated, the grey-haired man. Why was the boy so important? Clement checked his watch. Two hours at least before he would be in Cambridge.

Crossing the forecourt at Cambridge Railway Station, Clement walked outside to queue for the bus. Twenty minutes later he walked into the St Andrew's Street Police Station. Sergeant Kendall nodded in the direction of the stairs and Clement went straight up. He knocked at

Morris's door then went in. Reg was sitting in the chair in front of Morris's desk.

'What did you learn, Clement?' Reg asked, standing to greet him.

'Plenty. You?'

'I've set up a couple of trigger cameras around Hitcham Hall.'

'I'm not sure I know what that means, Reg?'

'A battery operated camera on a pressure switch. If the switch is depressed, it will trigger the shutter. Much like a pressure detonator but instead of an explosion, it takes a picture. I change the film every night. That way, we see who's involved. First roll of film was interesting. I have a lovely picture of Hugh Armstrong arriving by boat at *The Bridge* pub at Waterbeach. He took a suitcase from the river. No prizes for guessing what that contained.'

'Arthur, did you recover the suitcase in the pond at Ramsey?'

'Yes. It contained a wireless,' Morris said, indicating for Clement to sit down.

'So why take the parachute all the way to Waterbeach to dispose of it?' Clement asked.

'Can't answer that for certain, Clement. Perhaps it was just that it's a long way from Ramsey. Given the Cam's current, it wouldn't be long before the suitcase was washed out to sea and never seen again. At least we've found all four suitcases and we know what each held.'

'Has the Lagonda been moved?' Clement asked.

Morris shook his head.

'Do you have the men to keep it under surveillance?'

'Sergeant Kendall has volunteered to do whatever is necessary.'

'It would have to be watched day and night.'

'Especially night,' Reg added. 'Car's too noticeable to move in daylight.'

'And the boy, Reg?' Clement asked.

'Not a sign of him. That's not to say he isn't there. I just haven't seen him nor has he been in any of the photographs.'

Clement sighed. The boy's welfare worried him. 'Anyone else in these photos of yours, Reg?'

'Just Armstrong and his henchman, the one you call the Scot.'

'Do we know who he is?'

Morris shook his head. 'Now we have a photo I'll make some enquiries and let you know.'

'And the grey-haired man?'

'He's there, Clement,' Reg said. 'Comes out for a smoke every so often then goes back indoors. But he's there. Are you any further advanced?'

Clement told them about Albrecht Haushofer. 'And I think I can confirm the identity of the man in your mortuary, Arthur. His name is John Nicolson. He's from Shetland. He has a sister who worked in Glasgow until about a year ago. Her name is Ailsa Hazelton and apparently she moved to Cambridge.' Clement looked at

Morris. 'Could you check to see if you have anything on her?'

Morris reached for the telephone and asked Kendall to look into it. 'Are you suspicious about this woman, Clement?'

Clement told them about the conversations he'd had with the gravedigger at Sighthill, with Nicolson's former employer at the stonemason's yard and the conversation with the woman at the rear of Twenty-Five Devonshire Gardens.

'What's the glue, Clement? What binds them all together?' Reg asked.

'Freemasonry.'

Reg snorted. 'Boys pretending to be men. More cloak and dagger than the real thing.'

'Are you sure, Clement? Morris asked. 'Sounds more like the Nordic League to me. Or the White Knights of Britain.'

'Who?' Reg asked.

'Far-right groups, Reg, but I thought they'd disbanded before the war,' Clement said. 'I do recall they used various organisations as fronts for their network. It could be that the Freemasons are unwittingly harbouring a secret resurgence within their ranks.'

'So what's it all about?' Reg asked.

'I hope I'm wrong but…' Clement paused, reluctant to voice his concerns, 'I think they are going to attempt a coup.'

'What! When?' Reg asked.

'Soon.'

'You informed Winthorpe?' Reg asked.

Clement nodded, stifling a yawn.

'You look done in, Clement. Have you eaten and slept?' Morris asked.

'I'm alright, Arthur. Would you mind though if I were to stay here in the police station for a few hours?'

'I think it's the safest place for you at present, Clement. I'll get Sergeant Kendall to open a cell for you, should you wish to rest, and I'll brief him about keeping the Lagonda under surveillance. And we'll see what we can find out about this woman Ailsa Hazelton. The meeting room is at your disposal, if you need it.' Morris reached for the telephone.

Clement stood and walked towards the door to the meeting room, Reg behind him. Morris was on the telephone giving instructions to Kendall.

'How are you, Clement?' Reg asked, closing the door behind him.

'Getting too old for this, Reg, if you want the truth.'

'Doesn't seem to stop you though.'

Clement smiled but his face and neck were sore and he felt old. Was it pain or the guilt he felt about young Michael? He thought about Bill Hayward looking after the boy and the telephone call with the initials *W.C.* Did that call concern the boy or was it something unrelated?

'Penny for them, Clement?' Reg asked.

'Thinking about Michael. Why do they have him, Reg? What possible reason could they have for taking an innocent child?'

'Kidnap's usually about a ransom,' Reg added.

Clement frowned. With educated and highly success-ful businessmen like Armstrong, and the enormous amounts of money the Abwehr had intended to pour into the coup, Clement didn't believe this organisation to be short of funds. He looked up at Reg. 'Do we know what Michael's father does?'

Reg shook his head.

'When do you change the film in those cameras of yours?'

'Midnight. I leave Cambridge from Jesus Lock around eleven and row to Baits Bite Lock. I can lift the boat out of the water there and carry it to the other side of the lock then row the next stretch on to Horningsea. That's where I tie it up then do the rounds via Hitcham Hall and Waterbeach, then back to Horningsea. I'm back in Cambridge around three in the morning.'

'Do you ever see anyone? Here or at Trinity Hall steps?'

'No. And I don't use Trinity Hall steps. I 'borrow' a boat further downstream then return it. Never the same boat twice though. What is it, Clement?'

'Stick to your routine. Then I'll meet you on the jetty at *The Bridge* at midnight tonight. I'd like a closer look at Hitcham Hall. I want to see if the boy is inside.'

'You have a death wish now?'

'It's not only the boy. I think someone else is there.'

22

Wednesday 11th June 1941

It was well after ten o'clock when Clement and Morris drove out of Cambridge, heading north. The long twilight had gone and a strong moonlit night was drawing in. About half a mile from Waterbeach, Morris slowed the police vehicle, pulled off the road and switched off the engine.

'After I've gone, Arthur, drive back to Hitcham Hall and hide the car, then take up a position where you can see the entrance gate. I'll join you there as soon as I can. And Arthur, if you see anyone, don't engage with them on your own. They are extremely dangerous.'

Morris nodded.

Clement stepped out of the car and closed the door. He ran the half mile to Waterbeach. *The Bridge's* distinctive silhouette stood out against the night sky as he approached it from the Clayhithe side. He crossed the bridge. He hadn't passed anyone. Neither had he seen any cars. Creeping through the rear garden of *The Bridge*, he crouched behind a low shrub, the jetty in his sight. He checked his watch. It would soon be midnight. The moon was near full and the bright nocturnal light cast long shadows over the jetty and grass. Clement waited, his gaze fixed on the immediate area, particularly the jetty and public house. Nothing stirred but he needed to know if anyone was in the vicinity. Hurrying across the grass, Clement checked the front of *The Bridge* then crossed the road and ran down the bank into the narrow, wooded area. Running along the path, he stopped at a gate that separated the copse from a ploughed field. In the distance, the high roofs of Hitcham Hall poked above the surrounding trees. Pulling the binoculars from his coat he checked the fields between himself and the Hall, but he saw no one. Returning to the road he ran back across the grass at the rear of *The Bridge* and lay under one of the overhanging shrubs to wait for Reg to arrive, his binoculars in his hand. Five minutes passed before he heard the sound of oars in the water. A minute later he heard the sound of a boat hitting the pylons. Clement put his binoculars into his coat pocket and reached for his knife. A man dressed in black with a pack over his shoulder stood on the jetty.

'Reg!' Clement whispered, stepping from behind a willow.

Reg spun around. Without speaking he joined Clement under the low growth. 'Anything happening?'

'Morris has the Hall under surveillance from the front. I said we'd join him outside the gate.'

'I've got a camera there too. I'll get this one and set up the next. Back in five.'

Reg scurried across the grass, darting between the trees' elongated shadows. Within minutes he was back. He tapped his pocket to indicate it held a roll of film. 'We using the boat again?'

'Too slow. I don't want to leave Morris alone for too long. He doesn't have a weapon and wouldn't stand a chance if he got into difficulties. Can you leave the boat here?'

'An hour or two won't hurt. But I should get it back before daylight.'

'Right.'

Together they crossed the road and ran back through the copse then, jumping the gate, headed south-west towards Hitcham Hall and Morris.

'What did Whitehall say?' Reg asked.

'A few things I told them came as a surprise. And they didn't know just how sophisticated and involved this network is. You know, Reg, recruits have been enlisted and intelligence gathered for years. Most likely from before the war. And it's widespread. Scotland, Cambridgeshire, Oxford...' Clement paused.

'Universities?'

'And quite possibly schools.'

'Student networks? It hardly seems possible.'

'Hitler Youth!'

'Hitler Youth attend our schools?' Reg said.

'Exchange programmes, Reg. There were plenty of foreign students here before the war. And not just any school. Good schools. I've seen the former headmaster's papers at St Edward's and those exchange programmes included young German students, right up to just before the outbreak of war.'

'You are talking boys of what, ten, twelve?'

'And older. Perhaps girls too. Who better, Reg? They would have lived and studied in the area for six months or more. Befriended locals. We are not talking about in-quiring, logical minds, Reg. These young people have been indoctrinated since birth. What better way to learn about your enemy than from very close quarters. They'd do anything for the Führer.' Clement visualised Hugh Armstrong with his disingenuous smile.

'So what are you saying, Clement?'

Clement stopped running. 'Dear Lord. Hugh Arm-strong!'

Reg stopped. 'What is it, Clement?'

'Good schools.'

Reg stood facing him.

'Hugh Armstrong, Reg. He could also have been in the Hitler Youth or at least had German students billeted with them. And he was a Wykehamist.'

'A what?'

'A student at Winchester College. *W.C.*, Reg.'

23

Thursday 12th June 1941

The moonlight was strong, a colourless pastiche of illusion and reality that lit up the fields and where the flickering shadows of swaying trees provided places of concealment. Clement stared at the ground beneath his feet. His mind churned about this network of traitors and spies that crossed county and foreign borders. Everyone from aristocracy to labourers, and even schoolchildren. It had taken years of preparation down to the last detail. No wonder the man on the porch at Hitcham Hall had said it would go ahead with or without Armstrong and Haushofer. It really was unstoppable. Through the trees, Clement could see the tall rooftops of Hitcham Hall. Five minutes later, the large stone pillars at the gate came into view.

'The camera's behind the gate post,' Reg said.

Clement waited, his gaze fixed on the trees and shrubs beside the road and the long driveway into the property. His ears strained for any sound. Two minutes later, Clement heard running feet. He drew his knife, hunching beside one of the tall, stone gateposts. From across the road, Morris was running towards him.

'Any comings or goings?' Clement asked Morris.

'None. You?'

'No one. Reg is with me.'

Reg reappeared beside them, another film in his pocket.

'What now?' Reg asked.

'Arthur, would you be willing to drive in and knock at the door?' Clement said.

Morris paused. 'In for a penny, I suppose, Clement. What's your plan?'

'Say you wish to speak with Hugh Armstrong. Say it's urgent. If you can get inside, that would be ideal. I want to know who's there. But don't take any risks. Police questions only.'

Morris nodded then returned to his car. The engine started. Pulling onto the road, Morris drove slowly past Clement and Reg and into the property. A minute later Clement and Reg ran through the gate, and keeping to the shrubs at the side of the driveway, approached the house. Off to the left, Clement could see the high-roofed barn where he'd been held and where Hector Armstrong had died. What remained of the large double doors were blackened from the flames.

251

Clement crouched beside a large oak, Reg beside him. He could see Morris's car. Taking his binoculars from his pocket, Clement watched as Morris switched off the engine and got out. Slowly, Morris walked to the front door and rang the doorbell. Clement kept his binoculars focused on the porch. Several minutes passed. No one came. Morris rang the bell a second time. Still no one came.

'Stay here, Reg, and watch,' Clement said, handing him the binoculars. Clement ran the short distance to where he'd secreted himself before beside the front porch and where Morris still waited. Morris rang the doorbell a third time. With his back to the house, Clement scanned the area in front. No cars. No lorries either. And no guards patrolling the fields. Given what had happened at Hitcham Hall, Clement would have thought, at the very least, a guard would have been posted at the front door or at the main gate. Despite the hour, the eerie stillness of the place was unnerving. Clement couldn't shake the feeling that someone was inside. He pulled his Welrod from the holster under his coat, his senses on high alert, and moved closer to where Morris was standing.

Morris backed away from the front door and stood facing out under the porch. 'You're taking a risk, Clement,' Morris whispered, not moving from his position.

'Go back and get into the car, Arthur, as though you're driving away. Then park it just beyond the trees at the curve in the drive,' he said. 'Stay in the car but keep the front door to the house in view.'

'Right. Where will you be?'

'In the house.'

'And Reg?'

'He'll be with me directly.'

Clement stayed by the porch as Morris drove away. As soon as Morris had gone, Clement moved to the corner of the house. He reached for the Welrod, his ears straining for any sounds from within.

A minute later, he signalled Reg who joined him at the side of the house. Reg dropped his pack on the ground and withdrew his Sten gun, assembling it quickly then swinging the pack over his shoulder. Together, they crept along the side path. Clement checked the windows above their heads but the curtains remained drawn. He paused at the back corner of the house and peered around the edge. No guard stood there either. In the strong moonlight, he saw washing still hanging on the line. Isabel. He paused, his mind racing. He had never believed the girl was involved with the group for anything more than domestic duties but did the presence of washing indicate she was still there? Clement thought back to his home in Fearnley Maughton. He knew Mary never left washing out at night. Something to do with damp. Had Isabel been sent home? Or was she in the house?

Hunching low and running forward, they squatted by the rear door, Reg keeping his Sten up across his chest, his finger poised by the trigger as Clement reached for the lock-picks and rotated the barrel. Within seconds they entered the house.

Clement lingered by the door and waited. No one came. He slipped inside, Reg following him. Reg checked the blackout curtains then flicked on the torch and scanned the room. It was the scullery and kitchen. The room was long and narrow with two doors leading back into the house. Everything looked tidy and no dishes or foodstuffs were left out. Clement crept towards one of the internal doors and gradually opened it. Beyond was a large dining room. Silently closing the door, he went to the other and opened it. This door led into a hall. Leaving the rear door unlocked and the internal door ajar, they tiptoed along the corridor. To his right were several doors. He opened each in turn until he found the one to the cellar. Opening the door, Reg waited at the top while Clement descended. It smelt damp and musty. Clement shivered, forcing the memories of the last time he was imprisoned in a cellar from his mind. He flashed the torch around the dark space but no one was being held there. He checked the walls and floor but there wasn't another way out. Hurrying back upstairs, he rejoined Reg in the hall. Together they checked the front rooms. Standing by a window that faced the front of the house, Clement pulled back a curtain and stared out into the night. He pulled the binoculars from his coat and trained them on the driveway. In the moonlight he could just see Morris's car parked beside the drive, under the large oaks.

Leaving the front room, he checked the next room; Armstrong's study. It was an elegant room with a large ornate desk in the Napoleonic style. A bust of Adolf Hitler sat on the desk. Clement glanced at Reg who, Clement felt, would like to have broken it. He then checked the desk drawers but they yielded nothing of interest. He stood, his gaze slowly taking in every aspect of the room. He couldn't shake the feeling that someone was there. Yet the house and the rooms, other than where Isabel worked, looked vacated; as though it had all been packed away and the house closed up, but his skin prickled with anticipation. They left the room, crossing the hall. Opposite was a sitting room. Here large dust cloths had been draped over the furniture. Whoever was now in charge of the group wasn't intending to return any time soon. Clement walked into the hall. Nothing. Lifting his leg, he placed his foot on the lowest stair. Reg close behind him.

A light, fierce and blinding, flashed into his eyes from the top of the stairs. He shielded his eyes from the intense glare with one hand and slipped the catch on his Welrod with the other. In that second, Reg swung around and crouched behind the stairs, his Sten in his grasp. That no one had fired at him told Clement that, whoever it was standing at the top of the stairs, it wasn't Armstrong. Armstrong wouldn't hesitate to shoot. 'Show yourself or I shoot,' Clement threatened. He waited two seconds for a response then let off two quiet thuds into the side wall hoping that whoever stood above him on the upper landing wouldn't return fire. A scream followed.

'Isabel?' Clement shouted.

The girl screamed again, dropping the torch. Clement heard her pounding footsteps as she ran back along the corridor. A door slammed shut.

'Isabel? We don't mean you any harm,' Clement shouted, cautiously climbing the stairs. He moved slowly along the corridor towards the back of the house. 'Are you alone in the house?'

Silence.

Clement repeated his question. 'I'm coming in. You're safe. I mean you no harm.'

Clement kicked the door, the lock shattering. The girl screamed again.

'Isabel? Don't be afraid.'

'I thought you were dead,' she stammered.

'Is anyone else in the house?' Clement asked.

'Just me,' she said, hysteria taking hold.

'How many people were here, Isabel?'

'Six. Five if you don't count Sir Hector.' She paused. 'You killed him, didn't you?'

'I didn't mean to. I was just trying to escape and he came into the barn as it blew up. Did Mr Bainbridge go with them?'

'Who?'

'Mr Bainbridge,' Clement repeated. 'I saw him with the important visitor,' Clement said.

'I don't know who you mean. I don't know anything,'

the girl sobbed.

'Isabel, has the important man with grey hair gone with Mr Hugh Armstrong?'

She nodded, her whole body visibly shaking.

'Do you know where they've gone?' Clement said, his voice calm.

Isabel shook her head. Tears were streaming down her face and Clement could see that the girl was terrified. 'I don't know. Really. They've gone. That's all I know.'

'How did they leave? By car? Or lorry, perhaps?' Clement said his voice soft.

'Mr Hugh took the visitor in the sports car. The others went in the lorry.'

A noise, like the sound of a chair falling over, crashed onto a wooden floor somewhere further along the corridor. Clement shot a glance at Reg. 'Isabel, who else is in the house?' he demanded.

Isabel stood trembling, her whimpering unintelligible.

Clement nodded to Reg who ran along the corridor and kicked open a door further along the corridor.

'Clement!' Reg called.

Clement grasped hold of Isabel's right arm and pulled her along the hall. He knew if it had been Armstrong in the room he would have come out shooting. Someone was held captive there. Clement opened the door and shone the torch into the darkness.

24

Reg cut the ropes. 'You alright, lad?'

The boy's eyes were wide and mistrustful.

'Do you remember me?' Clement said, kneeling down so the boy could see his face clearly. 'I came to your school with Superintendent Morris.'

The boy nodded.

'My friend, the policeman, is outside. Come with us now. Do you have a coat?'

'He can't leave,' Isabel said. 'I'll be in terrible trouble if he isn't here.'

'I think you should come with us too, Isabel,' Clement said, standing, his hand on the boy's shoulder.

'Leave the boy where he is!'

Clement heard the voice. It was a voice he knew. He spun on his heel. His eyes fixed on the pistol levelled at him. He looked into the face of Gabrielle Warrender, his housekeeper. Her blue eyes were like steel, her square jaw fixed with determination and hostility. Seconds passed and neither spoke. Clement saw she was wearing a thick travelling coat and he realised that she had been left behind to take the boy somewhere. Then Clement saw it, the thin blue line in the weave of her coat, repeated every six inches or so. He'd seen it before in the trousers of the dead man in Morris's mortuary; the thick, hand-spun cloth, the same pattern with a single thread of blue.

'The boy is innocent. It's me they want, Ailsa. Or is it really Gabrielle?'

The woman laughed. She cocked the gun. 'Don't think for one minute *your* life means anything at all. Insignificant people don't matter.'

Clement kept his eyes on her. 'Did you kill the porter at Trinity Hall?'

The woman smiled. 'It was so easy. And they arrested you!'

'Why did you kill him?'

'I told you, insignificant people don't matter. He knew too much and he was seen talking to you. Besides, he knew about the boy.'

'Why do you want him?'

'While he is with us, his father will do as we require.'

Clement kept the eye contact between them. Had Bill Hayward really died because of him? Or was she just trying to unsettle him? Either way, he felt some degree of guilt for the man's death. In his peripheral vision he saw that Reg had quietly withdrawn his knife and was holding it by his side.

'Why don't you let Isabel go then. She's of no use to you.'

'Not while the boy is here.'

'Where are they taking him?'

Outside, Clement heard the sound of a vehicle on the gravel drive.

The woman smiled. 'Your end has come, Reverend Wisdom.'

They heard the sound of a car door slam. Then the front door opened, a cool breeze wafting up the stairs.

'That will be Mr Armstrong come for the boy. Isabel, go and bring Mr Hugh here.'

Clement stared at the woman as Isabel ran from the room. 'Aren't you interested in how your brother died?'

'My brother died years ago.'

'I'm not talking about Bill.'

She paused but Clement saw the fleeting reaction in her steely eyes. 'I have no other brother.'

'I think you do. Another brother named John. He is currently in the police mortuary in Cambridge waiting for his family to give him a decent burial.'

'Then he'll be waiting a while. He was a traitor. And he died as one.'

Clement saw the hatred in her eyes. He didn't understand it. Had she meant her brother was a traitor to their cause or was it to Nazi Germany? Clement heard the footsteps on the stairs. 'And what are you to Hugh Armstrong?'

'A patriot and loyal servant to the League,' she said, her finger moving to the trigger. Reg lunged forward, taking her around the neck and pulling her backwards. The gun in her tight fist discharged into the ceiling. Clement turned the boy to face him and held him tightly as Reg drew his knife across the woman's throat. The footsteps on the stairs had stopped.

'Is there a back way out?' he whispered to Michael.

The trembling boy nodded. Opening the door, Clement peered out, back along the corridor. The front stairs were a distance from the back bedrooms. A door, usually closed, divided the front bedrooms from the servants' quarters at the rear. A light had been turned on downstairs. Clement tiptoed along the corridor to the dividing door. In the glow of the light below, he saw Armstrong's shadow on the wall, a pistol in his grasp as he slowly and noiselessly climbed the stairs. Clement beckoned behind him to Reg who carried the boy along the corridor to the rear stairs. Clement joined them. Descending the servants' stairs, they hurried to the scullery at the rear of the house. Isabel sat wide-eyed on a stool by the stove. Clement signalled with his finger against his lips for her to remain quiet. 'Go home, Isabel,' he whispered. For one second, he wondered if he should take her too but he could see she was paralysed with fear and there was no time for remonstrations. He believed Armstrong was unlikely to harm her, simply because she was of no significance to him.

Leaving by the kitchen, they crept around the house in a wide arc and crouched by a fence in the adjacent field. The front of the house was in the centre of his vision. Clement took his binoculars and trained them on the house. The Lagonda was parked on the driveway, turned around and ready to leave. Clement estimated it would only be a few minutes before Hugh Armstrong found the woman's body and that the boy was no longer in the house. Not that Clement thought Armstrong would be dismayed by the woman's death. The boy, however, was a different matter.

Clement kept the binoculars on the car. Armstrong, Clement guessed, had returned for the boy and the Lagonda had only two seats. But it didn't mean that Armstrong had returned to the house alone. The Scot could still be in the vicinity. Clement closed his eyes for a second. Why, if the boy was still of value to them, had he not gone in the lorry with the others? Why was it necessary for him to be transported in the car? Was it possible the lad was to be traded with someone? Clement couldn't think about it now. The boy's immediate safety was all that mattered and Clement needed to get him away from Hitcham Hall. Reg reached for the binoculars, scanning the driveway and gardens for Morris's car.

'He's not there, Clement!' Reg said.

'What?' Clement felt his stomach churn. 'Check

again, Reg.'

'I could go and look, if you'd like?'

'No. I can't lose you as well.' Clement paused. 'We take the boy with us to the boat.'

Reg picked up Michael, and carrying the lad on his back, they headed out across the fields.

As Clement ran he wondered what had happened to Morris. It wasn't like him to change a plan. Did that mean Armstrong, or more likely the Scot, had either killed or taken Morris? Was Morris a hostage now? Clement glanced up at the boy on Reg's shoulders. Was Michael more important than Clement had realised? He remembered the woman's words about the boy's father. What role did Sir Cedric Hasluck play? No man would trade his son for an unknown policeman? As Clement ran he realised Armstrong's intent. Morris was to be traded but the trade wasn't with Michael's father. It would be he, Clement, who would be forced to choose; Morris or the boy.

Clement checked his watch, his mind racing. They struck out over the fields, weaving their way from fence to fence or through wooded areas. The gate into the copse adjacent to *The Bridge* was ten feet away when they heard a shot. Clement stopped and turned. He thought of Morris. 'Keep running!' Clement said, hoping the gunshot was a bluff. Clement believed that while he had the boy, Morris would remain alive. Jumping the fence they crossed the road and went straight to the river but Clement knew what lay ahead. Armstrong intended a confrontation and when it happened it would be personal and deadly.

Crossing the narrow woodland path, they waited by the road. Jumping the fence, Clement ran into the rear gardens of *The Bridge*. He saw no one. He signalled Reg. Drawing his Welrod, he watched the road and inn as Reg and Michael joined him by the sprawling trees. Together, they ran across the grass to where Reg had tied up the dinghy.

'Clement, you stay with the boy and row the boat to Horningsea. I'll get the film from the camera by the gate at Hitcham Hall and meet you there. That should tell us what happened to Morris.'

'Agreed. And Reg, be careful.'

Reg smiled and disappeared into the night.

Minutes later, Clement put the oars into the rowlocks and started to row upstream.

'Are you alright, Michael?' Clement whispered.

The boy nodded but Clement could see fear and exhaustion. The lad had seen enough malevolence for one lifetime and Clement wanted to get him to safety as soon as possible. 'Just sit tight there for a few more minutes. Once we are safe you can tell me all about it.'

Clement leaned into the rowing, dipping the oars carefully into the running water, his shoulder pain the least of his concerns. From time to time he turned around, hoping to see the spire of St Peter's. Half an hour later, it appeared. He smiled again at Michael. 'Nearly there,' he whispered. But his mind was on Morris and Armstrong and what lay in store. Pulling hard on one oar, Clement rounded the dinghy so that it came up beside the timber platform.

Tying the dinghy to the jetty, he stood and stepped from the boat, his eyes firmly on the shore and the hill above the jetty. Assisting Michael out of the dinghy, he and the boy hurried up the grassy bank towards the dark edifice of St Peter's Church, his senses on high alert.

Standing beside the old stone church with Michael beside him, Clement waited at the corner and peered around to the church's front door and its covered porch. Crouching low, they ran towards it and hid beside a pillar. Clement scanned the scene before him. Large trees dotted the graveyard. It was dark. A light wind was rustling the leaves in the large trees. Odd shadows flickered over the headstones. Beneath one of the trees, he saw the silhouette of a man. Clement waited, his ears straining for sound. Nothing. The figure hadn't moved. Clement stared at the scene for what seemed like minutes. He knew from the size of the man it wasn't Armstrong and although he couldn't be sure, he didn't think it was the Scot either. The trees swayed and leaves continued their rustling but something about it wasn't right. As the seconds passed Clement had a growing sense of unease. He put his arm around Michael. No matter what this man wanted, Clement knew he couldn't expose Michael to further danger. Yet Clement was unwilling to leave the boy alone. He studied the figure. Pulling his Welrod from its holster next to his chest, and holding the boy firmly, Clement tiptoed forward.

'Show yourself!' he said in a low voice. The figure remained, unmoving. Clement felt the realising shiver. The sight was spellbinding. He slipped the catch on the pistol. His eyes flicked around: the church, the trees, the headstones. He and the boy were vulnerable now. With his eyes as wide as possible, and his ears straining, he advanced towards the figure. Five feet from the man, Clement froze. His hand covered the boy's face.

Clement felt his heart almost stop. He stared, his eyes wide, his brain frozen in horror. Reg was tied to a tree trunk. A myriad of questions screamed to be answered. Was he alive? Was he wired? Was Hugh Armstrong waiting in the graveyard ready to detonate a fuse? Clement felt the breeze on his face yet he felt hot. 'Stay here, Michael,' Clement whispered, his voice almost inaudible. Crouching beside the boy, he turned the lad's face away from Reg. 'Hide behind that headstone there and don't come out, no matter what you hear or see. I'll be back for you and that's a promise,' Clement whispered into the boy's frightened face, his hands gently holding the lad's shoulders. He saw the boy slip behind the stone, then Clement stood and slowly advanced. He stared into the face of his old friend, comrade and neighbour, but he knew Reg was dead. Clement began to shake. A rope bound Reg to the tree. It wrapped around his torso and was drawn tightly around his neck. Reg's tongue protruded from his open mouth and his face was swollen and smeared with blood. Clement felt the breath leave

266

him and nausea well up. He swallowed. No time. No time for horror or grief. Clement could almost feel the sadistic presence of Hugh Armstrong. He needed to think; to act rationally. If Armstrong was nearby, then his car was also. Clement crouched behind a nearby headstone and gulped in air, trying to quell the rising panic. Glancing back to where Michael had hidden, he could just see the boy seated behind the tombstone, his leg's drawn up. For now Michael was safe. Waiting only a few seconds, Clement ran towards the adjacent stone building that bordered the graveyard. Barrels stacked outside reminded Clement it was the public house, *The Crown and Punchbowl*. No lights were visible. He ran along the northern side of the building, crouching at the corner. In front of him was the sealed road. Parked by the inn's front door was the Lagonda. Clement stared at it. No one was in the vehicle. No one was anywhere. Reg had been placed so that he would be found. And not just by anyone. Clement's heart pounded as he crept up to the car and ran his hand over the bonnet. Warm. He looked around. Nothing. Yet he sensed Armstrong, waiting, watching, the ever-present sneer. Clement knew he had to make a decision. He could use the car to get Michael to safety. Clement put his hand on the car door. Surprisingly it was unlocked. He hesitated. Was it wired, a delayed detonation? He swung the car door wide and jumped back. Nothing. Sitting inside the car, he remembered a skill Reg had taught him while in Scotland. His hand reached under the dashboard, his fingers searching for the wires.

The engine roared. Quickly he leapt from the vehicle, returning to the corner of the inn and crouched in the shadows, his pistol in his grip. From the side of the blackout curtains he saw a light go on. Minutes passed but no one came outside.

He waited a full minute. Surely the sound of the car starting would bring someone, he reasoned? If not Armstrong, then certainly the publican. No one came. Clement stood. He intended to drive the Lagonda to the edge of the graveyard then get the boy. He waited a further minute than dashed for the car. Pulling the door closed after him, he put it into first gear and drove around the corner into a lane that ran down the southern side of the inn, past the graveyard and back towards the river. In the muted glare of the headlights, Armstrong stood in the centre of the road, a pistol held at Morris's head.

25

In the strong moonlight, Clement could see that Morris's face was one of sheer terror. Clement shifted his gaze to Armstrong. There he saw the maniacal sneer; ruthless, devoid of human compassion.

Clement pulled on the hand brake, put the car in neutral and got out of the vehicle, leaving the engine running and the door wide. He stood facing Armstrong, the open door like a shield between them. Below the level of the car window, Clement gripped his Welrod. 'It's me you want, Hugh. Why don't you let the Superintendent go?'

'Where is the boy?'

'What boy?'

Armstrong laughed. 'You must think we are fools! We have been planning this for years. Not you or anyone can prevent it from happening now.'

'What *is* happening, Hugh?'

'Beyond anything you can imagine.'

'If it cannot be prevented now, why not tell me?'

'I think you'd like that. All neat and tidy. Your friend, by the way, is dead. But I think you know that, too.' Armstrong nodded in Reg's direction. 'He's not very well mannered, is he? Used all sorts of obscenities. His pack,' Armstrong said, kicking the bag at his feet. Clement recognised it immediately.

He swallowed hard. As much as the sight of young Armstrong revolted him, Clement couldn't divert his eyes. Before him stood pure evil, far worse than sadism, Armstrong had been brainwashed with twisted ideology at its most depraved that made him capable of anything. Despite every belief Clement held dear, he wanted to kill Armstrong. That, too, was what Armstrong wanted; for him to lose control, to lash out. If he did, Morris would die instantly. Stay calm, Clement told himself, his eyes flashing to Reg's pack. Clement lowered his hand. Still clenching the Welrod, he hid the weapon behind his right leg and took a step sideways, running on pure adrenaline.

Armstrong reached for Reg's pack and threw it towards him.

Clement reacted immediately, hurling himself sideways, rolling away from the car and towards the low shrubs that grew by the wall of the inn.

Hugh Armstrong laughed aloud. 'So you knew what was in it then?'

Clement glanced at Morris who stood rigid with fear. Clement stood slowly, his eyes fixed on Armstrong.

'Put the weapon down!' Armstrong shouted, pushing the tip of his pistol into Morris's right ear. 'Do it or your friend here dies!' Armstrong pulled back on the safety catch.

Clement tossed the Welrod forward. It landed about six feet from where he stood and about ten from Armstrong. Keeping his eye on Armstrong, Clement shot a glance at Reg's pack only a few feet away.

Armstrong had seen his eyes dart to the bag. 'Look inside, if you are sceptical about it. You'll be disappointed,' Armstrong added with mock insincerity. 'You see I have taken the grenades and a few handy little gadgets, like knives and timer switches, plastic explosive and fuses. Nothing left now. So here is where you will die, Reverend Wisdom. With your friends. All together. And already in a graveyard. Convenient, don't you think?'

Keeping his eyes on Armstrong, Clement slowly reached for Reg's pack.

'Go on! Look! I told you, it's empty!' Armstrong shouted.

Clement squatted by the bag, and with both hands opened the pack. Just as Armstrong had said, it was empty but Clement saw the edge of a notebook left in the side pocket. He swallowed. It was his only chance. If something went wrong, Clement knew he and Morris were dead men. Slowly, he reached in, his hand grasping the device. Keeping it within the pack, he selected red and slid his thumbnail along the edge hoping it would be enough to activate the fuse. He then stood and took a step forward towards Armstrong, carrying the pack.

'Not a step closer or your friend here is dead.'

Clement stopped. 'Release Morris. It's me you want.' Clement flicked a glance at Morris. 'Release him! Or shoot me. But if you shoot me, you will never know where I've hidden the boy.'

Armstrong's smile widened. 'Why would you do that?'

'Because I have nothing to live for, Armstrong. Like you, my family is dead. And also like you, we fight for a cause. Different causes, but we honour them with our lives if necessary.'

Clement saw Armstrong's smile falter but the eyes were fixed on him, the pupils wide and unblinking. Clement watched those wild eyes that stared back. The smirk had faded, the game of cat and mouse was over. Now it was just death or survival. No henchmen, no authority figures, just the two of them.

Armstrong's grip on Morris slackened and Morris broke free, running forward towards Clement.

'Now, the boy or you die!' Armstrong said, his pistol now levelled at Clement.

Clement stared at Armstrong. He said nothing.

'Where is the boy!' Armstrong shouted.

'I'm here.'

Clement swung around in horror. Michael stood in the middle of the road, facing them.

'Come here,' Armstrong yelled at the boy. The lad

moved forward. Armstrong's wild eyes shifted to Clement. 'Move and I kill him!' Armstrong pointed the pistol at the frightened child.

Clement froze.

Michael walked forward.

As soon as Michael passed him, and while Armstrong's attention was on the boy, Clement seized the moment. Throwing himself forwards, he grabbed his Welrod that lay in the dirt and fired a single shot at Armstrong. Armstrong saw the move and without aiming, returned fire. Both shots missed their targets. The boy stood rigid as Morris ran forward and grabbed Michael. Armstrong swung around and let off three more shots. Morris went down, grasping his arm, the boy now unprotected. Armstrong moved his pistol wildly, from Clement to Morris then to the boy. Armstrong ran forward and grabbed Michael with one arm, then ran towards the Lagonda. Clement raised his Welrod, aimed carefully and pulled the trigger. The bullet hit Armstrong's shoulder. Clement heard the dull thud as the bullet tore into Armstrong's flesh. Armstrong fell, dropping the boy, and lay on the ground, screaming. Clement stood and rushed for Michael. Scooping him up in his arms, Clement ran for the car.

'Climb into the back, Michael and stay down!' Clement got into the car and pushed open the passenger door. 'Morris!' he shouted from the car. 'Get in! Hurry man!'

Morris struggled to stand, his body swaying. He staggered towards the car, clutching his injured and bleeding arm. Collapsing onto the passenger seat Morris managed to pull the door closed. Swiftly engaging gear, Clement backed up the lane towards the High Street as a door into the inn opened and the Scot emerged. Clement could still hear Armstrong screaming as he turned the car onto the road from the lane. In the rear-view mirror, Clement saw the Scot bending over Armstrong. Two seconds later, the notebook detonated.

26

Clement drove fast. Morris was losing consciousness, his head falling backwards.

'Stay awake, Arthur. Once we are away from here, I'll bind that wound.'

In the early dawn light, Clement saw an open farm gate and, slowing the car, pulled into the field and switched off the engine. Getting out, he went to the other side and opened the door. He could see from Morris's ashen face and the amount of blood on the door that Morris was bleeding heavily and losing consciousness fast. Clement pulled his belt from his trousers and wrapped it around Morris's arm, drawing it tight above the wound.

He needed to get Morris to a hospital and the boy to safety. Things were happening too quickly. Questions brimmed and flowed through his brain. Why had Morris not warned them? And what of Reg? How had Armstrong caught Reg? Don't think about it now! he told himself. Morris was his priority and for the boy's sake Clement needed to stay in control and make the right decisions. He blinked, forcing the horrific images of his friend from his mind. No matter what he knew he had to do, the appalling image of Reg was like a photographic negative that refused to disappear from his mind's eye.

'Where is your home, Michael?'

'Wilstock House. It's near Lode,' Michael said. 'My parents are away,' the boy added, tears falling down his cheeks.

'You've been very brave, Michael. I'll look after you. You can stay with me for now.'

Morris groaned.

'Stay with me, Arthur. Tell me what happened?'

'I'm not sure,' Morris murmured, his breathing thready. 'Just came from nowhere. Smashed the side window. Dragged me from the car. Hit me. I don't know what happened then. I woke up in *The Crown and Punchbowl*.'

'And Reg?'

'I don't know where he is.'

The image flashed again. 'He's dead.'

'I'm sorry, Clement.'

'Hang on, Arthur. Take deeper breaths. Won't be long now.' Clement got back behind the wheel and drove off, fast. He glanced across at Morris as they sped south. The man was white. Clement checked the rear-view mirror. No one was following. 'Not far now, Michael. You'll be safe soon.'

'I want to go home,' Michael said through the tears.

'I'll try to call your parents from the police station and ask them to return. You say they are in Portugal?'

'Yes.'

'Do you know why?'

The boy shook his head. 'No.'

'What about your uncle, Michael. Perhaps you could stay with him again?'

'No! He hates me! He only likes his books.'

'Why do you think that?'

'Because he told me to go with them. He said I'd have fun at a farm. I didn't. They locked me into that room. Only Isabel talked to me.'

'The man in the dinghy with you, the night you left Trinity Hall College, was that your uncle?'

'No. I don't know who he is. He hit me.'

Clement glanced at Michael then Morris. 'I'm not taking you back there, Michael. Don't worry. You can stay with me but I must get Superintendent Morris to a doctor.'

Clement sped through the Cambridge streets, heading for St Andrew's Street. As soon as Morris was in safe hands, Clement decided to call Johnny. He would locate Michael's parents but until then, Clement decided, Cambridge Police Station was the safest place for himself and the boy.

'What did you say your father does?'

'He works for the government. They go away a lot. Papa flies the plane.'

'Is your father in the Royal Air Force?'

'No. He doesn't wear a uniform. But he flies everywhere.'

'Does he fly himself to Portugal?'

'Sometimes.'

'Does he fly to other places, as well as Portugal?'

'Yes. They went to Germany once before the war.'

'Do you know why?' Clement asked.

Michael shook his head. The boy paused. 'I've met Winston Churchill.'

Clement flicked a glance at Michael; the boy's importance was becoming all too clear.

'Does your father work in London?'

'Yes. In a big building near Westminster Abbey. He's been to America!'

Clement stared at the road ahead, his foot firmly on the accelerator.

Clement drove the Lagonda into the police compound. Running into the station, he called aloud for the constable on duty. Within minutes, Sergeant Kendall had Morris inside the police station and the ambulance sent for. Taking the boy with him, Clement went to the meeting room on the first floor. He walked to the window and looked down at the street. Minutes later he heard the ambulance siren. Below him, Clement saw Morris being stretchered to the rear of the ambulance and put inside. It drove away. Clement turned to face

Michael. 'You've been so brave. You must be tired. Now that Superintendent Morris has gone to hospital, I'll ask Sergeant Kendall to find you something to eat. And perhaps he can find a place for you to sleep.'

'No. I want to stay with you.'

Clement smiled. He'd never had his own children and he didn't really know what to say to the little creatures but perhaps the shared experience had formed a bond between himself and the lad. Clement went to the telephone and spoke to the constable on duty.

A short time later, Sergeant Kendall arrived with a tray of tea and some sandwiches. 'Only for special visitors,' he said to Michael. 'I'll arrange a stretcher bed for you lad, so you can sleep. You must be done in. I'll put it up in here, if you like.' Kendall left the room.

'He's a very caring man, Michael,' Clement said. 'Would you like to stay with him while I attend to a few things?'

Michael nodded. 'But you'll be back?'

'Yes.' Clement tucked the lad into the stretcher and sat near the window sipping his tea. He felt exhausted, beyond anything he'd ever experienced. He glanced over to the boy who was already drifting off to sleep. Clement understood the effects of adrenaline withdrawal.

A soft knock at the door made Clement look up. Sergeant Kendall entered carrying a fresh pot of tea. 'Thought you may like a top-up, sir. How is he?'

'You're very kind. How is it you're still here, Sergeant? You were on duty late last night. Have you been here all this time?'

'Yes. I tried to get a message to you about the Lagonda leaving Tenison Street but you'd all gone. Thought I should stay on, just in case.' Kendall's gaze shifted to Michael. 'He's seen things no ten-year-old should. I have a lad about the same age. You always worry about them. War and childhood, they just don't go together, do they?'

'No, Sergeant. Would you do something for me?'

'What's that, sir?'

'Go to Horningsea. Soon. A very brave man has died there. He's tied to a tree in the graveyard of St Peter's church. It's a tragic and horrific sight, so please go before morning's light. While you are there it may be a good idea to question the publican. Find out what happened to Armstrong and the man with him, the Scot.'

Michael turned in his sleep.

Clement sighed. 'This poor child needs a safe place for a few days until his parents can be located.'

'I've been thinking about that, sir. A police station is no place for the lad. He can stay with Mrs Kendall and me until his parents come. My boy would be happy as Larry if he had a playmate.'

'You are a kind man, Sergeant.'

'You leave it all to me, sir,' Kendall said, and left the room.

In the stillness, Clement glanced across at Michael but Armstrong's whereabouts worried him. While Armstrong remained at liberty, the boy was in danger. In his mind Clement visualised Armstrong writhing on the ground. Dead or alive, the Scot would have taken him away. Hitcham Hall was the likely place. At least now, the Lagonda was safely in the police yard and no longer available for Armstrong to use. Clement's mind drifted to the suitcases in the car's boot. Reg had referred to them as Trojan horses. Now that the car was in police hands, he could make a thorough search of the cases and their contents. Standing, Clement tiptoed out of the room and went downstairs, then out to where the car was still parked.

Walking around to the boot, he sprang the catch. Lifting each suitcase out, he closed the boot and carried them back to the meeting room upstairs. Opening the door quietly, he glanced at Michael who was still asleep, then gently placed the cases onto the table. He ran his fingers along every surface and edge, feeling for wires, then opened them, lifting the delicate tissue wrappings out and tearing each open. Both cases still contained the evening apparel. With all the items removed from the case and from their wrappings, Clement ran his hand over all the surfaces and along the inside edges of both cases. He felt the ridge under the lining in both suitcases. He reached for his dagger. Carefully he sliced along the bottom edge of the lining. Lifting the fabric with the tip of his blade, he saw a large folded sheet of stiff paper. Grasping the corner between the tips of his thumb and forefinger, he slid it out. He could see from the corners it was a blueprint. Placing it on the table, he cut the lining fabric in the second suitcase. As with the first, another blueprint was concealed there. Pulling it out gently, Clement unfolded both then laid each on the table, placing them side by side. He stared at the prints.

Before him were two maps of Britain. One was of the country's entire electricity network with the location of every substation in every county clearly marked. Clement stared at the document, his jaw dropping. His gaze shifted to the other blueprint. This one showed, in detail, the telephone and radio communication networks across Britain. Even bus stops and church spires were labelled, along with the names of rivers and bridges.

'Dear Lord! This must have taken years to compile,' he whispered, thinking of exchange students on bicycles. Britain's entire infrastructure recorded in detail and now about to be in the hands of the nation's enemy.

Clement slumped into a chair and, leaning into his hands, covered his face with both palms. He needed to think. He knew what they intended. And from what he'd seen, it had the potential to be successful. Time was critical but what would trigger the coup? It had to be an event so momentous that it was guaranteed to be broadcast to the nation. He needed to speak to Nora or Johnny. Clement paused, his head still resting in his hands. Armstrong. Was he alive? If he was, Clement reasoned, he wouldn't be content to lie in some remote farmhouse recuperating. He would want to be where the uprising was to take place. Clement went to the telephone. He waited while the number was connected.

'Miss Cunningham, is Johnny in?'

'Not yet, Major. Can I help?'

'I need to know, as a matter of real urgency, where Michael Hasluck's parents are and what exactly his father does in government.'

'Where are you, Major?'

'Cambridge Police Station.'

'I'll do my best. But wouldn't the boy's school be quicker? They would have this information.'

Clement heard the words.

'Major? Are you still there?'

'Yes…' Clement paused. 'Miss Cunningham, do you have the headmaster's name on file?'

'I understand you've met him. The school should be able to give you this information also.'

'Please, Miss Cunningham. This is important.'

'Very well. We called the school recently when you telephoned Superintendent Morris to remove the boy. We'll have it here, just a minute.'

Clement heard her place the receiver on a table. He had to wait no more than a few minutes. 'His name is Hetherington. Arnold Hetherington.'

'Don't involve the school at all, Miss Cunningham.'

'As you wish. I'll be in touch when I have the information about the Haslucks.'

Clement sat in the chair facing the large window that overlooked St Andrew's Street. Michael still slept on the stretcher bed beside him. Outside, he heard a vehicle pull up. Standing, he went to the window and looked out.

Below, he saw a large police vehicle with a black windowless hearse behind it. His heart sank but he couldn't face Reg yet. His anguish and grief would have to wait.

Ten minutes later there was a soft knock at the door and Kendall came in. 'Sergeant Naylor is downstairs, sir, when you're ready. Also, I spoke to the publican at *The Crown and Punchbowl*. He was held at gunpoint and not freed until sometime after the explosion. The Scot is dead. Died at the scene. According to the publican, a priest came with the two young men and took Armstrong and the deceased man away. The publican says he was instructed to remain inside the inn for an hour after they'd gone. When he did venture outside, he saw debris and a large amount of blood on the gravel drive.'

'Thank you, Sergeant,' Clement said. He let out a long sigh. The Scot was dead but Armstrong lived, although injured. Clement turned to the window and stared at the bright sunlit morning as images of Reg flashed again in his mind. Salty tears stung his eyes. Taking his handkerchief from his pocket he blew his nose. As exhausted as he was, he couldn't rest. Not while Armstrong's whereabouts remained unknown. Clement began to think. Armstrong would know he'd search for him. Therefore, Armstrong would avoid all the places Clement knew about. 'Where would you go?' Clement whispered.

He wondered about the Abbey School. If he were correct about A.H. initials, Hetherington could be hiding Armstrong, but how likely was it that Ramsey would be the starting place of a coup? Clement shook his head.

Ramsey wasn't central enough, nor important enough. Neither, really, was Cambridge. He felt certain that wherever the coup was to take place, injured or not, that was where Armstrong would be.

The telephone on the table rang.

He jumped from the seat. 'Hello?'

'Major?'

'Yes, Miss Cunningham.'

'Michael's father is Sir Cedric Hasluck, a senior public servant with the Foreign Office. He and Lady Ellen Hasluck are currently in Portugal.'

'Where would I find Corporal Hughes currently?'

'Here.'

'I'll be on the first train.'

27

Clement hung up. He glanced at the clock. All being well, he could be in Whitehall before two o'clock. His eye hurt. And he needed sleep. But this couldn't wait. Closing the door to the meeting room, he returned downstairs and found Sergeant Kendall. 'Any news about Superintendent Morris?'

Kendall nodded. 'He's through the surgery. The doctor said that while he lost a lot of blood, none of the bones were damaged so he's hopeful that Superintendent Morris will have the use of his arm although there may be some nerve damage. He'll have his arm in a sling for a while.'

'That is good news. You'll look after the boy? He still isn't completely out of danger, Sergeant.'

'I'm about to go off duty, sir, so I can take Michael home with me now. He'll be right as rain, Major Wisdom.'

'I need to go to London, Kendall. Could one of your constables drive me to the station?'

'You really should rest. It was quite a night for you, sir and your injuries aren't yet completely healed.'

'You are probably right, Sergeant. I've no doubt that I must look unkempt but I cannot rest until this is done.'

Kendall reached for a set of keys. 'You're in no fit state to travel on the trains. I'll have a constable drive you to London.' Kendall paused, his voice almost a whisper, 'Mr Naylor is downstairs, if you'd like to see him before you go.'

Clement fought the tears. 'Not yet, thank you.' He cleared his throat. 'Did you find anything on him, I mean in his pockets?'

'Something in particular?' Kendall asked.

'Rolls of undeveloped film.'

'Nothing, I'm afraid.'

As he and the constable left the building, Clement cast his eye towards the Lagonda. He wondered if any-one would attempt to break into the police station to access the vehicle. Surely Armstrong would surmise the blueprints had been found but Clement wasn't taking any chances. He returned to the duty desk. 'Sergeant Kendall, please make sure that the Lagonda is securely locked up here. No one is to take it anywhere or have access to it for any reason.'

'Understood, sir,' Kendall replied.

The constable drove the police car quickly through the back lanes of Cambridgeshire. Clement sat beside him in the front seat. Neither spoke. As they left the pastures of the countryside, the afternoon light was bathing the fields in the vibrant glow of a summer's afternoon. Just after half past twelve they entered the northern outskirts of London and forty minutes later the constable pulled the car into Whitehall Place. Thanking him, Clement hurried towards the familiar entry.

'Good afternoon, Major,' Nora said, her hands still hovering over the typewriter keys. I believe you know Miss Cunningham?'

Clement smiled. 'I apologize, ladies, for my appearance.'

'They are expecting you. Just go straight in,' Nora smiled.

Clement knocked on Johnny's door and entered. A group of men looked up as he walked in. The number of people seated in Johnny's office surprised Clement. Johnny stood. Clement thought his old friend's face looked strained but then he realised his probably looked worse. *C* was standing by the window. Sitting to one side of Johnny's desk was Colonel Gubbins, although from his uniform Clement could see he was now a brigadier, and another man in plainclothes sat in a chair facing the others. Clement wondered if he should salute. To him, the gesture seemed out of place. Glancing at the faces, he decided against it. Two empty chairs sat on the other side of Johnny's desk. One would be for *C*, the other, he guessed, was for him.

Johnny indicated the chair. 'Clement, let me introduce you. Brigadier Gubbins you know.'

'Sir,' Clement said, his eyes going to the other man.

'And this is the Minister for Economic Warfare, Dr Hugh Dalton, Clement.'

'Sir.'

'Be seated, Major. I understand you have encountered some problems,' *C* said, returning to his chair.

Clement sat as instructed.

'Captain Winthorpe has brought us up to date with events. So what brings you here so urgently, Major?' *C* said.

Clement glanced around the group. 'Three things, sir. Hugh Armstrong has disappeared. He needs to be found. Wherever he is, that is where the coup will take place.'

'And the second?' *C* said.

'A small boy is central to everything. Right now, he is in the safe care of Sergeant Kendall of Cambridge Police. Michael was kidnapped to ensure his father did as this group require. May I ask why Sir Cedric is in Portugal and what exactly he does for our government?'

'Sir Cedric liaises with both industry and government. He has been instrumental in us sourcing vital raw materials for the manufacturing and hardening of steel components for our munitions and aircraft factories. He's in Portugal because they have large deposits of tungsten. Needless to say, the Germans are also after these resources.'

'I understand Sir Cedric Hasluck flies himself to these meetings?' Clement asked.

'That's correct,' Dalton replied.

'Was he there recently?'

'He is there currently,' C said.

'With respect, sir, I don't think so.'

C reached for the telephone on Johnny's desk. 'Get me the Foreign Office.'

Clement looked at the faces in the room as telephone lines were being connected. A minute later C spoke, 'I need to know exactly where Sir Cedric Hasluck is?'

Some minutes passed while C listened. He rang off, his hand still holding the telephone receiver. He depressed the dial tone buttons and spoke again with an operator. 'Get me our embassy in Lisbon.'

Clement glanced at the men in the room. All were grim-faced and no one spoke. Clement didn't really know if Hasluck had been the other man in the lorry. It was a hunch. A strong one but a hunch nonetheless.

'I wish to speak with Sir Cedric Hasluck, Sir Stewart Menzies speaking,' C paused. 'What! Why weren't we informed?' C rang off. Everyone in the room waited.

'He isn't there. Left Lisbon over a week ago.'

The room was silent.

Clement thought back; six days ago he and Reg had seen Michael taken by boat from Trinity Hall steps. He'd been transferred from the college to Hitcham Hall. That had also been the morning Clement had been kidnapped and imprisoned in the cellar of Caius College. In his mind, Clement heard Sir Hector's voice telling his son to bring the other one. Clement now believed that man to have been Sir Cedric. He had flown Haushofer out of England sometime between February and May; most likely landing in Portugal on one of his many trips to negotiate tungsten contracts there. Clement's thoughts raced. If Hasluck had flown Haushofer to Portugal, then his son, Michael, was kidnapped to compel Hasluck to fly another; the grey-haired man he'd recently seen at Hitcham Hall.

'Of course!' Clement said.

'Major?' *C* said.

Clement explained.

'So who is this grey-haired man?'

'I don't know.'

'Do you know who they are waiting for?' *C* asked.

'I don't know that either.'

C looked across at Johnny and Dalton. 'Perhaps you should be made aware of something, Major. It's classified as Most Secret and carries that security level.' Menzies paused. 'But, it has a bearing on the current situation. We are aware of several members of our own upper classes endeavouring to bring about peace through negotiated talks with the Nazis. The Prime Minister is aware of it but believes it is completely misguided and has chosen to keep it secret. Even a member of our royal family is involved, so needless to say, we must tread carefully. We know that some of these people met with

Haushofer and Rudolf Hess in both Spain and Portugal between February and April. We also know that Hasluck flew them there. That much you are correct about. But, are you really expecting us to believe that a senior member of our royal family would be involved with murderous thugs like this Hugh Armstrong?'

Clement swallowed hard. 'I think they are being manipulated, sir. They may have good intentions but they are being subverted. The real purpose is total control through a coup d'état. The Nazis and some influential Englishmen, through the resurgence of the Right Club and Nordic League, and by using the Freemasonry network, do not intend a negotiated peace. And they never have.'

'Well what do they want?' Dalton said.

'Nazi rule, sir. They want Britain to be controlled from Berlin and for life under British democracy to be eradicated. They are completely ruthless and prepared to do anything to bring it about. I know they intend to free Rudolf Hess. And I believe it is their intention to assassinate the Prime Minister. And, he may not be the only one.'

'And you've come to this theory because of one dead man in a field in Cambridgeshire?' Dalton said.

'Yes,' Clement said. His mind was racing but it was all he could say.

'Who was this man?' *C* asked.

'His name was John Nicolson.'

Gubbins sat forward, his hands gripping the armrests

of his chair, his eyes fixed on Clement.

Clement felt the piercing stare. He told them what he knew about the dead man with the faint blue thread in his turned-up trousers that matched his sister's coat.

'So that's what happened to him,' Gubbins said. 'He was one of mine, Wisdom. He worked for me in a highly secret capacity. He's been missing for several months. He made his last contact with us five months ago from his location in Norway. He said he was working on infiltrating a Nazi-led, non-military invasion of Britain. That was his description. He was given complete autonomy to go wherever he deemed he needed to be. And he preferred to work alone.' Gubbins looked directly at Clement. 'He said he already knew some of the people involved so he would be the best person for the job. When his transmissions ceased, we assumed he was either captured or dead.'

Clement looked at Gubbins. 'Somehow his infiltration was discovered and that must be why he was chosen to make the rendezvous with Haushofer, who shot him. Michael Hasluck witnessed Haushofer in Armstrong's car. Had Superintendent Morris and I not gone to the school to ask questions, the boy may not have been kidnapped. But as we did, the headmaster, who I believe is also a member of this group, became aware that young Hasluck had seen something and so the boy was taken which guaranteed Sir Cedric's continued cooperation.'

'If Hasluck flew Haushofer out of England in late April, why was his boy kidnapped six weeks later? It doesn't make any sense,' Dalton said.

'Perhaps Michael's kidnap was initially only a threat to compel Sir Cedric to return Haushofer to Europe. But when Hetherington told them what Michael had seen, and that we knew about it, that threat became reality and Sir Cedric continued to be manipulated,' Clement added.

'So where is Hasluck now?'

'I don't know.'

The tension in the room was almost electric. Johnny twiddled a pen while C paced the room. Gubbins and Dalton waited. No one spoke.

Clement looked out the window behind Johnny's desk. A barrage balloon floated above the city. 'What airfield would Sir Cedric use to fly in and out of England?'

'One close to his home would be my guess,' Johnny said.

'They're waiting for someone,' Clement said. 'The man with grey hair said that Teddy would be here soon.'

'Who's Teddy?' Johnny said.

Clement shook his head.

'So where's this revolution to take place?' Dalton asked.

'Find Hugh Armstrong and we'll know the answer to that,' Clement said.

'I think we all know what a successful coup would mean for us,' Dalton said.

C looked at Clement. 'Can you think of any place where Hugh Armstrong would go? Somewhere familiar to him. Somewhere where he is known and where he considers he will be safe?'

Clement stared at the portraits on the wall for no other reason than to rack his brains. He was tired. He gazed at the paintings around him, the stern faces of long-dead generals and admirals. Where would Armstrong go?

Clement leaned forward in his chair, his mind overflowing with thoughts. 'Does the Prime Minister have any official engagements in public places in the next few days?'

'What are you thinking, Wisdom?' Dalton asked.

'For this coup to work, Mr Churchill needs to be eliminated.' Clement paused, his mind was racing, trying to recall everything he'd overheard the grey-haired man say. He visualised Bainbridge and the man on the porch at Hitcham Hall. 'They intend to replace him with Hess.'

'Dear God!" Dalton said.

Johnny pressed the button on the small wooden box on his desk. 'Nora, will you get the official calendar and bring it in straight away?'

Ten seconds later Nora entered the room, the heels of her shoes like a drum-roll on the floor. She placed the large book on Johnny's desk. Everyone waited while he leafed through the pages. 'Here it is, Friday 13th June.' He looked up at them. 'Mr Churchill is to hand out bravery awards to the fire wardens of Southampton.'

'My God! That's tomorrow!' Dalton said.

'Where precisely?' C asked.

'Winchester.'

28

Clement sat in the car. His Welrod was in a holster around his chest and his Fairbairn-Sykes knife in its scabbard attached to his left leg. Beside him was Johnny Winthorpe. No one sat in the front with the Secret Service driver.

Clement stared through the window as the car drove west through the streets of London. In the mild early-evening light, Clement hardly saw the rubble that lay over footpaths and the row after row of boarded-up buildings. Clement cast his mind back to Christ Church Mayfair where he'd been on the first night of the Blitz last September. He'd gone to London to see Gubbins and he'd joined the covert Auxiliary Units. It was the beginning of his clandestine life. While it was less than a year ago, it seemed like a lifetime. So much had happened. He reached, almost unconsciously, to the wound over his left eye. He couldn't remember exactly when he'd received it. Everything was connected yet seemed jumbled. At least the boy was safe in Kendall's custody.

'Eye giving you trouble, Clement?' Johnny said quietly to him. 'You really should get those stitches out. Perhaps you should find a doctor in Winchester.'

'I'm alright, Johnny. Thank you for asking...' Clement paused. 'Johnny, there is something I need to do after this is all over. That is, if I'm still alive.'

'Name it?'

'Reg Naylor. I need to see he is taken back to Fearnley Maughton and buried at *All Saints* there.'

Johnny nodded. 'Gubbins will write to the widow.'

The car left the outskirts of London heading west. 'How far is Winchester?' Clement asked.

'About eighty miles. It shouldn't take us too long, even with the roadblocks.'

'Where exactly are we going?' Clement asked.

'I have arranged for us to billet at an almshouse known as the Hospital of St Cross just south of Winchester. We'll formulate our plans there.'

'Who else knows?'

'Not many. Because we cannot be certain that this will be the event where they attempt the assassination, it's only a small force; myself, you, and *C* will be there tomorrow, along with two special duties officers. I have four snipers joining us who will be placed at various points where the Prime Minister will be seen.'

'Does the Prime Minister know he's the bait?'

'Yes. He's quite excited by it, in fact. He actually said

that there is nothing more exhilarating than being shot at without result. Let's just hope he's right.'

Clement laughed. 'He's certainly courageous.'

'He's not unprotected, despite his bravado. In addition to ourselves, there will be Inspector Thompson, Churchill's personal bodyguard who never leaves his side. It is risky, though. There are just so many places where an assassin could hide.'

'What's the plan then for tomorrow?'

'Mr Churchill will arrive in Winchester at half past ten. He is to attend a service of Morning Prayer in the Cathedral at eleven. Then there is a reception in the Great Hall where firemen from Southampton will be presented with bravery awards. He is due to leave Winchester around two o'clock.' Johnny shook his head. 'He wishes to walk from the Cathedral to the Great Hall. We have advised against this, but he's insistent. The snipers will be placed along the route but it's still very dangerous. An assassin could take a pot-shot at him from anywhere. Or approach him in the crowd. Why, even one of the firefighters, who would be very close to him, could be his assailant. The recipients of the awards have all been vetted, of course, but we must expect the unexpected. Actually, I'll be pleased to see him leave Winchester.'

'It may not be tomorrow.'

'Exactly. So until they make their move, it's a game of watch and be prepared for anything. It's all we can do.'

The car turned south-west, skirting Windsor and making for Reading before turning south to Winchester.

Clement gazed through the window. He'd missed the countryside, although for Clement nothing would compare to the rolling green fields of the South Downs and the white chalk land of East Sussex.

'Was Hasluck really in Portugal for tungsten?'

'Yes. It's very important to the war effort. Lisbon is an interesting city, Clement. Of course, we have a long relationship with the Portuguese. Currently it's its proximity to Spain that makes it a hotbed for spies. Many in the Spanish government are pro-Nazi and Portugal being neutral makes it a safe place for many to do business there for all sorts of reasons.'

'So Hasluck is a spy?'

'No. Not really. He is there for the tungsten contracts but he does some work for us from time to time. While there, he mixes in interesting circles, so who better to keep an eye on things for us.'

Clement pursed his lips. He thought on what a father would do for a son. Would it include consorting with the enemy? Almost certainly. So why was Michael left at Hitcham Hall and not taken with the others in the lorry? It plagued Clement. The boy was to be traded, of that Clement had been certain. Had he been kept back solely as a trade to make Clement choose between the boy and Morris? Clement sat up. He stared through the window at nothing in particular, his mind desperately grasping his thoughts as they rushed around his brain forming disconnected threads. Armstrong couldn't have known he and Reg were in the house until after he had seen Morris in the police car on the drive. Therefore, Armstrong intended to trade Michael with someone else. 'I know I'm thinking aloud, Johnny, but bear with me. Armstrong came back to get the boy from Hitcham Hall because his father…' Clement leaned forward in the seat. 'Turn the car around, Johnny. We must get back to Cambridge as quickly as possible.'

'What?'

Clement paused, his mind on fire. Johnny was staring at him. 'Sir Cedric was in the lorry with me. Of that I'm sure. But he hasn't been all this time at Hitcham Hall.' Clement ran his hand through his hair then turned to face his old friend. 'Sir Cedric brought the grey-haired man into England. He's doing another flight. He's bringing someone else into the country, tonight! Most likely this Teddy person. The boy was to be handed over to Hasluck on Hasluck's return from Portugal and on the safe delivery of this Teddy. But we have the lad. They'll kill Hasluck once he's of no further use to them. And they'll meet at Hasluck's home, Wilstock House, which is where the trade is supposed to have happened. Michael told me it's near Lode. That's near Cambridge, isn't it?'

Johnny leaned forward and tapped the driver on the shoulder. 'How long to get to Cambridgeshire?'

'Top speed, sir, and with roadblocks, about four hours.'

Johnny slid back on the seat. 'If you're wrong, Clement, if we miss the ceremony tomorrow and Churchill is killed, it will be more than a court martial for both of us.'

'Can we get a message to Sergeant Kendall at Cambridge Police Station? He could meet us there with a force of men.'

'Stop in the next village, driver, at the first telephone box you see.'

Less than thirty minutes later the car pulled up beside a phone box near the village of Datchet and Johnny jumped out. Clement waited in the car. He saw Johnny make two calls. Minutes later, Johnny opened the car door and got back in.

'Nora tells me that there is an airfield at Bottisham about five miles east of Cambridge. It's a Royal Airforce base as well as a training airfield, so if Hasluck uses it, he and many others would be coming and going all the time and no one would think it odd. I also spoke with Cambridge Police. The constable there said he'd get a message to Sergeant Kendall. They'll arrange to have a team watching the airfield around the clock for any non-military aeroplanes arriving this evening. But we should consider that Hasluck may have already landed. The airfield staff there will know. Sergeant Kendall will meet us in Stow Cum Quy, a village just on the Cambridge side of the boy's home. Apparently Wilstock House is a large property, a former abbey on the road between Cambridge and Lode just passed Stow Cum Quy.'

'He's there, Johnny. Sir Cedric will fly this person into England, and Armstrong will be there to greet him.'

29

Twilight was nearly gone when the car pulled off the road and Clement woke. He'd slept nearly the entire journey back to Cambridgeshire. 'Where are we?'

'We're in the village of Stow Cum Quy, quite close to Wilstock House.'

'Has Kendall arrived yet?'

'Due momentarily.'

They waited. Within minutes, a low glow of shielded headlights appeared.

'This should be him now,' Johnny said as the vehicle slowly came towards them then stopped.

Clement and Johnny got out, quietly closing the car doors. Standing by the road Clement shook hands with Sergeant Kendall.

'Someone wanted to be here,' Kendall said, indicating the police vehicle's rear seat. Clement looked in. Morris sat there, his arm propped on pillows.

'I had to come,' Morris said. 'Clement, Sir Cedric's plane arrived this evening around five.'

Clement turned to Kendall. 'Is the boy safe, Sergeant?'

'Right as rain! My boy and young Michael get on like brothers,' Kendall replied.

'Could you station your men around the perimeter fence. They should apprehend anyone leaving the grounds of Wilstock House but on no account are they to go into the grounds. And Kendall, warn them, these people are dangerous and may be armed.'

'I understand,' Kendall said and went to speak to the constables gathering by the roadside.

'Do you know anything about Wilstock House, Superintendent?' Johnny asked.

'I've been there twice,' Morris said. 'Once recently to enquire about the boy but I didn't go inside. The other time was about six months ago to investigate a burglary. It's a large house. Not one of the great houses but still big. Made of stone and it has a very long drive. It isn't completely straight so you cannot see the house on approach.'

'Good,' Johnny said. 'And the gardens at the front?'

'Lots of large trees with some open grassed areas. There is another gate along the drive that leads into a wide gravelled area in front of the house. The front door is to the left side, as I recall.'

'This burglary; connected to this, do you think, Superintendent?' Johnny asked.

Morris frowned. 'Can't be completely certain but I shouldn't have thought so. Someone had smashed the glass in one of the dining room windows. Nothing of any consequence was taken and they were quickly apprehended.'

'Do you remember anything of the layout of the house?' Clement asked.

'Once through the front door, the hall turns to the right and continues along to a wide stone spiral staircase at the end. I have never been up the stairs, but downstairs leads to the kitchens and rear of the house. The break-in happened in a dining hall on the lower level. The rooms on the ground floor are the formal rooms plus a sitting room and a room used by Sir Cedric as his study. I spoke to him there after the incident.'

'Any other rear access into the house? Side doors?' Clement asked.

'Unknown, I'm sorry, Clement. There is a formal garden to the side of the house and the window in the study overlooks this area, as would the sitting room. I know nothing about the other rooms on this level.'

Kendall rejoined them. 'One of the lads tells me there's a second gate further along the road. I've sent them to watch it. If anyone comes out there, they'll be stopped.'

'So we approach from the front as there's no time for scouting the area first,' Clement said. 'Kendall should drive in and knock at the door. Johnny, you and I will secrete ourselves either side of the front door. As soon as it's opened, we enter and take whoever opens the door as hostage to lead us to Hasluck. Do you have any weapons on you, Johnny?' Clement asked.

'Same as you.'

'Do you want any of my men secreted in the grounds, Clement?' Morris said.

'I'd rather not, thank you, Arthur. They don't carry weapons, besides which, if your men are seen, it would alert anyone in the house to our presence.'

Returning to the cars, they slowly drove the half mile to the front perimeter fence of Wilstock House. Clement could see the large ornate gates about a hundred yards in front. They parked, leaving the Service driver with the car. Kendal pulled up beside them in the police vehicle and Clement and Johnny got in.

Ahead, the gate was open. No one spoke. Kendall turned into the drive. The car crawled past expansive lawns and well-established trees. In the light of the near-full moon, what should have been a verdant and tranquil scene looked grey and foreboding. They passed the second gate. It too was open. Kendall slowed as he drove through a thicket of overhanging trees and low shrubs.

'Keep driving, Kendall, slowly. Don't stop in case we are being observed. Major Wisdom and I will leave you here. Ready, Clement?' Johnny said, his hand on the car door handle.

Clement opened the car door on his side of the vehicle at the same time and they fell out of the vehicle, rolling over the gravel and scrambling into the shrubs at the side of the drive as Kendall drove slowly on. Looking up, Clement saw Johnny on the other side of the drive. Seconds later Johnny joined him. Crouching under the foliage, Clement reached for his binoculars. Ahead, Clement could see a large stone mansion; the front entry, just as Morris had described, was to the left. Clement scanned the area, checking windows and a path that led down the right side of the house. All was quiet and still. That there were no guards worried Clement. If Hasluck was there with someone important, surely Armstrong would have posted his henchmen in the grounds? Clement saw the police vehicle stop, then the headlights were switched off. They had ten seconds.

They ran forward, the sound of the police vehicle's engine still idling covering the noise of their footsteps on the gravel.

Clement leaned into the stone wall beside the front door as Morris slowly got out of the police vehicle. He carried a walking stick and moved slowly towards the front door, mounting the steps with notable difficulty.

Clement reached down and withdrew his knife.

The door opened and a man appeared.

Clement and Johnny rushed forward as Morris stood back. Clement held his knife at the man's throat.

'Who are you?' Clement whispered.

'The butler, sir,' the man whispered back. 'There's no

one here, sir. Sir Cedric and his family are not here.'

Clement moved the blade. 'Anyone else in the house?'

'No one,' the man said.

'We'll just check for ourselves,' Johnny said. He nodded to Kendall who had joined them in the house. Kendall and Johnny ran down the corridor. 'I'll go up, Kendall, you down. Back here in five.'

Morris backed away, returning to the car as Clement continued to hold the man at knife point. 'What's your name?'

'Cosgrove, sir.'

'Cosgrove. You may not believe this, but we are with His Majesty's Secret Service. Where is Sir Cedric?'

'He left this afternoon, sir.'

'Who was with him?'

'I cannot say.'

'Cannot or will not?'

Clement maintained his grip on the frightened man. 'You're hiding a man who's committing treason to save the life of his son. His actions, though understandable, are misguided. His son, young Michael, is in my care now not theirs. So there's no need for either you or Sir Cedric to remain complicit or to protect these people. Now I repeat, where is Sir Cedric?'

'How do I know you have young Master Michael?'

'I can describe him. I know his liking for expensive cigarettes has landed him in much trouble. I know he was removed from this house by his uncle then taken into Caius College in Cambridge where he was handed over to a man called Hugh Armstrong, a neighbour from Horningsea. I also know Michael attends the Abbey School in Ramsey. And, I know there is a button missing from his purple school jacket on the right-hand cuff. I know he has a ready wit to match his quick tongue. He is also a frightened but brave young lad who has seen enough evil for one lifetime. And he won't have to see any more because he's now safe and well away from these traitors. I also know that a grey-haired man was brought here last night. You may not even have been permitted to see him but you will have taken him food and pressed his clothes. You may even have had to purchase him new evening clothes.'

Cosgrove's eyes widened. 'How did you know that?'

'Because we've been watching him for some time and we have Mr Hugh Armstrong's Lagonda in safe keeping.'

'I never saw his face. I saw him get out of the car with Mr Armstrong so I know he was here.'

Clement slackened his grip on the man and lowered his knife slightly. 'And Hugh Armstrong? Was he here as well?'

Cosgrove nodded. 'Yes. I swear to you, I never saw their faces.'

'Their faces! Did Sir Cedric have other guests?'

'Yes. Nine others. Two arrived late yesterday, a priest, Father Rathbourne and another man. There were two young valets with them.'

308

'Was Sir Cedric here at the time?'

'No. I received a telephone call from him telling me to expect Mr Armstrong and some guests. I was to provide them with whatever they needed and not to ask questions.'

'When did Mr Armstrong arrive?'

'Yesterday, sir, along with the next guest to arrive, the grey-haired man. Mr Armstrong had been injured and was wearing a sling. It was for the older man, this grey-haired man that I was asked to purchase evening clothes. Not an easy task at present.'

'Was there to be a celebration of some kind?'

'Apparently.'

'Is it being held here?'

'Not that I'm aware of, sir. Sir Cedric wasn't in any mood to celebrate.'

'Why was that, do you think, Cosgrove?'

'I met him at the door as usual. I've never seen him so anxious, so I knew something wasn't right and there was someone else sitting in the car. He told me to leave the hall and remain on the lower floor until he rang for me. I thought Sir Cedric's behaviour was all rather odd but I did as instructed and left the hall. I returned downstairs via the upper floors.'

'Well done, Cosgrove. What did you see?'

'There were, in fact, three people sitting in the rear seat, waiting in the car. After a few minutes, Sir Cedric went back outside. He opened the rear car doors and a man and two women got out. They preceded the man into the house. Then the Master brought his guests in and took them straight upstairs.'

'Did you see their faces?'

'No. They were all wearing hats and heavy coats. But I thought...'

'Thought what, Cosgrove?'

'I thought there was something familiar about one of the ladies.'

'Who did you suspect it was?'

'The Mistress, sir.'

'Did you hear any of them conversing?'

'No.'

'Did the guests stay in their rooms upstairs?'

'No. They joined the others in Sir Cedric's study.'

'How long were they here?'

'No more than an hour during which time I took tea and sandwiches for ten to Sir Cedric's study.

'Ten?'

'Yes. Sir Cedric met me at the door so I did not enter the room. He took the tray and told me to remain downstairs. Under no circumstances was I or anyone in the household permitted to leave the lower floor for two hours.'

'Ten people you say? Do you know the identities of any of them?'

'Sir Cedric, of course, Mr Armstrong, Father Rathbourne, the priest from Cambridge and two young men who came with him, possibly the Mistress and four unknown guests, one of whom was a lady.'

'How did Father Rathbourne, the other man and the two young men get here, if they didn't come with Mr Armstrong?'

'I don't know for sure. There was no car. So they and the young valets must have come on foot or by boat.'

'Boat?'

'While there's no road between here and Horningsea, there is a walking path. It connects to the towpath from Cambridge at Bait's Bite crossing. It's near the old Biggin Abbey ruin.'

Johnny ran down the corridor. 'No one upstairs but two of the bedrooms have been used.'

Kendall joined them. 'Only servants downstairs. They seem pretty frightened.'

Clement turned to Cosgrove. 'Thank you for your assistance.'

Johnny and Kendall looked at the butler then at Clement.

'I'll tell you in the car,' Clement said.

Running outside, they got in and Kendall drove away from the house.

'Arthur, do you know what sort of aeroplane Sir Cedric has?'

'I have no idea, Clement. Why?'

'Perhaps, before we leave here for Winchester, we should see if Sir Cedric's aeroplane is still at Bottisham.'

'Your reason, Clement?' Johnny asked.

'I'd like to know if it can carry up to ten people including the pilot.'

'Ten?' Johnny asked. 'Hardly likely, Clement, that it would seat any more than two or possibly four.'

Clement told them about his chat with the butler.

'How far is it to the airfield, Morris?' Johnny asked.

'It's close. Five miles at most.'

Kendall slowed then stopped the car by the boom gate into Bottisham Airfield. A corporal stepped forward and Morris proffered his warrant card.

'Would you know, Corporal, if Sir Cedric Hasluck's aeroplane is still here?' Morris asked.

'It is, Superintendent. Although Sir Cedric isn't. He took a Hudson out on an evening demonstration flight. I can let him know you wish to speak with him on his return, sir.'

'Is it a large aeroplane, Corporal?' Clement asked.

'Large enough, sir.'

'How many would it carry?'

'It usually carries cargo, sir, for our French friends, if you understand me, so moderately large. It could take up to eight people.'

'Was anyone with him?'

'Six in all, including himself. Said they were from the Ministry checking out the aeroplane's uses as a personnel transport aircraft.'

'Did he supply names?'

'No, sir.'

'Anything unusual about any of them?'

The corporal paused. 'There were two ladies with them. I thought that was odd.'

'Did you recognise them?' Clement asked.

The corporal shook his head. 'Other than Sir Cedric, I didn't recognise any of them. They were all wearing hats. One of the ladies even had a veil so I didn't see any of their faces. Now I think about it, the one with the veil seemed to be rather anxious about something. I noted she was being supported by one of the gentlemen. Probably had never flown before.' The corporal paused. 'And another thing; when I said good evening to one of them, he didn't answer. Only Sir Cedric spoke. I thought it rather rude at the time, but it takes all sorts.'

'Other than Sir Cedric, can you describe any of them?'

'Sorry, sir. Although two of them were quite tall.'

'You're sure it was six and not ten people?'

'Just the six flew.

'Where is Sir Cedric's car, Corporal?' Clement asked.

'Not here, sir. One of the men in the second car drove it away.'

'There were two cars?'

'Yes, sir.'

'Did you see any of the people who didn't fly?'

'Not really, sir. As I recall, one man got out and opened the rear door of Sir Cedric's car for the others to get out but then he got into the driver's seat and drove away. There may have been two or three others in the second car. As they didn't get out of the car, I couldn't really be sure.'

'Anything physically unusual about this man? Like a limp, or stooped posture?'

'Nothing, sir.'

Clement smiled. Clement guessed the men in the car were Rathbourne and his two watchdogs. And what of Bainbridge? Was he also in the car? Clement thought about them leaving. Was it because they were no longer needed; sent away to await further instructions? Could they still be in the vicinity?

'Did Sir Cedric inform anyone of his destination?' Johnny asked.

'It's a demonstration flight, sir. He takes off and lands here.'

'When did he leave?'

The corporal checked his watch. 'Well now, he took off over three hours ago. I think I had better notify Wing Commander Osborne that the plane is overdue. Can't have ministers of the Crown and their good lady wives going missing.'

Clement took his SIS identity card from his coat and showed it to the man. 'Corporal, we will speak to Wing Commander Osborne. Please get an immediate message to your wireless operator to send out a coded message to all airfields requesting any sightings of this aeroplane. This is extremely urgent and a matter of national security. We need to know exactly where this aeroplane is. And tell the wireless operator to check all airfields, especially those around Winchester.'

30

Wing Commander Osborne strode towards them. He had the demeanour of a man woken from much needed sleep. 'This better be important!'

Johnny reached for his identification. 'Wing Commander, I understand Sir Cedric Hasluck took a Hudson aeroplane out earlier this evening with several others on board. I believe it was a demonstration flight?'

Osborne studied the ID card before responding. 'That's correct. He had members of the government with him. It's an American aeroplane but it has some issues with propeller feathering...'

'Immaterial, Wing Commander,' Johnny interrupted. 'All we want to know is *where* this plane is, because it isn't returning here.'

'Impossible! Sir Cedric cannot just take an aeroplane for a joy ride, I don't care who they are.'

'Do you know who his passengers are?' Clement asked.

'As I said, government officials and two women. Didn't like that. Well, it's not the sort of thing to do, is it, to take wives along on wartime business.'

'Wing Commander, they are not government officials,' Johnny said. 'This is of the utmost importance. I have authority to require you to assist in this matter. We need to know where that aeroplane is and where it is heading. Once we learn this, I am ordering you to fly us there.'

Osborne's face took on an indignant scowl, his jaw set. Clement couldn't tell if it was due to someone in the Service issuing orders or annoyance that one of his planes had been stolen. 'You'd better come this way.' Osborne led them to a hut about fifty yards away. Inside, a sergeant was standing beside the wireless operator.

'Sir,' the sergeant said as they entered the hut. 'I understand from Corporal Bevis at the gate that these gentlemen want to know the whereabouts of the Hudson?'

'That's right, Sergeant,' Osborne barked.

'We have sent out urgent messages to all airfields within a fifty-mile radius of us here. A Hudson was sighted over Duxford just before seven this evening. It's heading south-west.'

'How long to fly from here to Winchester, Wing Commander?' Clement asked.

'Depending on conditions and other traffic in the air,

including the Luftwaffe, around an hour. Say two to be on the safe side.'

'When, exactly, did it take off?' Clement asked the sergeant but he didn't think the Luftwaffe would intercept this flight.

'Well, Sergeant?' Osborne demanded.

'Eighteen thirty-eight, sir.'

'How long to drive it, Johnny?' Clement asked.

'It's about two hundred and fifty miles or so from here. Add roadblocks, about five to six hours. But we won't drive it, Clement. Too slow.'

'I understand that, Johnny,' Clement said, his mind racing. 'Corporal Bevis said that four men and two women boarded the plane. That would be Hasluck, our grey-haired man, Armstrong, another and the women. He described two of them as tall. Father Rathbourne is stooped which Corporal Bevis would have noticed. Rathbourne, along with some others in a second car, most likely his two henchmen and Bainbridge, came with the group but they didn't fly. So where are they?'

'No longer needed?' Johnny said.

'Or driving to wherever Hasluck is landing. If this is so, then Hasluck will arrive first, which means they will wait at an airfield close to Winchester.'

'Or others unknown to us will collect them. Which means, we've lost them,' Johnny added.

Clement stared into the air, his mind alive with possibilities. Could they be meeting someone else? Other supporters? What Clement dreaded was that another senior Nazi or Nazis had entered the country. He stared at Johnny. He couldn't discuss it in front of these airmen. Regardless, there were no answers. One thing Clement felt completely certain about; that aeroplane would land somewhere and tomorrow Hugh Armstrong and his important visitors would all be in Winchester.

They waited in the darkened hut, listening to wireless static while airfields across the southern counties responded to the message about the Hudson. Minutes passed. The wireless operator tapped out his Morse coded messages. The atmosphere in the communications hut was electric. 'Any responses from airfields around Winchester?' Osborne asked the operator.

The operator shifted his headset off one ear and nodded. 'There are about thirty airfields in Hampshire, sir. However, I have sent detailed messages to five of the closest to Winchester: Eastbourne, Thruxton, Chilbolton, Frost Hill Farm and Middle Wallop. The last three are all within five miles of each other. There are two that haven't yet responded; Chilbolton and Middle Wallop.'

'How many miles from Winchester?' Clement asked.

Osborne walked towards the map on the wall. 'Both are no more than ten miles.'

The operator replaced his headset as the wireless crackled. He scribbled down an incoming message. 'That was Chilbolton, sir. No Hudsons have been sighted or have landed there.'

'Middle Wallop it is then,' Johnny said. 'If they have taken Middle Wallop, then we will go to Chilbolton.

Wing Commander, I must ask you to fly us immediately.'

'How many?'

'Just myself and Major Wisdom. And I need to use a telephone.'

'My office, I think,' Osborne said.

Outside, Clement walked back to the police car. Morris lowered the rear seat car window as Clement approached.

'Thank you for all your help, Arthur, and the repeated use of police cars. Captain Winthorpe and I will be flying out of here.'

'I understand. Take care, Clement. Let me know how things work out, would you?'

'Of course. And, Arthur, I'll be back for Sergeant Naylor, if you wouldn't mind keeping him till then.' Clement paused. 'Should I not return, I would ask you to contact Reverend Battersby in Fearnley Maughton. He'll see Sergeant Naylor is properly looked after.'

'Take care of yourself, Clement. I know this isn't the time or place but I want you to know it's been an honour to know you. You're a good and brave man. One I would hope to see again.'

Clement smiled and shook Morris's hand. What he'd said Clement found profoundly touching. Standing beside the police car, he shook hands with Sergeant Kendall. 'Thank you for all you've done and for looking after Michael. I'll be in touch when this is over.' Kendall got in and the police car drove away.

Clement strode across the grass to the tarmac and

reached for the rail on the small steps into the aeroplane. He had never been in an aeroplane much less flown in one and he wasn't looking forward to it. As the door closed, he felt the atmosphere around him become still, as if the air itself was holding its breath. It felt odd and unsettling. Within seconds he heard the engines start. The body of the plane rocked as the engines began to roar. Even if he'd wanted to talk with Johnny, the noise made conversation impossible. The plane began to move, slowly at first, with a rhythmic swaying and bump-ing of the machine as it taxied across the grass then onto the hard surface. It continued along what Clement guessed was the runway. Then it turned. The engines roared until the noise was thunderous, the plane station-ary yet pulsating with contained power. With the release of a brake, the plane hurtled forward down the runway, shaking and lurching. A minute later Clement felt the aeroplane rise, the feeling of weightlessness lifting him out of his seat and making his stomach churn. He wrapped a blanket around his legs, leaned his head against the metal struts and said a silent prayer for their safety.

Osborne's voice on the intercom roused him. They were due to land in a few minutes. His ears popped with the descending pressure. He checked his watch. The flight had taken just over an hour. The heavy bump on landing, although anticipated, was unexpected when it happened. The plane lurched forward, the brakes hard on, the body of the aircraft straining and swaying under what seemed like unnatural forces until it moved slowly along, finally stopping. He heard Osborne cut the engines. Two minutes later the door opened. Removing his restraining belt, Clement stood and followed Johnny and Osborne to the small door. Stepping onto a ladder, he climbed down onto the ground then glanced up at the night sky, thankful for the fresh air and endless stars.

Awaiting them not twenty yards away was a man standing beside a black car. 'Captain. Major. I am to take you to The Hospital of St Cross, just south of Winchester for the remainder of this night. They are expecting you. Then early tomorrow C will join you.'

Johnny turned to Osborne. 'Thank you, Wing Commander. We'll take it from here.' Johnny started to walk away, then turned. 'On second thoughts, Wing Commander, it could be a good idea for you to remain on base a day or so. Just in case you're needed. Have the plane refuelled and on stand-by. If you haven't heard from me or Major Wisdom in two days, you can return to Bottisham.'

Clement nodded to Osborne. He knew what Osborne was feeling and doubtless thinking. It was on a need-to-know basis and Osborne would know this, but Clement could see in the man's eyes the faint hope of further inclusion; to know what this night had all been about. Clement walked away with Johnny and they got into the waiting car. A minute later they were driving through Hampshire lanes, the overhanging trees just inquisitive shadows in the strong moonlight.

31

The car pulled into a small side road adjacent to a long, high flint wall. At the end of the road and to Clement's right, was a large gate. It was open. The car drove in and pulled up under an arch. A man wearing the distinctive collar of a cleric stood in a small doorway to their left. For Clement it was a welcome and comforting sight and a real contrast to the events of the past few weeks. In the late twilight, Clement could just see the silhouette of a church of some size through another archway in front of him. He and Johnny got out, the driver taking the car through the arch and out of sight.

'This way, Captain, Major,' the man said to them. They followed their guide through the arch and along a path to a long terrace of houses where another man dressed in maroon robes waited. Clement and Johnny followed this elderly man to an upper floor. There, two small bedrooms had been prepared for them.

'Long day, Clement. You need sleep. We'll talk in the morning.'

'Suits me, Johnny.' Clement closed the door on his little room. Secreting his weapons, he removed his boots and fell onto the bed. As exhausted as he felt, he couldn't sleep. Something still troubled him about the events of this night. He shook his head as though trying to clear cobwebs but the feeling of dread wouldn't leave him. Hugh Armstrong had said that nothing could stop *it* from happening now. Had he meant the coup or the assassination? Clement's mind drifted. He wondered how important men, knights of the realm and high-ranking government officials, could be involved in such matters. Clement thought about the level of secrecy and complexity required to bring about such a coup. It would require hundreds of people, not just the small group he had seen, and there would have to be extensive planning, with a chain of command and a highly detailed plan that could be adapted at short notice. That would require a communication network. His mind went to the blueprints and the network of Masonic Lodges around the country. People would have been placed over many months or possibly years, in readiness to respond. Ready to take up certain key positions all around the country, including replacing the Prime Minister. Clement shuddered. The thought that Rudolf Hess may become Britain's Prime Minister was not just unthinkable, it was totally repugnant. In one stroke, the entire country, her empire and commonwealth, as well as all her armed forces personnel currently spread all over the globe and indeed every ship, aeroplane and all weapons would be in the hands of the Nazis and controlled from Berlin. In his mind he heard Churchill's words about a new Dark Age from which no one would escape.

Light streamed through the crack between the curtains. Clement reached for his watch: six o'clock, Friday the thirteenth of June. Remembering where he was, he stood and rubbed at his whiskered face. There was a soft knock at the door. Clement opened it expecting to see Johnny. An elderly man stood there holding a basin and jug. Clement held the door wide for the man to enter. He placed the basin and jug of warm water on the stand along with some shaving equipment, smiled at Clement and left. Not a single word had been spoken. 'Thank you,' Clement said, closing the door.

Half an hour later he descended to the lower floor where another man dressed in black robes took him to a nearby building. In the early morning light Clement could see the large church clearly now. Its beauty was surprising and there was a palpable serenity about The Hospital of St Cross.

The adjacent building was medieval in style with a short flight of steps worn over the centuries that led inside. There, his guide stopped by a door and indicated for him to enter. Inside was a small medieval Great Hall complete with paved floor, musician's gallery and a central fireplace. A steep staircase led up the side of the hall to a room at the top. In front of him, Johnny sat at a long refectory table, eating a hearty meal of eggs and thick bread.

'Morning, Clement. Sleep well?'

'Not really, thank you, Johnny. Where are we, exactly?'

'The Hospital of St Cross. About a mile south of Winchester. Marvellous, isn't it?'

'Another world,' he said. Another century, he thought. He looked at the eight chairs around the long table. 'Others joining us?'

'Yes. At seven. In addition to you and me, C will join us along with Inspector Walter Thompson, Churchill's personal bodyguard, two SIS men and the four snipers.'

Over breakfast, Clement shared his thoughts about the blueprints and his theories concerning the coup.

'I think you're correct, sadly, Clement. The safe houses have already been changed and everyone on our list of trusted employees from cleaners to drivers, even casual observers, have either been replaced or in some cases arrested. Not even the Masonic Lodges have escaped our attention. Whatever happens, today will be a turning point in history one way or the other. If it ends the way we hope, no one will ever know anything about it.' Johnny reached down and opened his briefcase. Pulling out a map of Winchester, he spread it over the table. Clement stood staring at the layout of the old city. Fifteen minutes later the tall figure of Inspector Thompson entered the room. Beside him was *C* as well as six deter-mined-looking young men.

'Good morning, sir,' Johnny said as *C* took a seat at the table. 'Clement, these men are the snipers; Robert, George, Gordon and David. And this is Inspector Thompson, and Majors Thomas Mollineux and Benja-min Greaves from our office.'

They took up seats around the table, the large map of Winchester on the table before them.

While Clement had never been to Winchester, the inner city layout was straightforward and uncomplicated. For the most part, the inner town was grouped around the High Street with the railway station and the old Great Hall of the long-gone castle at one end and the Bishop's ruined palace and river at the other. The Great Hall was all that remained of the thousand-year-old seat of the Wessex Kings. The imposing structure sat on a hill which gently descended away through the town towards the river. Between them, on the southern side of the town, was the Cathedral. It was set back from the High Street and occupied a flat, central position.

Clement fixed his gaze on the streets to the south of the Cathedral. 'Where is Winchester College?' he said aloud.

'Here,' Johnny pointed.

'Close to the Cathedral, isn't it?' Clement said. 'If they're no longer at the airfield, then they will be at the school.' Clement looked at the location of the school and its proximity to the Cathedral. His mind sorted and sifted facts and suppositions. 'What time is the service at the Cathedral?'

'Eleven,' Johnny said.

'How long has today's presentation of bravery medals been known about?' Clement asked.

'It'll be listed in the calendar. The Prime Minister has multiple engagements every day, so it will have been scheduled months in advance,' *C* said.

Clement continued. 'If Mr Churchill were to appear in public at such an event, would the Foreign Office know about it?'

'Of course, Major.' *C* said.

'Then, Sir Cedric Hasluck would have known the date months ago?'

The room was quiet.

'You think they're here?'

'Yes. Sir Cedric will have been told his son is here in Winchester to guarantee his continued co-operation.' Clement checked his watch. It was already after eight. 'We need to find Hugh Armstrong.'

Johnny stood. 'If he remains uncaught by the time the Prime Minister arrives in just under three hours, it's watch and act. We will place you, Robert, here in the Great Hall.' He jabbed a finger at the map. 'I'll arrange for you to be seated at the front where you will have an uninterrupted view of the proceedings and where you can be as close to the Prime Minister as possible. Then you, George and Gordon, take the High Street. Following the church service, Mr Churchill will walk across the square in front of the Cathedral, then into Great Minster Street, past St Lawrence-in-the-Square under the arch to the Buttercross and up the High Street to the old Westgate arch then to the Great Hall.' He traced the route on the map. 'Gordon, you take up a position at Westgate and George you move into place at the Buttercross where Mr Churchill will turn left. David, you wait beside the entry to St Lawrence-in-the-Square and follow Inspector Thompson through the arch towards the High Street staying behind them. Move with Mr Churchill up the High Street in a circle around him. Greaves and I will be in the cathedral forecourt among the crowd. Clement, you take inside the Cathedral, watching the people who have been invited to attend as they arrive. Mollineux will be in the house next to the Cathedral which has a window overlooking the front, here, behind this high redbrick wall. It's very high, so too high for Armstrong to scale or for Mollineux to drop down. If he is needed, he would have to leave the house by the front and cross the lawns to the south of the Cathedral. So Mollineux, keep your eyes out for any signal from either myself or Major Wisdom.'

'Is there another way out of the Cathedral?' Clement asked.

'Yes, the southern door. It's about halfway along the nave of the church. The door will be closed but not locked as there will be many people attending. The town is excited about the Prime Minister's expected arrival, so people will be everywhere.'

'Please remember, everyone,' *C* said. 'This is a public event. Do not show your weapons unless needed, it will only cause alarm.'

'Good luck everyone,' Johnny added.

At nine o'clock they left by car. The Service driver took them into the city and they went to their designated places.

Clement walked along a short street and entered the cathedral precinct. A wide grassed area with large trees was at the front and side of the ancient building. It was a quiet, calm day and the weather was pleasant. Clement breathed in the warm summer air. Such a beautiful city. People were gathering and the noise of the excited crowd was escalating. Clement moved slowly among them, his eyes darting to each face. He crossed the lawns surrounding the Cathedral. All around people were beginning to find vantage places near cordoned-off areas. Clement moved past them and standing under one of the trees in front of the great Cathedral, studied the front façade. There were three entry doors at the front, the central one larger than the other two. Above them was a narrow balcony of sorts. Leaving the forecourt, he wandered towards the doors. Attendants stood there, stopping people from entering without an invitation. Clement showed the man his SIS card.

He walked in; the quiet sanctity of the place was awe inspiring. Checking his watch, he walked once around the entire nave, taking in every nook and chapel which could conceal an assassin. Climbing the steps mid-way along the nave side-aisle, he turned left to the main aisle. Taking it, he returned down the full length of the building, returning to the front. As he approached the main door, he saw a tiny, narrow door just to the right of the front entry. He looked up. Above him was a ledge surrounded by a balustrade. He walked up to the attendant.

'Where does that lead?' He pointed to the narrow door.

'To the triforium. It's a gallery mostly used by musicians. It's not in use today.'

'Is the door locked?'

'Yes.'

Clement looked across at the narrow door. Regardless, an assassin could unlock it as quickly as he could. Clement walked over and turned the handle. It was locked. He turned and walked along the northern side, checking and watching for anything unusual. Walking beyond the crossing he walked into the Choir, then crossed to the southern aisle again and walked slowly back towards the front. At the southern door he stopped. It was a large double door of considerable height. It too was closed. He thought it unlikely that Armstrong would use it to gain entry. The door looked heavy and would make a noise when opened. Clement turned again, this time re-entering the Choir. Looking along the reserved seats for special guests, he stopped.

He stared at the seats, his eyes wide, and his heart began to pound so loudly he could hear it pulsating in his ears.

Now he ran. Ignoring the rebuking crowds, he ran as fast as he could down through the Choir, down the steps and along the main aisle. People stared at him aghast as he ran towards the front door. He stood at the entry, frantically scanning the gathering crowd. People were already standing behind ropes waiting and cheering. In the distance near to where he knew the man named David was positioned, Clement could see the official party walking down the path towards the Cathedral. Churchill was in front, his hat held high on his walking stick. Inspector Thompson was behind to Mr Churchill's left. Clement turned. Mollineux stood in the window of the red-brick house that overlooked Cathedral Square. Clement signalled his alarm. He scanned the front of the cathedral forecourt, his eyes searching for Johnny and Greaves but it was already too late.

At that moment, a black car drove into the precinct and stopped by the Cathedral's front door. The Dean met Mr Churchill in the forecourt and they both approached the vehicle. The Prime Minister stopped. As an attendant opened the rear door of the vehicle, the King got out. Next the car's other rear door was opened and the Queen stood in the morning sunshine, waving and smiling to the people. Clement spun around, his eyes turned upwards to the narrow balcony above the entry doors. From his position directly below the balustrade, he saw the barrel. Waving his arms, he signalled to Mollineux who threw open the window and, levelling his rifle on the window sill, fired. As Clement rushed into the Cathedral, he heard four short bursts of gunfire.

Clement went straight for the narrow doorway that led to the triforium. It was unlocked. Outside, he heard screaming. He knew Walter Thompson would be with the Prime Minister but the unexpected arrival of the King and Queen had taken the crowds by surprise. Everyone, of course, except Hugh Armstrong. Clement ran up the spiral stairs to the triforium, his eyes frantically searching for the gunman. He spun around. A door to the outside of the cathedral façade was open. He looked through the narrow window to the external balcony but Armstrong wasn't there. Fifteen feet from where Clement stood, another small door was open. Below Clement was mayhem. He returned to the triforium where he had a panoramic view of the Cathedral's interior below him. His eyes rapidly scanned the jostling, panicked crowd below. He watched the flow of the people, rushing for the front door. One figure was pushing his way in the opposite direction.

Clement ran down the narrow spiral staircase, forced his way through the crowds and headed for the southern door. Just as he left the cathedral building, he saw the blond hair and bowed gait of Hugh Armstrong running across a lawn, his injured right arm tucked close to his chest. He turned left, skirting the Deanery. Beyond was The Pilgrim's School but Clement knew where Armstrong was headed. Over his shoulder Clement heard someone call his name. He turned and saw Johnny about fifty feet behind him. Running on, Clement ran towards

Kingsgate and turned left. Once through the arch, he again turned left. Before him on his right were the high flint walls of Winchester College.

Clement ran on, his rapid pulse pounding in his ears. He prayed all the students had been given the morning off to attend the service. If Armstrong was cornered in the school, Clement didn't want to think what he would resort to doing.

As he entered the college, Clement ran past the porter's lodge and into the outer courtyard.

'Did you see a tall, blond-haired man run through here?' Clement said, flashing his SIS security card.

'He went into Chamber Court, that way,' the porter said, pointing.

Clement ran on but stopped under the arch before the inner courtyard and peered around the corner. Diagonally across the wide paved courtyard he saw Armstrong run to some steps in the opposite corner.

Clement ran back to the porter as Johnny joined him.

'What's in the corner of the next courtyard, where there are some stone steps?'

'That's Hall,' the porter said. 'Where the boys take their meals.'

'And nothing else up there? No other doors or way out?'

'There is a dumb waiter to the kitchen. It's not large but it isn't unknown for boys to use it as a prank. Suspension, of course, if caught.'

Clement and Johnny ran across Chamber Court towards the stairs which spiralled up, turning left to a closed heavy wooden double door at the top of the steps. It was bolted shut.

Taking his Welrod from his shoulder holster, Clement pointed it at the lock and fired. The muted sound ricocheted around the masonry but the door remained bolted from inside. Clement fired again. This time the timbers splintered. Through a gap he could see a long heavy wooden beam had been placed across both doors on the inside barricading them shut. Clement knew it would take too long to break the thick timber beam. He ran down the steps then turned left into the passage beneath. On the wall in front of him was the most bizarre painting he'd ever seen. It had the body of a man with the head of a pig and donkey's ears. Ignoring it, Clement pushed his way into the kitchens and past the astonished staff then ran towards the dumb waiter at the end of the room. He heard its gear turning.

Johnny was beside him.

Clement held his weapon aimed at the dumb waiter. Johnny opened the door. Inside was a hat and scarf and a note. Johnny tore it open.

'Look for me where the heroes lie. Heil Hitler.'

'How did he get out?' Johnny asked one of the kitchen hands.

'He ran through there,' a cook said, pointing to a door.

'Where does it lead?' Johnny shouted.

'It's a service door for food deliveries,' the man said.

'Is there a chapel or school graveyard inside the college?' Johnny demanded of the bewildered cook.

'Yes. Seventh Chamber Passage. It's in the corner, across the quadrangle,' the man said.

They left the kitchens and returned to the quadrangle. 'It could be a trap, Johnny!'

'Only one way to find out,' Johnny said, running. Their footsteps echoed on the hard surface.

They crossed Chamber Court and entered Seventh Chamber Passage, then paused and edged their way forward into the cloisters. Moving slowly, they heard loud voices, both male, then scuffling. Clement and Johnny paused, secreting themselves behind two stone pillars. A shot rang out; the sound sudden and deafening inside the confined stone surfaces.

Clement crept around the edge and peered along the cloisters in both directions. A man's body lay on the flagstones. Johnny moved forward but Clement put out his hand. He shook his head. 'Doesn't mean the killer isn't still there. Besides, he's got one more shot. Three at the Cathedral, two just now.'

'Last one for himself, perhaps?' Johnny whispered but Clement didn't believe it. Armstrong wouldn't take his own life; he would want a martyr's death. Clement edged his way forward.

'Who's dead, Clement?' Johnny asked.

'I don't know. I can only see his feet. I'm guessing it's Hasluck.'

Ten minutes passed. No noise. No further shots.

'It's over, Hugh,' Clement called. 'You didn't kill them.'

'Yes, I did. I'm a perfect shot, Pa taught me. I don't miss.'

'You did this time.'

A long silence ensued. 'Then it's your fault! I had to shoot with my left hand but I know I got that usurper. I saw him wince. And that cow of a wife. I saw the Dean wrap his arm around her. She was falling so I must have shot her.'

'The King has a graze to his right arm, that's all,' Clement said, hoping it were true. 'And the Dean was protecting the Queen. She is perfectly fine.'

'You're lying. It doesn't matter now anyway.'

'Why is that?'

'There you go again! Having to have everything all neat and tidy.'

'Hess won't be joining you, Hugh. And the others have surrendered.'

'You're lying!'

'Is Sir Cedric dead?'

'Yes.'

'You killed him?'

'Yes, I killed him. Out-lived his usefulness.'

'Who did he fly into the country?'

'Lots of people.'

'Last night, I mean.'

'Well now, that would be telling.'

'The coup won't happen now.'

Silence.

Clement heard the cynical laughter, then a shot rang out, hard against the stone walls. He stood and edged his way around the pillar. Armstrong's body lay sprawled on the hard stone. A grey-haired man stood over Armstrong, a pistol in his grip.

Clement levelled his Welrod. 'Who are you?'

'Sir Samuel Hoare. British ambassador to Spain,' the man said, lowering his pistol.

From the corner of his eye Clement saw Johnny inch forward, his Welrod pistol in his hand.

'I have nothing to do with this murderer,' Hoare was protesting.

'Stay where you are. Where are the others?'

'Waiting in the Chantry.'

Clement glanced back at Johnny. 'I'll stay here with him. Get *C*,' he said, then added half under his breath, 'and Johnny, make it as quick as you can. I don't trust him.'

Johnny nodded and vanished.

Clement kept his eyes fixed on Hoare. 'We'll wait here until Sir Stewart arrives.'

'This is outrageous! I've told you who I am?' Hoare was shouting.

'Yes, you've told me and right now, I don't care much. What's more, I don't know if you are just a foolish man or a traitor. So, stay where you are, Sir Samuel, while we wait for Sir Stewart Menzies.'

Clement stared into the man's glowering eyes. He waited, his Welrod still levelled at Hoare.

Clement heard running feet. Keeping his gaze on Sir Samuel, Clement stepped over Armstrong's dead body then moved slowly towards Hoare, so he could see who was approaching. He held his Welrod steady.

C approached. 'Thank you, Major. I'll take it from here. Where are the others, Hoare?'

'In the Chantry.'

'Who, exactly is there?' *C* asked.

'Lord Halifax, Lady Armstrong and Lady Hasluck.'

'Captain Winthorpe, bring Lord Halifax and the Lady Armstrong here. Tell Lady Hasluck to wait where she is. Reverend Wisdom can look after her.'

'I'll fetch them, sir,' Johnny said and disappeared back along the passage.

'Would you come this way, Sir Samuel?' *C* gestured back along the cloister to the Chamber Court beyond.

'This is an outrage, Menzies! Who is this?' Hoare said, pointing at Clement.

'Not now, Hoare. We'll discuss your part in today's events later.'

'What events? I'm here only to speak to Winston. Privately!'

'I think not. The attempt on the Prime Minister's life has been unsuccessful.'

'What!'

'As was Hugh Armstrong's attempt to assassinate their Majesties, King George and Queen Elizabeth.'

338

Hoare's face remained stern and indignant. 'I know nothing about assassinations. It's preposterous to suggest that I, or Lord Halifax, would have any involvement with an attempt on the King or Queen's life. And as far as Winston is concerned, I may disagree with him but I could never condone murder.' Hoare turned and pointed at Armstrong. 'There is your murderer.'

'When you've finished, I have an aeroplane nearby at my disposal. You and Lord Halifax will be flown to Lisbon, then you will return to your posts as soon as possible. I will arrange for Lord Halifax's passage to America from Lisbon. As for Lady Armstrong, I suggest she returns to the south of France for the duration of the war. Captain Winthorpe will escort you all to the aeroplane.'

'This way, sir,' Johnny said. He nodded and smiled to Clement on leaving the cloister.

C turned to Clement. 'Thank you, Major. Would you see to this?' *C* pointed at Armstrong's body. 'And would you also attend to Sir Cedric. You are perhaps the best person for this anyway. Also, please see that Lady Hasluck is taken home.'

'Sir.'

'I will speak to the porters in the lodge here and arrange for two hearses to come to collect the deceased,' *C* said. 'And Major. Take two days off then I'll see you in my office in Whitehall on Monday morning.' *C* turned to leave then stopped and held Clement's gaze. 'I'm sure I don't need to remind you, Major, that everything you have seen and heard here today is top secret. This includes the identities of all the people involved. I remind you also that you have signed the Official Secrets Act and I would be forced to take it very seriously if this was to be breached. You do understand me, Major?'

'I understand,' Clement said, replacing his Welrod. He watched *C* go. He squatted beside Hugh Armstrong and rolled his body over. The bullet had entered his chest almost directly over his heart. Congealing blood had pooled around his body. Clement stood and stared at Armstrong, a man who had caused such carnage. Or was he its victim? Sacrificed by others more important? Clement walked through the ancient cloisters to the small Chantry and found Lady Hasluck. Entering the tiny sacred place, he saw her sitting alone. He walked silently up to her and sat beside her.

'Lady Hasluck. My name is Reverend Wisdom.'

The frail woman looked up, her tearful eyes wide with fear and apprehension. 'Is he dead?'

Clement nodded. 'So is Hugh Armstrong. It's over now.'

Lady Hasluck bowed her head. 'It's my fault. It's all my fault.'

'Why do you say that Lady Hasluck?' Clement asked.

'She was always there. Helena, I mean, Lady Armstrong. Every time we were in Lisbon she came. I never knew why she befriended me. She invited me to join them in Caen. I was flattered, I suppose. I'm not really like them. I don't mix easily with people. She even introduced me to the Duke and Duchess of Windsor. I was swept off my feet. She asked all sorts of questions about Cedric and I was too flattered to see what she was doing.'

'Did Lady Armstrong learn that your husband owned an aeroplane?'

'Yes. And what he did for the government. Don't you see, it's my fault he's dead.'

'You mustn't blame yourself. Many people have been manipulated and deceived by these people. Your husband was a very brave man. As indeed is your son.'

'You know Michael?'

'I do. He's being cared for by a very kind family,' Clement said, thinking of Kendall. 'But now he needs his mother.'

Clement escorted her to the front entrance of the college. 'I'll arrange for your husband to be taken back to Cambridge. The driver here will take you home.'

Clement waited at the college until both hearses had removed the bodies of Sir Cedric Hasluck and Hugh Armstrong. Remembering the map of Winchester, he walked back through the town, past the Cathedral and across the grassy lawns. The crowds had gone. There was no sign of anything untoward having happened. He walked towards the Buttercross in the High Street and found a place where he could have something to eat and be able to sit for a while. An hour later he walked up the hill in the late-afternoon sun towards the railway station.

32

Monday 16th June 1941

Clement climbed the well-known stairs to the third floor. He'd read all the weekend newspapers and this morning's but there hadn't been a single reference to either Sir Samuel Hoare or Lord Halifax. Rather, the tabloids had said that a network of terrorists had been uncovered and the ringleaders arrested. There was nothing about treason or murder. He knew it was what the Service did best; maintain authority and no sensationalism. He smiled at Nora Ballantyne and Joan Cunningham as he approached them.

'They're inside,' Nora said.

Miss Cunningham smiled.

Clement nodded. When he'd last seen *C* at Winchester College, Clement felt that his boss intended to conceal the truth about Hoare's and Halifax's involvement, if not with insurrection, then at least with consorting with the enemy in secret meetings during wartime. These were acts of treason. But instead, Hoare and Halifax, along with the Lady Helena Armstrong, had been whisked away, out of the country and away from any impeachment. The only reference to Winchester in the newspaper were happy pictures of the King and Queen giving out bravery awards in Winchester's Great Hall with a smiling Prime Minister. It appalled Clement that censorship would mean that the truth would not be told and none of the influential people would stand trial. It reinforced his opinion that such lowly members of the Service such as himself were, indeed, expendable and that the Official Secrets Act conveniently suppressed unwanted or undesirable truths. In Clement's opinion, senior members of the British establishment appeared to have one rule for themselves and another for everyone else. Or perhaps the web of secrecy in Freemasonry at influential levels had kept the truth from being revealed. Either way, it had helped to cement his decision.

Johnny smiled as Clement entered the office and sat down.

C was seated in front of Johnny's desk. 'Thank you for coming, Major. You will be interested to know that the King and Queen are well and have returned to London. The King has a slight graze to his arm but otherwise is unhurt. The Queen was unharmed. Mr Churchill also. Mr Thompson will have a sore shoulder for some time but he is alive. And Sir Samuel Hoare has returned to his post in Spain as has Lord Halifax to America. The Lady Armstrong will be watched for the rest of her life. I don't think they'll give us any trouble in future.'

'Am I permitted to ask why there will be no prosecutions?'

C frowned. 'Much of our work, Major, goes unreported. That way we avoid scandal and sensational gossip. When no real harm is done, life returns to something approximating normality which, given our current circumstances, is the best outcome for everyone concerned.'

'Sir Cedric Hasluck was murdered, sir. And his wife and son terrorised.'

'Yes. A tragedy.'

'And Lord Halifax?'

'Has returned to America, as I said.' *C* stood and walked towards the window. 'It is, of course, entirely possible that some of these people didn't know what Sir Hector Armstrong and his cronies were attempting to do. It is also conceivable that they'd been told that they were there merely to meet secretly with Churchill and that the meeting would take place sometime after the ceremony.'

'Sir, with respect, I overheard Hoare talking with Bainbridge. It's my opinion that he was very much involved.'

'And it is my opinion, Major, that Sir Hector Armstrong had been very clever. If anything were to go wrong at the last minute, these prominent people would have been used as ransom to guarantee safe exit out of Britain for Armstrong and his family. If the uprising had been successful, well, these well-meaning people would know they'd been used and protest their innocence.'

'Am I permitted to know what you and Sir Samuel discussed?'

'No.'

A palpably tense silence ensued.

Clement felt a surge of injustice, or was it disillusionment. Perhaps both. 'So the war goes on.'

'Yes.'

'And Hess?'

'Is at His Majesty's pleasure. He won't be going anywhere anytime soon.'

'Why did he come to Britain?'

'Partly personal; to put things right between himself and Hitler with whom he'd lost some influence. Hess read the British opinion of war with Germany incorrectly, largely due to organisations like the Right Club and some zealous members of the Nordic League as well as the secret peace talks that were being conducted by well-meaning but misguided members of our own aristocracy. Don't upset yourself about this business, Major. Nor about the people involved. They will be watched. While it will never be publicly known, you have done your country immeasurable service.'

Clement left the War Office. He walked to King's Cross Station. Despite what *C* had said, or rather not said, about the men involved, Clement's resentment was barely suppressed. Good but inconsequential people had been murdered and a child traumatised but their stories would never be told. They were as much sacrificed as any soldier on the battlefield but with none of the honours. As Clement approached the railway terminus, he was almost running. Not because he was late. He just wanted to be gone from the machinations of Whitehall and the Service in particular.

Finding a seat in a compartment, his hand reached up to feel his newly acquired clerical collar. It made him feel normal again. He closed his eyes. Even the cut above his eye had repaired and the stitches removed by an SIS doctor in Harley Street. His hand reached into his coat pocket and he felt the eye patch. It would be the only tangible reminder of recent events. One duty remained. Until this was done he couldn't truly rest.

Morris was at Cambridge station to meet him. 'How are you, Arthur?'

'Mending every day,' Morris said. They walked through the station to the street outside where a constable waited by the police car. Clement sat in the rear beside Morris as they drove through the streets of Cambridge, heading for St Andrew's Street.

'Thank you for this,' Clement said.

'How will you take him?'

'The Service is providing a car and a hearse. They'll be here at midday.'

'A sad duty, Clement. How did it go in Winchester?'

346

'Hugh Armstrong is dead. As, unfortunately, is Sir Cedric. Armstrong killed him.'

'And the others? The grey-haired man?'

Clement visualised Sir Samuel Hoare and Edward Frederick Lindley Wood, first Earl of Halifax, known to his friends as Teddy. 'There were no others, Arthur, just misguided fools.'

'What?'

'Some well-known men became involved in something they shouldn't have. So nothing will be said and they won't be convicted. Armstrong killed Sir Cedric Hasluck, Ailsa Hazelton killed Bill Hayward, and a Nazi called Albrecht Haushofer killed John Nicolson so there is no one left to accuse. And the war goes on.'

'I see,' Morris said at length. 'You will be saddened to learn that we found the body of a young woman inside Hitcham Hall. I'm guessing Hugh Armstrong shot her.'

Clement glanced at Morris then let out a long sigh. 'Evil man! We heard a shot after Reg and I left Hitcham Hall with young Michael. Her death was so unnecessary. She was completely innocent. I should have taken Isabel with us.'

'You weren't to know what Armstrong would do. You're not responsible for her death.'

But Clement would always feel the guilt. The car drove into the rear yard at Cambridge Police Station and they got out. There, already waiting, was a Service car and a hearse. Kendall was standing beside the driver.

Sergeant Kendall approached Clement. 'Sergeant

Naylor is already inside, sir,' Kendall said, indicating the hearse.

'Thank you. Thank you also for your part in recent events and for looking after Michael Hasluck. He's with his mother now, I presume?'

'He is indeed. My boy has been invited over any time he wants to play with the lad.'

Clement smiled. Standing beside the car he shook hands with Morris.

'Thank you, Arthur.'

'Clement, despite the obvious cover-up, which I can see has upset you, I repeat what I said at Bottisham Airfield. You are a brave and decent man. Better than many of our so-called *betters*. Perhaps, after the war, if we're both still here, we could meet again at *The Trout* in Godstow?'

'Of course. Thank you again, Arthur.' Clement smiled and got into the car. He waved to Morris as the car left Cambridge. He felt it unlikely that he would ever see Morris again.

The car drove quickly through Cambridgeshire heading south. Clement wanted to see the landscape he treasured; the open fields of crops, the hedgerows, the tranquillity of the luxuriant green and cool, shady glades of large oaks and elms. East Sussex was his home county and the village of Fearnley Maughton was where he had spent the happiest years of his life. He breathed it in like a prodigal son, drinking in the sight of the undulating country of southern England, the rolling fields of pastures dotted with villages and the white chalk land. Returning to Fearnley Maughton was a vision he'd cherished. But not now. And not like this. He sat alone in the rear seat of the SIS-supplied vehicle. Behind him, a hearse carried the body of Reginald Naylor. Every time Clement thought about Reg, he saw the mutilated body of a loyal and dear friend.

Just on dusk, the cars pulled into the graveyard of *All Saints,* his former church. He stepped from the car. Reverend Battersby greeted him. Clement saw Battersby's shocked reaction to his appearance. Gone was the old Reverend Clement Wisdom. What was left was a hollow man.

'Clement. Welcome home,' Battersby said, his voice low.

'I can't stay long. Just for the burial.' Clement turned and looked at the lychgate. He knew what was down the lane. The Rectory, his former home and the police station where he had first met Arthur Morris. Clement frowned, suppressing the emotion, a wave of sadness washing over him as he remembered Doctor Phillip Haswell's house. Beyond that the village and all the people he now couldn't face. They would want to know where he'd been and to ask about Mary. As much as he longed to see them, he couldn't. He turned away.

Battersby conducted the quiet service beside Reg's grave, Clement the only mourner. He gave five pounds to Battersby who promised to arrange a headstone for the man. Clement had written the inscription:

Here lies the mortal remains of
Reginald Naylor,
Resident of this village
who died in the service of his country, June 1941

Clement shook hands with the elderly cleric and returned to the car. During the trip back to London he closed his eyes and wept.

33

Tuesday 17th June 1941

Johnny was at his desk when Clement entered the office.

'Please sit down, Clement. I am instructed to inform you that you have been awarded a Distinguished Service Order and a citation from the King. It's a very great honour.'

Clement struggled to smile then reached into his coat pocket. He handed a letter to Johnny.

'Clement?'

'My letter of resignation, Johnny.'

'I don't think that's possible, Clement.'

'Regardless, Johnny, you can lock me up if you wish, frankly I don't care, but I will not do any more work for the Service.'

Johnny leaned back in his chair. 'You have done an

amazing thing, Clement. Perhaps you don't realise just how important and pivotal your involvement has been. Because of your diligence in putting the pieces together, a network has been exposed, a certain coup thwarted, and a serious if not psychopathic Nazi sympathiser and murderer eliminated; and Deputy Führer Rudolf Hess remains in custody. Not to mention you exposing serious flaws in our recruiting of people and selection of safe houses.'

Clement nodded. 'And Walter Bainbridge?'

'Picked up yesterday in Liverpool trying to board a ship to America along with Rathbourne and his two accomplices. They've been charged with treason. It may interest you to know that Bainbridge had his own network of informants. One of whom was an elderly academic you may have seen on buses around Oxford. He reported to Bainbridge on a regular basis.'

'Was John Nicolson really Gubbins's man?'

'Yes. Special Operations Executive. Gubbins recruited him in Norway. Nicolson had set up a ring of informants along the coast there and was getting intelligence as well as people who'd upset the local Gestapo out of Norway by boat to Shetland. It was thought Nicolson was in hiding or missing, most likely dead.'

'And the scar on his upper arm?'

'It wasn't done to remove a tattoo. It was done so that Nicolson could pretend he'd been in the Hitler Youth. Just part of a necessary deception.'

Clement stared at Johnny. Deception. It was what the

Service did well. 'Do you know Johnny, while you, and just about everyone here, knows everything there is to know about me, I know almost nothing about you. Other than that we were at seminary school together a lifetime ago, I don't even know where you were born or grew up.'

'It's not something I talk about. But it's no secret.'

Clement laughed.

'No truly. I was born in Singapore. My parents were missionaries there.'

Clement stared at John Winthorpe. He wasn't sure if he believed him.

Johnny reached for an envelope on his desk. 'I have a request, from Brigadier Gubbins.'

'Oh?'

'Given what you learned about the Shetland connection, Gubbins would like you to go there. There are plans to set up a regular network between Shetland and Nazi-occupied Norway.'

'I've just resigned, Johnny.'

Johnny reached forward and grasped the note. He then tore it up, stacked the pieces in an ashtray on his desk, and set fire to them. 'Yours is a secret position, Clement. Until the war is over, I'm afraid resignation isn't an option.'

Clement leaned back in the chair. 'Then there is something I want from you first.'

'Name it.'

'I wish to inform Reg's wife Geraldine about his

death. No details, of course. But I will not allow such a brave man's death to be conveyed by telegram to the other side of the world.'

'Are you saying what I think you are saying?'

Clement genuinely smiled for the first time in days. 'I wouldn't know what you think, Johnny.'

'Goes with the job, Clement.'

'Yes. I know it does.'

'Perhaps it can be arranged. Gubbins won't be happy.' Johnny paused again. 'However, the operation Gubbins is setting up in Shetland will take a few months to organise. Its activities are, of course, top secret, but they can only be operated in winter when the North Sea is shrouded in darkness. Norway and Shetland have very long hours of daylight in summer. So, this gives you time to see the widow. I'll let you know when I've booked your passage and by which routes. You'll have to travel on commercial ships, I'm afraid, via America. The crossing is not without danger, Clement, but God willing, you'll get there. I'll see if I can get you flown to the west coast of America. That should shorten a long voyage a little. As there is no war in the Pacific, at least not yet, you can quite safely travel on to Australia in merchant vessels. I'd be interested to know what you think of the place. I hear they are a rebellious lot and rather dismissive of authority. Courageous though. We have some in the RAF. In the meantime, I'll arrange for you to rest and recuperate in the Peak District again.'

'They don't have an aristocracy in Australia, do they?'

'No. Some good men but no upper class.'

'Good. I think I'll like it there then.'

Clement thought Johnny looked slightly bewildered but nothing further was said. Clement stood up and shook Johnny's hand. He smiled to the ladies as he left the third floor. Descending the steps to the ground floor, he stepped out onto the footpath outside Number Seven Whitehall Place. He sniffed the air then crossed the road. As he walked towards the railway station, he glanced up at the windows high above the ground where he knew Johnny and C had their offices. 'Good bye, Johnny,' he whispered. He had no intention of ever coming back.

Acknowledgements

I would like to thank my editor, Janet Laurence, my publisher Ian Hooper and proof editor Andrew Bridgmont. Also special thanks to my husband Peter and to my whole family for their encouragement and support and to the following people who so kindly assisted me with information:

To Jill and John Wadsworth from Wistow. Robert Bullen for his local knowledge of the Cambridgeshire fenland. David Anderson for his reminiscences of The Abbey School and for his farming knowledge.

Hector Gordon and George Charlton for their local knowledge and information on farming practices.

Jason Edwards, Porter at Caius College, Cambridge and Paul Magison, former Porter at Caius College.

Christine Turnbull, for allowing us to cross her land to access the towpath at Bait's Bite.

To our guide at Anglesey Abbey, Barbara Constable and to John Lunt for his friendship and information about The Hospital of St Cross near Winchester.

Thank you to the Winchester College Guide and all the college Porters and finally, last, but not least, thanks to the Ramsey Agricultural Museum, Cambridgeshire, England.

Author's Note

There are numerous historical events in this fictitious work. Research about Josef Jakobs was obtained from newspapers of the time at The Ramsey Agricultural Museum, Cambridgeshire and from numerous online sites and small references in Masterman's excellent book on the Double-Cross system. This book, as well as other online sites, including declassified MI5 files from The National Archives at Kew provided information on other German spies and some Double-Cross spies; Karl Richter, Wulf Schmidt known as TATE and a Welshman, Arthur Owens known as SNOW. Latchmere House in Richmond was indeed the place where MI5 interrogated captured German spies and the commandant there was a Colonel Stephens.

Secret peace talks took place in 1941 between January and April in Portugal and Spain. According to Heinrich Stahmer, Albrecht Haushofer's agent in Spain, those present at these clandestine talks included Haushofer, Rudolf Hess, Sir Samuel Hoare, British Ambassador to Spain, and Lord Halifax. Other talks took place in Switzerland and Sweden but these do not form part of this story and are therefore not included here. **While the inference in this work of fiction is that Sir Samuel**

Hoare and Lord Halifax were involved in insurrection, this is entirely fictitious. Likewise, their involvement in a fictitious coup d'état in Britain in 1941 is not meant by the author to infer any actual treasonous acts on their part.

The mysterious flight of Rudolf Hess took place on 10th May 1941, a year to the day after Churchill became Prime Minister. Hess landed in a field in Scotland near the home of the Duke of Hamilton and was captured almost immediately. It is believed the reason for his ill-fated flight was that Hess wished to negotiate peace between Britain and the Nazi government. Hess was convinced, and in some cases rightly, that many of the upper classes in Britain would be predisposed to assist him to this end.

There are references to other historical facts, namely; that tungsten or wolfram was mined in neutral Portugal where there was fierce competition between Britain and Germany to purchase this raw material used for hardening steel. Also, there is a reference to the Shetland Bus, as it became known, which had its beginnings in the spring of 1941. For five years it carried people, munitions and money in the winter months between Shetland and Norway. This was no mean feat as Nazi aircraft were always on the look-out for these little ships and the North Sea is a ferocious place in winter when the trips were usually made under the cover of darkness. Many brave men gave their lives to this part of the war.

There is also reference to several right-wing groups

that formed in Britain in the pre-war era. These include The Right Club, The Nordic League and the White Knights of Britain.

Three fine schools are referred to in the book: The Abbey School in Ramsey, St Edward's in Oxford and Winchester College in Winchester, as well as two Cambridge colleges, Gonville and Caius and Trinity Hall. Events in this work that took place in these colleges and the people employed at these educational institutions are entirely fictitious.

Likewise, Hitcham Hall is fictitious but Anglesey Abbey, a National Trust property in Lode was used for the location of Wilstock House.